The Wisdom
of the
Olive Tree

A Novel

Corey Stewart

**Canoe Tree
Press**

The Wisdom of the Olive Tree

Copyright © 2022 by Corey Stewart

Printed in the United States of America

Paperback ISBN: 978-1-959096-28-3
Ebook ISBN: 978-1-959096-29-0

Canoe Tree
Press

4697 Main Street
Manchester Center, VT 05255

Canoe Tree Press is a division of DartFrog Books

For my children.

Prologo

The olive tree stands alone, away from her sisters and brothers in the grove. Her trunk is gnarled and hollow, emptied by time and trauma, but somehow she—and I am sure it is a *she* despite what the gendered language of Italian might say—remains standing, and still yields fruit.

I watch as Oliver curls himself into a perfect crescent at the base of the tree and tucks his tail under his chin. He exhales audibly and rests his muzzle on his paws, knowing that for as long as it takes me to drink a cup of coffee, nothing is expected of him other than casual vigilance.

"How old do you think that tree is?" I ask when Porter appears.

His mouth twists in thought. "The house is from the 1500s, and I wouldn't be surprised if the tree was here first. They typically live several hundred years."

"How is it still producing olives? The trunk is barely there."

"That's where I found Oliver, did I tell you? I came over one morning about a week after I bought my place, and there he was, waiting for me."

Hearing his name, Oliver lifts his head and thumps his tail against the ground.

"There's a tree near Trevi that's supposed to be almost two thousand years old," Porter continues, bending to scratch Oliver's ears. "They have a parade for it every year."

"The Saint Emiliano tree," I say. "I read about it."

"I have no clue who Saint Emiliano was."

"The first bishop of Trevi. During the persecution of Christians in the early 300s, he was tied to that tree and beheaded," I tell him. "They call the tree *il saggio signore* because it has seen so much history."

"That's what I want to be called, too. The wise old man."

"I think you might have a few years to go, huh?"

"You could start practicing now. Just saying."

I smile at him before returning my gaze to the tree.

Amazing, that something so damaged can remain standing, much less bear fruit.

But she does.

And maybe, despite all that's happened, I will, too.

Uno

Dear Mia,
Last night I lay awake thinking about everything that led me to Italy. All of the highs and lows of my life, the twists and turns I never could have anticipated.

I was reminded of an old toy called Bozo Bop, a big industrial-plastic bag with Bozo the Clown's face and a weight in its base. It reeled backwards when you punched it, then rocked back to upright. That's all there was to it. No bells, no whistles. Just punch, reel, return, repeat.

In a lot of ways, my life has felt like endless rounds of Bozo Bop. Up for a couple of years, then *wham*, knocked flat again. The problem is, after your accident, I couldn't get back up. And I began to see how easy it could be to just stay down. So I made deals with myself every day—*If it still feels this bad tomorrow, I'll end things*—and somehow the days brought me here, to this

1

big stone house on the line where Umbria touches Tuscany on the map, with a man I once knew thirty years ago sleeping down the hall.

And as I was lying there, dreading another sleepless night, I realized something. I'd never talked about what happened to you, or what came after. And my whole life, whenever I was searching for clarity, whether I was starting a project or trying to make a decision, the first thing I needed to do was put the facts into a narrative. Somehow that process sorted the jumble in my brain and allowed me see what needed to be done, and when.

Oliver raised his head off the pillow when I swung my feet to the floor.

"Come on," I told him, pulling a ratty gray sweater over my head.

I padded down the hall to Porter's room and rapped softly. When he answered, I opened the door a crack, but Oliver pushed past me and leapt onto the bed.

"Sorry. Were you asleep?"

"No, not yet."

"Can I talk to you?"

"Of course. Sit down," Porter said, scooting sideways and patting the space he created. "Move over, Ollie."

"Do you remember when we went to see *Fried Green Tomatoes* in Chapel Hill?"

Porter nodded. "Sure."

"Remember after Buddy dies, when Idgie's living out by the river? There's this line Ninny says about Idgie, that a heart can be broken but still keep on beating."

"I remember when Buddy died, yeh."

"That's how I feel, Porter. I'm completely broken inside, but I'm still walking around. My brain doesn't work right anymore, but I'm still going through the motions, even though nothing makes sense."

Porter reached out and scratched the top of Oliver's snout, making his lip curl to reveal his teeth.

"I hope Oliver and I make sense, at least."

I was quiet for a minute, pulling a loose thread from the cuff of my sweater. "I was thinking that maybe if I could talk through what happened to Mia, it would help."

"Sure," Porter said, nodding slowly. "I read a lot of stuff on the internet."

"I mean what it was like for me."

Porter nodded.

And so, perched on the edge of Porter's bed in the small hours of the morning, I talked for the first time about the day.

It was a beautiful spring day, one of those sunny, cloudless rarities that causes Londoners to pour into the parks. Unbeknownst to me, you and Devon and Salma were celebrating the unseasonably warm weather by skipping school. You'd taken the Tube to Tottenham Court Road, where you met up with a kid named Jacob, one of Devon's friends. As you were leaving the station, you stumbled and stepped off the curb into the street. A bike courier racing to beat the traffic light hit you, propelling you forward several feet through the air. Your head hit the pavement, and in that instant, your life on Earth was over.

Salma was hysterical, incomprehensible, when she called, and I nearly hung up, thinking it was a prank. A police officer pried the phone from her hands, and that's when I heard Devon screaming your name in the background. When the officer told me where the ambulance was taking you, I dropped the phone and ran out the door and into the street, nearly colliding with a taxi.

Your father raced into the hospital, a phone pressed to his ear, while I was still at reception begging the nurse to let me see you. You hated small spaces and would be scared in an MRI, I told her, and I needed the doctor to know that you were allergic to morphine and penicillin. She shook her head and told me it wasn't possible to see you, that you were being evaluated. I remember being struck by that word, *evaluated*, as if it was possible that you were anything less than perfect.

What happened? Crawford demanded, gripping my arms so tightly that there were fingerprints in my skin for weeks afterwards. But I could only repeat what the nurse had said.

When the doctor approached, followed by the hospital chaplain, your father let go of me to shake the doctor's outstretched hand and I crumpled to the floor.

The press was a giant, frothing mass outside the hospital when we left hours later. Your father swatted microphones out of his face and pulled me through the crowd to George, who was standing next to the car with his chauffeur's hat over his heart. I slid across the back seat, followed by your father, and George drove us home in silence.

You were not the first person to have been killed by a cyclist in the city of London that year, and your accident quickly became fodder for the groups pushing for tougher laws and steeper penalties for bike riders. I didn't care about any of that, and I deeply resented the co-opting of our pain. I told your father to have someone from his firm threaten litigation, to keep your name out of their mouths and press releases, but I don't know if he did. I doubt it.

The CCTV footage was all over the news. I watched it once before shutting the television off for good. The four of you exited the Tube station, laughing, and Jacob playfully shoved Devon, whose hand you were holding. Devon knocked into you and lost his grip on your hand, and you stumbled into the street. The bike struck. You flew to the edge of the camera's view. There was a pause, your friends frozen in shock, and then Salma disappeared in the direction you'd flown.

It was a chain of events that could never make sense.

Everyone was devastated. Your friends, our friends, our neighbors, your teachers. My uncle David flew over and he, and someone at your father's office, made all the arrangements. The house filled up with flowers, big, elaborate, cloying bouquets that I dumped in the bin out back, unable to bear the smell of lilies since I was a kid, and trays of food and bottles of Scotch from your father's colleagues crowded the dining room table. The mothers of your school friends and my editors and the ladies I knew from various writing groups came with books and cards and gifts and tea.

Your friends huddled in a clump in the sitting room. Poor Devon, who was inconsolable, and Salma, who looked like a ghost, white-faced and drawn, and Jacob, who introduced himself and burst into tears. I knew I should hug him and tell him it was okay, that no one blamed him, but I couldn't make myself speak, and it was my uncle David who came and put his arm around Jacob and ushered him away. I said hello to your friends and accepted their hugs, but I couldn't bear to look at those faces that I'd watched grow from children to young adults, and went upstairs.

Your father decided not to prosecute the cyclist. He announced this about a week after the funeral, when it was just the two of us and the walls were echoing with silence. We were sitting at opposite ends of the dining room table, an ocean of mahogany and grief and untouched Thai food between us, and he informed me matter-of-factly, as if we were discussing mango sticky rice or the weather, that there wasn't any point to ruining the cyclist's life, too.

I was livid. I wanted that twenty-six-year-old idiot, who'd thought it was so important to get to where he was going that he'd ignored the rules of the road, to suffer. I wanted him to think about you every day, and to know the pain his decision had caused. I wanted to extinguish the joy in his parents' lives just like he had extinguished the joy in mine.

But your father didn't ask me what I wanted. And when I told him I would never forgive him for making that decision without consulting me, he looked at me wordlessly, pushed his chair back from the table, and left the room.

We just unraveled, your father and I. The problems that had been percolating between us, the disconnect I'd been so studiously avoiding addressing for years, made it impossible for us to reach across the yawning gap between us. I lay down in your room the night of the accident, and I never went back to our bed. Your father started leaving even earlier and staying even later at the office, and I drifted around like a ghost, ignoring my email and my cell phone and letting the mail pile up on the entryway table.

One day about three weeks after the accident, I managed to pull on clothes and go to the market. Graciela stripped your bed and put the sheets in the washer while I was out, erasing the scent of you that lingered there. When I came home and discovered what she'd done, I fired her on the spot. She left the house in tears and called your father, who rehired her.

I felt as though my skin had been removed and the world was acid and salt. The only thing that made the pain bearable was constant movement, so every morning I laced up my tennis shoes and walked, putting one foot in front of the other without ever noticing where I was going or where I'd been, and only returning home when my hips hurt so badly that I couldn't take another step. I'd pull myself up the stairs by the banister and sit under the shower where my tears could join the water swirling down the drain. The only evidence I ever saw of your father during that time were dirty highball glasses in the sink.

Early one morning, the phone rang as I was tying my tennis shoes. Reporters still called occasionally, but even worse than their asinine questions were the sympathetic friends who called with well-meaning invitations, as if I gave a damn about a trendy new restaurant or what was playing in the West End. So I let the machine pick up, as I always did. But when the tone sounded and the caller cleared his throat and said, "Beth? It's me," I froze.

I hadn't spoken to Porter since the day we ended our engagement in a parking lot full of cigarette butts and recrimination thirty years earlier. I hesitated, my shoelaces suspended in my fingers, then lunged across the sofa just as Porter was saying goodbye. He was in Italy, he said. He lived there, had been there for two, almost three, years already. He'd stumbled across an article I'd written in a travel magazine and had been curious about what I was doing and where I was and had Googled me the day before. But instead of bylines, he'd found dozens of articles about the accident. He'd read them all, then found David's phone number online and placed a call to Chapel Hill. David had given him my cell number, but it went straight to voicemail, so he'd called the house phone.

Was I okay? Could he come see me? Was there anything he could do to help?

No, I wasn't okay, I told him. No, he couldn't come visit. But yes, there was something he could do. He could call me again the next day.

And he did.

Porter was a lifeline. He didn't ask anything of me, just told me stories about his life in Italy while I cried on the other end of the phone. At first, his calls delayed my walk by half an hour, then by an hour, and then I started to do simple tasks around the house with the cordless phone pressed to my ear, folding laundry, dusting, and loading the dishwasher while he talked about what he was working on. When we hung up, I'd start walking.

"I don't know anything that's going on in the world," I said one morning, the phone tucked between my chin and shoulder while I rinsed out the coffee pot. "I don't watch television. I don't listen to the radio. I haven't read a paper in months."

"I don't think you're missing much," Porter said.

"You're the only person I talk to. Graciela hides whenever she sees me."

"What about Crawford? Don't you talk to him?"

"I never see him."

"What do you mean?"

"He's at work. And then he's... he's with someone else. I'm assuming he talks to them, not me."

"What do you mean, he's with someone else?"

"He's....involved with someone."

"He's having an affair? Jesus, Beth."

"For a long time, I think," I said. "I found out right before Mia—before the accident. I thought if I left him alone he'd come back because we had a family, but now...."

Porter was quiet while I cried.

"Why don't you come down here?" he said finally. "I think a change of scenery would do you good."

"I can't," I said, looking down at the jeans I'd cinched to my hips with one of Crawford's old neckties. "I'm not well."

"I know that," Porter said. "I know you're not well. That's why you need to come. You said Crawford is at the office all the time and you're not working right now. So come Monday morning and leave Friday afternoon. You'll be back in time for the weekend and he probably won't even notice you're gone."

"I don't know...." I set the coffee pot on the counter and wiped my hands on my jeans while I walked into the sitting room.

"It will be good for you. It's really summer here. Hot and sunny. I'll buy the ticket and arrange a car to the airport, and all you have to do is throw some things in a bag and get in the car when it comes, okay? Or don't pack, it doesn't matter. I have lots of clothes. I'll pick you up in Rome. I'll be right there to get you."

I glanced at my face in the mirror above the fireplace. My eyes were black-ringed and sunken into my skull and my hair looked thin and matted.

"I don't think I'd be much fun."

"I don't need you to be entertaining, Beth. I just need you to get in the car when it comes."

I looked out the window, at the black cabs splashing down the street, and pulled my sweater tighter around my body.

"Okay," I said. "Okay. I'll get in the car when it comes."

I left Crawford a note on the kitchen counter, telling him that I was going to Italy for a week to get away from London. Early the next morning, he tapped on the bedroom door.

"Have a good trip," he said, and then walked away.

I never mentioned Porter, and Crawford never asked exactly where I was going or who I was seeing. I think he was just relieved for me to be gone. I emailed from Italy to tell him I was staying a second week, and then a third, and he wrote back *okay* both times and that was as much conversation as we had about it. After that, I didn't even bother to email.

Porter was solicitous and gentle from the moment he met me at the airport. He seemed to want nothing more than to move me, like a plant that needed tending, from one sunny spot to another. He cooked three meals a day, took me on long walks, and built a fire at night in the bedroom he'd made up for me even though he must have been sweltering in his own room down the hall. Every morning he met me in the kitchen, extending a cup of coffee and asking if I'd slept while Oliver thwacked his tail against the cabinets.

One night, after I'd pushed the food he'd made around on my plate for an hour, Porter reached across the table and tucked a strand of hair behind my ear.

"Just leave the dishes and come upstairs in a few minutes, okay? I have an idea."

I scraped my dinner into the compost bin and rinsed the plates before going up. Porter was in the bathroom, kneeling next to the enormous stone tub. Steam fogged the windows and little sprigs of fresh lavender floated on top of the bath water.

He looked up at me and shut off the taps.

"There is a clean robe on the hook there, and a towel on the chair. The hot water will be ready to go again in a couple minutes, if you need to reheat." He stood up. "I thought the lavender would help you sleep, maybe."

I nodded. "It's great. Thank you."

"I'll just go clean up the kitchen, okay? If you need me, just holler."

I nodded again.

"Okay," he said, turning to leave. "Try to relax."

"Porter?"

"Yeh?" He stopped in the doorway.

"Stay?"

Porter didn't respond. He reached for the towel on the chair and held it up while I slid my jeans to the floor and took off the two pairs of socks and the long-sleeved t-shirt I was wearing and climbed into the tub, where the water came up to my armpits. I wrapped my arms around my legs and bent my head onto my knees, closing my eyes and inhaling the lavender-scented steam that rose from the bath.

Porter knelt next to the tub. He moved my hair to the side and began to wash my back.

"I can count your ribs," he said softly.

I didn't respond.

"You still deserve to eat, you know. She would want you to eat."

I tightened my arms around my knees and turned my head away from him, sobbing.

"You were a good mother, Beth. Nothing will ever change that."

"Except that I'm not a mother anymore. I'm not anything."

"Yes, you are. You will always be her mom." His voice caught and made a small choking sound. "That's why you have to live. You owe that to Mia."

I turned to look at him. His eyes were full of tears.

"I can help you live, okay?" he said. "Let me help you, Beth."

I couldn't answer. I just bent my head over my knees again and cried.

Going to Italy and staying, first for one week and then two, and then four months, wasn't so much a step forward as it was a soft, slow slide into the past. I hadn't seen Porter for thirty years, but he was as familiar to me as the scar on my knee.

As comfortable as it was, though, and as good as it felt to be with someone who cared, it wasn't my real life. I knew I couldn't stay.

"You saved my life," I told Porter. He was sitting with his back against the headboard, one hand resting on Oliver's head, wearing a Pink Floyd t-shirt that was threadbare from decades of washing. "But I have to go back to London and figure out my next step."

"Why?"

"I feel like when I left London, I left her, too."

Porter's brow furrowed. "What do you mean?"

"London is where we lived. It's where my memories of my daughter are."

"Well, the great thing about memories is that they're portable. And I don't think you ran away from anything, Beth. I think you did what you could to save yourself."

"I have to go back. I can't keep hiding here."

"You know, when you got here, you were a walking skeleton. How come Crawford didn't notice that you were wasting away?"

I didn't respond.

"You said he's been having an affair for what—a couple years? What in the hell are you going back to, Beth?"

"I don't know," I said. "That's what I have to figure out."

Porter was quiet for a long time. Finally, he said, "Well, I'm not going to try to talk you into staying if you want to leave. I respect you too much to do that. But I don't think it's a good idea."

"I know," I said.

"Why don't you stay in here with us tonight? See if you can get some sleep. Move over, Ollie."

Oliver lifted his shaggy head off the pillow, looked at Porter and then at me, then put his head back down and started snoring again.

Porter patted the narrow space between them and I climbed in.

Due

Oliver usually stuck close to Porter, riding shotgun on the tractor and trotting next to him through the fields, chasing the magpies and rabbits who dared encroach on his territory. But if I was in the kitchen, Oliver liked to stretch out in front of the oven on the rug, where he could Hoover up anything I dropped and taste test whatever I might be cooking. That's where he was when Patrizio, Porter's neighbor, burst through the kitchen door this morning.

I was trying to scrub burnt risotto off the bottom of a pot when he materialized, causing me to yelp, drop the pot into the sink, and step backwards onto Oliver, who was so used to Patrizio's surprise appearances that he couldn't be bothered to bark or get up.

"*Stai calma, Elisabetta*," Patrizio said, his eyes twinkling.

Patrizio lived in the house at the far edge of the field with his twin brother, Alberto. They worked the fields with Porter and made wine from his grapes. I'd gone to their house once with Porter a few days after I arrived in Italy, to drop off some empty glass jugs. There was a faded sign tacked to the front door.

"What does it say?"

"*Citofono rotto. Urlare ding dong*," Porter read. "It means 'The doorbell is broken. Yell ding dong.'"

Alberto was quieter and more reserved, but Patrizio had starbursts of white lines around his eyes from years of laughter. The brothers had been born in the house they still occupied, and aside from brief stints in the military, had never felt the urge to travel more than a few miles from home. There had been wives at one point, Porter told me, but he'd never been able to figure out whether the women had died or simply left.

Every time I'd ever seen Patrizio, he was wearing the same thing, plus or minus a jacket and scarf. Threadbare brown corduroys, a nubby tan sweater, olive-green field boots, and a green wool cap that barely contained his unruly mass of gray curls. This morning he was also accessorized with a woven basket tucked under his muscular arm.

"*Guarda*," he said, setting the basket on the counter next to me and removing his cap. He gestured towards the basket with a flourish and watched intently as I slid the rubber gloves off my hands, unfolded the green linen cloth, and lifted a mushroom out of the basket.

"*Fantastico!*" I said, inhaling the scent of damp soil.

Patrizio exhaled and beamed like a proud father.

"*Hai trovati i funghi in Maremma?*"

"*Ma dai*," Patrizio said, shaking his steepled hands in front of his chest, conveying his profound regret that he couldn't answer my question about where he had found the mushrooms because some information was just too precious to share.

I motioned for him to sit down at the kitchen table and turned to fill the battered steel Bialetti coffee maker and set it on the stove. While we waited for the coffee to perk, Patrizio told me about the mushroom-hunting expedition. Did I understand the skill required to hunt mushrooms? Did I know the dangers that lurked on the forest floor?

"*Ci sono vipere.*" He wiggled his hand in front of me and told me that Alberto had only narrowly escaped being struck by a viper when he reached down to move a clump of vegetation aside.

I shuddered at the thought as I poured the coffee. Patrizio wrapped his brown leathery mitts around the cup I set in front of him and reminded me that not only were there vipers, there were also poisonous mushrooms that could kill a grown man with one bite. Luckily for me, he said, I lived next door to two of the most knowledgeable mushroom men in all of Italy. "*Quindi non preoccuparti.*"

I assured him I wasn't worried. "I'm just thinking about the vipers. Wouldn't it be safer to use a rake?"

I wasn't sure I knew the right word for rake and did a little pantomime to indicate what I meant, but Patrizio definitely understood because he made a horrified face and launched into a speech that seemed to cover a lot of territory. From what I could gather from his rapid-fire Italian, using any implement other than a skilled and gentle hand was a disgrace, the French knew nothing about mushrooms, and too many Germans were buying property in Tuscany. Just when I was beginning to regret that the doors were never locked, Patrizio tossed his hands in the air, as if conceding to the ignorance of people like me, and gave up.

"*Si, si, adesso capisco,*" I assured him, as penitent as Paul on the road to Damascus. *Forgive me, Lord. I was blind, but now I see.*

Patrizio visibly relaxed, satisfied that he'd made his point.

I transferred the mushrooms to the kitchen counter, then wrapped the loaf of banana bread that was cooling next to the oven in the linen cloth and tucked it into the basket. When I set the basket on the table in front of Patrizio, he sniffed the air like a scavenging bear.

"*È il pane alle banana?*"

I nodded.

Patrizio grinned. He stood up, scraping his chair across the tile floor, tucked the basket under his arm, patted Oliver's head, and quickly kissed my cheeks. "*Ciao, Elisabetta.*"

I gave up on the risotto pan while I cleaned the mushrooms, then sliced them and cranked thin ribbons of *tagliatelle* through the pasta machine.

Porter came in when I was chopping parsley.

"Was that Patrizio or Alberto I saw earlier?" he asked, leaning against the doorjamb to remove his boots.

"Patrizio. He brought you these mushrooms." I sprinkled chopped parsley over the pasta and set two bowls on the table while Porter washed his hands and Oliver took his position next to Porter's chair in anticipation of lunch.

"Did he tell you where he got them?" Porter asked. "Can I use this towel?"

"It's your house, Porter, you can use whatever you want. Of course he didn't tell me. I did ask, though."

"He would have been offended if you hadn't."

"These mushrooms were plucked from the jaws of a viper, by the way. Apparently Alberto nearly got bit."

Porter placed the towel next to the kitchen sink and walked to the table. He leaned over his bowl and inhaled as he slid into his chair. "Mmm. I thought I detected a whiff of viper."

"Just a hint," I said, "for flavor. And Patrizio made a point of telling me that he's pretty sure all the mushrooms are edible."

"Well, that's reassuring."

"Although I guess any mushroom is edible once, huh?"

"Sure," Porter said. "It's the second bite that's the problem." He spun his fork in the tagliatelle. *"Tonight...A sleepy Italian village..."*

"A charming Italian neighbor," I continued. *"A basket full of mushrooms. And a deadly plot to steal a Golden Retriever."*

Porter laughed and looked down at Oliver. "Are you sorry I didn't let Patrizio have you?"

Oliver lifted his ears and tilted his head.

"I didn't think so," Porter said, and forked a ball of pasta into his mouth.

"The bad news is, I gave him your banana bread."

"No!" Porter dropped his fork and clutched his chest like he'd been shot. "I've been thinking about it all morning! All of it?"

I grimaced. "I panicked. I'm sorry. I didn't have anything else to give him and the banana bread was right there."

Porter sighed dramatically. "I'm gutted. But I know he's happy."

About a month after I arrived in Italy, I saw bananas in the village market and remembered that Porter loved banana bread. I paid an outrageous price for a single, brownish-yellow bunch and cobbled the recipe together from memory out of a desperate need to do something, anything, to acknowledge Porter's hospitality. When Patrizio and Alberto came by to discuss the plans for the fields that same night, I put the coffee on and sliced the banana bread and retreated to the living room with a book. After they left, Porter told me the bread had been a huge hit.

"There's hardly any left. Patrizio took one bite and launched into an emotional story about the first banana he ever ate, which was in Sicily in the '60s," Porter said. "And Alberto said it was *buonissimo* and my wife was a good woman who deserved a crown."

"A crown?"

Porter nodded. "*Una donna buona vale una corona*. He's full of old sayings like that."

"Did you tell him I'm not your wife? That I'm a stray like Oliver, who showed up here after not seeing you for thirty years?"

Porter looked down at the scratchpad where he was calculating seed prices.

"No," he said finally, looking up and shaking his head. "The first part's none of their business, and I invited you, remember?"

"For a few days. And it's been almost a month and the neighbors think I'm a mail-order bride. They'll be scandalized when I leave."

"Is that your plan?" Porter asked. "To leave?"

"I can't stay here forever, Porter. You have a life, and I—"

I couldn't think of any way to finish that sentence.

"What I'm doing right now is my life. Sitting at this table, working out the planting schedule, and talking to you. That last part is a surprise, yeh, but as far as I'm concerned, it's the best part of it all."

"But I can't just barge in and insert myself into—" I couldn't think of how to finish that sentence, either, and just swept my arm around the kitchen and said, "All of this" and retreated to the living room with a book.

That was three months ago.

"I made chicken," I said, as Porter stabbed the last mushroom in his bowl.

"Excellent. I've been trying to fix the gates to the stalls. Some of the doors have pulled all the way off the hinges."

"I'll come out and help."

I made Porter an espresso while he finished lunch.

"Thank you," he said, throwing back the coffee in one gulp. He pushed his chair away from the table and took our bowls to the sink. "I'm tempted to take a nap now."

"You should."

"I need to get the gates done," he said, wiping his hands on a towel before moving towards the kitchen door. He leaned against the frame to tug on his boots. "Should we do something fun tomorrow? Go somewhere before you head back to London?" he asked. "Or have you changed your mind about that?"

I shook my head.

"Then let's go somewhere. I can get the gates done today if I have a reason to."

After washing the dishes and leaving them to dry on the rack, I refilled the risotto pan with hot, soapy water, then pulled on one of Porter's jackets and went out to the barn. He was lying on his side in the dirt using his body to prop up the wooden stall door that he was screwing into place.

"Could we go to Arezzo tomorrow?"

"Sure."

"Want me to hold up the gate?"

He nodded and I slid my hands under the dense wood and lifted the door. Porter rolled out from under it and knelt to screw the hinges into place. When he was finished, he jumped to his feet.

"That goes a lot faster with help. Only four more."

After the gates were secured, we found several other jobs that needed to be done in the barn and stayed out there until it was time for dinner. Porter fell asleep in his chair after we ate and only woke up when the book he'd been reading slid off his lap and hit the floor.

"You ready to go up?" he asked, yawning.

I nodded.

And thus began another sleepless night of searching for the life I used to have.

Tre

I don't know if you came to Arezzo when you were in Italy, Mia. It's not on the usual tourist path like Florence and Siena, and you and Salma had a whole country to cover, but maybe you did. I hope so. It's worth it, to see the wooden Cimabue crucifix in the Basilica of San Domenico and the porticos around the main square and the famous antiques market that happens every month.

Porter and I drove in early this morning, winding for nearly an hour along the two-lane country road and stopping for a cappuccino and a pastry before merging onto the *autostrada*.

"You're awfully quiet," he said, downshifting as we passed under the arched stone wall that surrounds the city. "What's on your mind?"

"London. I feel sick every time I think about it."

"Try not to think about it," he said, glancing at me. "Let's just enjoy today."

We parked in an underground lot near a market and pulled on our jackets for the walk up to the cathedral. The locals call the church, which looms over the city from its perch at the very top of Arezzo, the *Duomo*, but technically its name is *la Cattedrale di San Donato e San Pietro*.

"Jesus, I need to work out or something," Porter said as we reached the top of the steep *Corso Italia* and crossed the small piazza in front of the church. "I can barely breathe."

At the top of the stairs, he pulled on the oversized door of the church and gestured for me to walk in ahead of him, then let the door thump shut behind us.

"I'll be down in front," he said, squeezing my arm. "Take your time."

I picked up one of the brochures from the small wooden table at the back of the sanctuary to refresh my memory and started meandering around the perimeter of the church, looking at the paintings.

Every Italian town of any size has a church or twelve, and many of them are beautiful, but in my opinion, the Arezzo cathedral is among the best. It's made of sandstone, with painted ceilings, huge stained-glass windows, a diamond-patterned stone floor, and a fresco of Mary Magdalene by Piero della Francesca that's recently been restored, returning the vibrant green to her dress and the deep red to her robe. My favorite thing in the church, though, and the reason I'd asked to come back, was a small side chapel known as the *Madonna del Conforto*.

In 1796, Arezzo was rocked by a series of earthquakes, which, in turn, caused several fires. Legend has it that three locals were praying to a statue of Mary that stood in a tavern, asking her to bring an end to the destruction of their city, when suddenly the smoke-blackened statue became vividly colored, as if made of rubies and diamonds. The locals took this to mean that Mary was signaling her protection of Arezzo, and about twenty years later, they lugged the statue up to the Cathedral and placed it in the chapel dedicated to Mary the Comforter.

The first time I ever saw the chapel, I'd been in Italy less than a week. It was a cool and rainy day, common in London where the sky and the pavement so often blend together, but an anomaly in an Italian summer. As Porter and I walked into the church, I was inexplicably drawn to the chapel on the left.

There was something about the space that moved me in a way I still can't explain. It's visually striking, with the same vaulted, fresco-covered ceiling and arched windows and stained-glass as the rest of the church, but unlike the other chapels in the Cathedral, the *Madonna del Conforto* is lit by dozens of candles and silver gas lights that give it a dream-like quality. The gas lights are held by arms of iron that are twisted to look like flowers and vines, and cherubs spring out of the walls to hold the vines, as if they are lighting the way towards the marble altar. The effect is incredible.

That first visit, I was standing there, taking in the beauty of it all, when I spotted the della Robbia ceramics embedded in the walls and let out an audible gasp. I've never quite understood exactly how Luca della Robbia made his tin-glazed ceramics stand out against flat backgrounds the way they do, or how he achieved such incredible colors—the vivid lemon yellow and bright leafy green, and the pure, celestial blue of Mary's robe— but every time I encounter one of his works, I'm in awe all over again.

Totally overwhelmed, I took a seat in one of the pews in the chapel and bowed my head. I felt a hand wrap around the back of my neck, warm and supportive, and I had the sensation of being cradled and held, a feeling so strong that I turned around, expecting to see Porter behind me. But there was no one there. So I bowed my head again, and again the sensation came over me, and I began to shake and sob. After a few minutes, a feeling of peace washed over me and my tears stopped as suddenly as they'd begun.

The only way I can explain it is that sitting in that chapel so far from home and so utterly lost, I experienced the presence of God. Not just as an idea, but as a real, tangible, physical presence.

When I finally dragged myself out of the chapel that day, I found Porter standing down in the front of the church, admiring the fresco of Mary Magdalene. He looked at me without saying a word and stroked my tearstained cheek with the back of his hand.

Com'è bella e strana la vita e pensare che sono ancora qui con te, he said, his voice low and soft.

I'd repeated the phrase to myself, committing it to memory so I could look it up later.

How beautiful and strange life is, to think I would be here with you.

I was sitting in the chapel this morning, staring at the cherubs and wondering if I would ever have the chance to come back to Arezzo once I returned to London, when a woman came in and sat across the aisle. She was dark-skinned, wearing a long skirt with a dirty hem and a stained puffy jacket that swallowed her upper body, and she was holding a baby swaddled in so many layers that I couldn't see any part of it, but I could hear it mewling as the woman rocked slightly, staring straight ahead at the altar, and I had to swallow back the lump that formed in my throat. She reminded me of a painting I once saw of Mary who, rather than appearing beatific and serene, held the infant Jesus to her chest with an expression somewhere between fear and disbelief, as if she'd had a premonition of the excruciating events to come.

As I got up to leave, I stuck my fingers into the pocket of Porter's jacket and felt for the money left over from breakfast.

When I passed by the woman, I held out my hand. She reached for the money without looking at me, and a coin fell from my palm and clanged on the floor. I bent to pick it up, but the woman was faster, folding herself over the body of her baby and pinching the coin into her fingers. She nodded at me, the slightest dip of her chin, as I walked out of the chapel and into the sanctuary.

Porter was sitting in a pew at the front of the church, his arms folded over his chest and his eyes closed.

"Are you asleep?" I asked, sliding in next to him.

He shook his head. "Just resting my eyes. Ready to go?"

We walked the short distance downhill from the cathedral to the vaulted colonnade that forms one side of Arezzo's main piazza and found a spot at a table next to an outdoor heater. Porter ordered for us, and then started talking about the sheep he wanted to buy now that the stalls in the barn were fixed.

"Have you decided how many?" I asked.

"Depends how much pecorino you want to eat."

"Oooh, speaking of cheese, did you order the cheese plate? I wasn't paying attention."

He laughed. "I did, yes. And don't think I didn't notice how distracted you were by the waiter."

I slid my scarf off my neck and draped it over the back of my chair. "Slander. I was thinking about a woman I saw in the church."

"Let me guess. You gave her money?"

"Just the change from breakfast," I said. "I'm sorry. That was your money and I should have asked."

"Don't be ridiculous."

"No, I should have," I said. "But anyway, I think you should get a giant flock of sheep. How about fifty?"

"The barn's too small. Will you mind if they live in the house?"

"It's *your* house! But you said the downstairs was originally for animals, anyway. So, it would be like a historical restoration. You could apply for a grant," I said.

"Nice. I like that angle."

"But you have to promise you'll go old school. Flax robe, sandals, shepherd's staff, the works. And if one wanders off, go find it."

The waiter, who actually *was* distractingly good-looking, reappeared then with two wine glasses dangling from his fingertips, a bottle of wine tucked under his arm, a basket of bread, and a huge wooden board loaded with cheese and meat. He found room for it all on the table while explaining the different ages of the cheese, and informed us that the bread and jam had been made by his grandmother while the meat came from his cousin, a locally famous *salsiccatore*.

"You know," Porter said, after extending our compliments to the waiter's grandmother, who, we were told, would be out to say hello as soon as she finished the nap she was taking next to the oven, "I never got that story, about the lost sheep. One wanders off and the shepherd goes to find it, but why? He leaves ninety-nine sheep vulnerable to go find one."

"Yeh," I said, tearing my gaze away from the waiter, who was uncorking the bottle of wine. "Who was it that was described as ox-eyed?"

Porter wrinkled his brow. "Ox-eyed?"

"In literature. Someone with thick, long eyelashes and big brown eyes."

"I have no idea."

"He has ox eyes," I said, flicking my gaze at the waiter.

"Do you think he's aware of it? Should we let him know?"

I smiled and shook my head. "Okay, so you promise to hunt down the sheep that wanders away?"

"No, because that seems really dumb. A decent business plan would allow for the loss of—"

"It was Homer," I said, snapping my fingers. "Talking about Hera. Sorry, I just remembered. In *The Iliad*, Homer describes Hera as ox-eyed."

"Pretty sure I only read the Cliffs Notes."

The waiter finished pouring the wine and set the bottle in between us and left.

Porter held up his wine glass. "*Cin cin.*"

"*Saluti!*" I clinked my glass against his. "I toyed with being a Classics major, that's why I read it."

"Did you? I didn't know that."

"Before I met you. One semester and I knew I was on the wrong path."

"How?"

"By reading *The Iliad* and *The Odyssey*. About the sheep, though. They do have a tendency to wander."

"Okay, still, that story never made sense to me," Porter said. "I always just assumed that it was the guy's favorite sheep or something, and that's why he went after it." He lifted the small glass jar of jam and sniffed it, then picked up a spoon. "Ox Eyes said this came from their own fig trees," he said, smoothing a spoonful of jam onto a piece of bread and handing it to me.

"You have to read it with the other parable in the same chapter of the Gospel of Luke, about the woman who loses a coin," I said. "The shepherd has ninety-nine other sheep, and the woman has nine other coins, but they both go all out to find the one that's been lost."

"Sheep may be stupid," Porter said, "but they make damn good cheese."

"This *stagionato* is incredible. I don't understand how letting cheese get old makes it better, but wow." I reached for another piece and added it to the stack of cheese already teetering on top of my bread. "Remember when you had that aged steak at the restaurant in Pinehurst? The smell nearly knocked me out."

"I was a younger man then. I don't think I could handle aged beef now," Porter said. He held up his wine glass. "But how about this Brunello? We should go to Montalcino when you come back. Stock up for winter."

An image of the woman in the church flashed in front of me as I studiously avoided Porter's unspoken question. I doubted that she'd ever had a day to just enjoy her life, without worrying about where her next meal was coming from, much less the time or money to stock up on wine just for the hell of it.

"Are you going to explain what the sheep story means?" Porter said, interrupting my thoughts.

I finished chewing and took a sip of wine.

"You have to put it in context," I said. "The people who first heard that story would have placed a lot of value on a sheep or a coin."

"Because they were poor."

"Very. And so the point is that for God, who is not poor at all, each of us is just as valuable as the coin or sheep was to them. So valuable that the idea of letting one of us stay lost is unacceptable."

"I'm not sure I buy that," Porter said. "If God thinks we're so valuable, why does he let such terrible things happen to us?"

"Well, that's the question, isn't it?" I said slowly, lowering the bread and cheese masterpiece I'd been creating to my plate. "I've asked myself that a million times."

Porter reached across the table and patted my arm. "I know you have. That was a stupid thing to say."

I dabbed at my eyes, then put my napkin back on my lap and picked up my wine glass while Porter smeared another slice of bread with jam.

"By the way, it's out of style to refer to God as *he* anymore," I said. "Outside of Italy, anyway."

"Here," he said, piling prosciutto and cheese on top of the jam. "Eat this."

"Thanks." I added it to my plate. "For what it's worth, David would answer your question about bad things happening by saying that there is an element of chaos beyond our control that will touch each of our lives at some point. And because no one gets spared and we are all connected, we have to help each other." I leaned back and took a sip of wine. "He'd tell you about *ubuntu,* which I know you're dying to hear about."

"Should I drink more first? I feel like you're going to tell me, regardless."

"It's a Zulu idea of interconnectedness, generally summed up as 'I am because we are'," I told him. "David would tell you that *ubuntu* is why we have to forgive each other, because we're all flawed, and we all need each other."

"Hmm," Porter said, his mouth full of bread.

"And forgive ourselves, too."

Porter swallowed and said, "I suck at all that."

"David would say that we have to forgive ourselves because God forgives us, so if we don't, we're rejecting God's mercy and holding ourselves out as a higher tribunal than God, which is hubris in its highest form." I reached for the carafe and refilled Porter's water glass, then my own. "I think C.S. Lewis said that, actually, about the tribunal."

"Hubris in its highest form," Porter repeated. "I vote to add that to our list of band names."

"I'll put it on the list."

The waiter returned and presented a platter with a flourish. *"Ecco la carne grigliata,"* he said. The smell of grilled meat made my mouth water. Porter made room for the platter on the table and switched to Italian to ask the waiter for another bottle of water.

"Sure," the waiter said in English. "I find with my ox-eyes and bring to you *subito.*"

I buried my face in my napkin while Porter burst out laughing.

Quattro

Porter was sitting at the kitchen table with his reading glasses perched on the end of his nose, shuffling through a stack of mail, when Oliver and I came back from our walk yesterday.

"I was getting worried," he said, reaching out to pat Oliver. "You worn out, buddy?"

I hung up my jacket, unwound the scarf from around my neck and dropped it on the counter, and filled Oliver's bowl with water. When I placed the bowl on the floor, he dropped the stick he had been carrying for the past hour and put his entire snout in the bowl, blew a few bubbles, and then proceeded to drench the floor.

"Where'd you go?"

"Past the falling-down house and back," I said, reaching for a kitchen towel to dry the floor. "Not that far. Anything good in the mail?"

Porter shook his head. "Immigration nonsense."

"I thought you had that sorted?"

"I did. But someone's decided to make a problem."

"About what?"

"A youthful indiscretion. How about we take a drink out to the terrace? Think you'd be warm enough with a blanket?"

"Sure. I'll meet you out there."

I went upstairs and washed my face, then grabbed two blankets from the couch and joined Porter outside.

He was pouring a glass of wine that he handed to me, then poured himself one before dropping onto one of the lounge chairs. I placed a blanket on his legs and sat down on the other chair. As soon as I did, Oliver jumped up beside me, curled himself to fit next to my hip, heaved a great sigh, and propped his head on the chair's arm so he could look at Porter.

"I don't think anyone has ever looked at me with that much love," I said.

Oliver craned his neck backwards at the sound of my voice, then licked me and returned his head to the arm of the chair. Porter reached over and scratched his head.

"He knows you're unhappy," Porter said.

"I don't even remember how to be unhappy," I said, stroking Oliver's back. "I'm too lost to be any way at all."

"How do we get you found?"

I willed the tears that sprang to my eyes to stay put. Every day that I didn't cry counted as a victory, and so far, I hadn't cried.

"I have no idea," I said. "David says time will help."

Porter nodded. "He's right."

"It's been almost seven months."

"In the grand scheme of things, that's not very long. You've got to give yourself a break, Beth."

"What I've got to do is deal with the colossal shit show in London," I said. It still shocked me that when I'd gotten Porter's call, I'd simply turned my back on the ten-car pileup that was my life and walked away.

"I still don't understand why you think that's a good idea."

I shrugged. "Because he's my husband, Porter. That's my house. Those are my things in the closet, my furniture, my dishes and spoons. I can't keep wearing your sweatpants and pretending this is my life."

"Is that what you're doing?" He picked up the wine bottle, saw that my glass was still full, and refilled his own. "Pretending?"

"I cook and take walks with Oliver and I wait for you to need me to do something so I don't feel like the world's biggest loser, but the truth is, Porter, you're a better cook than I am and Oliver gets plenty of exercise without me. He's better company, too."

"I'm not the enemy here." Porter set the wine bottle on the table with a thud.

"I know. I'm sorry."

He was quiet for a minute. "Fine. We'll get a ticket online. I'll drive you to Rome and pick you up when you come back. How long will it take you to pack your stuff? A couple days?"

"I can't just—"

"You can get a lawyer online, too," Porter continued, as if I hadn't spoken. "Do the consultations on the phone. My lawyer's in Milan and I've only met him once. Everything else is on the phone."

"It's not that easy." I poked at a blister on the side of my thumb. I'd swept the terrace free of dog fur and leaves and my hands looked like I'd done hard labor.

"The airline will charge you for extra luggage but that's still the best way to get your stuff here."

"I just don't think it's going to be that easy."

"Sure it will. You just need to tell me how long you'll be in London. When you come back, we'll have my guy get going on the immigration paperwork for you, too. I've got to call him anyway, about this latest bullshit."

Porter made it sound so simple. Just fly back to London, pack up my belongings, and return to Italy where some rose-tinted version of *la dolce vita* would unfold. But what he was failing to take into account was that I'd had an actual life in London. A life that had once included a daughter and a husband, an assignment editor, friends and acquaintances and a house I loved. A life in which Porter was a distant, bittersweet memory.

"Can we table this discussion for another time?" I said finally.

"Sure. But you need to have a plan."

"That's what you're not getting," I snapped. "I can't make a plan, Porter. I can't even make a decision. I don't trust my judgment about anything."

"Including me? And the fact that I'm just trying to help you?"

I didn't answer and looked down at Oliver. "I forgot to feed him. Do you need anything from inside?"

Porter shook his head.

In the kitchen I scooped Oliver's kibble into a bowl, added a spoonful of olive oil and a parmesan rind I'd been saving for risotto, and washed the few dishes in the sink while he ate. When his bowl was empty, Oliver looked up at me expectantly, wagging his tail.

"I guess you want to go back out there, huh?"

He walked to the kitchen door in response.

We went back out to the terrace. As I passed the lemon trees I caught a whiff of citrus, and a memory came back like a knife.

"You okay?" Porter asked.

I nodded. "Just tired."

We sat in silence for another half hour, then Porter suggested we go in and watch a movie. I gathered up the blankets and he took the glasses and wine bottle inside and we met on the couch to watch a documentary he picked called *Team Foxcatcher*, about John DuPont, the heir to the chemical company fortune.

DuPont was a neglected kid, a lifelong misfit who moved from obsession to obsession. At one point, his obsession was wrestling, and he built a multimillion-dollar training facility on the family estate in Pennsylvania and offered free housing and financial support to the best wrestlers in America. But he became jealous of his wrestlers' camaraderie, and one day, fueled by cocaine and paranoia, DuPont went to the wrestler Dave Schultz's home and shot him dead, right in front of Schultz's wife. A jury sent DuPont to prison, where he died.

When the documentary ended, Porter grabbed his laptop. "I gotta know more about this. I mean, I think when DuPont was coked out of his mind and barricaded in his house, that would have been my cue to leave."

"Yeh, but they were all dependent on him," I said. "He was providing everything for those wrestlers and their families. Where were they going to go?"

Porter was quiet for a minute.

"You're right," he said finally, closing his laptop. "We all had to kowtow to Claire and The Colonel, too, because they held the purse strings. We could never complain, or even talk about what was really going on."

"Like what?"

"Like my dad. He was a mess, right? He needed help. But no one ever talked about it. They just left me and Ford to deal with him."

"We never really talked much about your family," I said, "back when we were—back then."

"I can see why my mom left him," Porter said, leaning forward to set his laptop on the coffee table. "But leaving me and Ford? I'm not even a parent and I can't imagine doing that."

"It's unfathomable."

"And after she left, it was like poof! She didn't exist. We couldn't even say her name in front of my grandparents. No one acknowledged the situation, much less explained to us what was going on."

"Did they actually say that, that you couldn't say your mother's name?"

Porter shook his head. "It was one of many unspoken rules. Like mandatory Friday night dinner."

"I always wondered—did you call them Claire and The Colonel to their faces?"

Porter nodded. "I think Claire would rather have been shot than called Grandma, and everyone called him The Colonel. His real name was George." Porter laughed lightly. "I had a stomachache every Friday morning until they died. I still do, sometimes."

"Because of the dinners?'

He nodded. "Ford and I would rush home from whatever sports practice we had and shower and dress and wait on the curb for my dad to pick us up and take us to the big house. If we were even a few minutes late, Claire would be furious." Porter took off his reading glasses and set them on the arm of the couch to rub his eyes. "We'd jump out as soon as my dad slowed the car down. He'd head to the Club and we'd race to the door."

"Your dad didn't eat with you?"

"He wasn't invited."

Sitting in their pressed khakis and navy blazers, Porter told me, he and Ford waited for the one thing they actually loved about dinner with Claire, which was the food Delia carried in on silver trays.

"The rest of the week we ate TV dinners, and I can't tell you how much I looked forward to that food. Roasts and vegetables and mashed potatoes... Delia was a better cook than most of the chefs I've worked with." He shook his head. "Of course, you couldn't say that in front of Claire."

"Why not?"

"Because in Claire's world, complimenting the Beef Wellington was like, I don't know, being Marlon Brando in a wife-beater screaming *Stella!* in the street. Totally over the top."

"Really?"

Porter nodded. "It would suggest you wanted more, and Claire never *wanted* anything. Which probably explains why my father was an only child."

I raised my eyebrows.

"There were lots of dinner rules, too. No talk of school, which I find utterly boring," Porter said, imitating his grandmother's lock-jawed speech. "No mention of people I cannot abide, which includes your father. And not one word about politics. I've lived through a World War and those horrid Asian affairs, and that's quite enough for one lifetime."

"So what was left to talk about?"

"Debutante balls. People at the Club."

"Oh, how fascinating."

Porter laughed. "Right? Then after dinner, Claire would go to her garden room and talk on the phone, and Delia would sneak us a second helping in the kitchen while she cleared the table, and then we'd go to The Colonel's library."

In the library, Delia would remove the old man's empty supper tray and replace it with a glass of port and his humidor.

"That humidor was gorgeous," Porter said. "Spanish cedar on the inside, walnut on the outside... When I was designing the bar at my restaurant, the look and feel of that humidor was what I based it on."

"I wish I'd seen your restaurant."

Porter nodded. "I do, too. Anyway, my job as a kid was to cut the cigar, and Ford got to light it."

Then, he said, the brothers would sprawl on the carpet while their grandfather smoked and regaled them with stories of the Confederate heroes they were named for.

"I'm lucky, because Porter Alexander wasn't that bad a guy, but did you know that Nathan Bedford Forrest went on to be the first Grand Wizard of the KKK?"

"Seriously? Poor Ford! But maybe people didn't make the connection since he was just called Ford?"

"It definitely could have been worse. Just think, my name could have been Stonewall Jackson Haven. Or Bloody Bill Anderson Haven."

"Your life was like a novel, Porter. Like *Gone with the Wind* meets *The Great Gatsby*. Mine was like...is there even a book about a middle-class family in central New York? I didn't even know anyone with a maid, much less one that lived in the house and cooked."

"That was just at the big house, though. At home it was just me and Ford and my dad. Our place was a disaster."

"Yeh, but you went to fancy schools and dances and stuff."

Porter nodded. "Sure. Cotillion. Everyone did."

"And debutante balls."

"Sure."

"My friends and I went to the mall. We hung out in people's basements."

"We did that stuff, too. And Ford and I always worked. I was a lifeguard at the Club, which was convenient for hauling my dad out of the bar every night." Porter looked at me. "And I think you know that I would have traded all the cotillions and the fancy school to have a dad I could respect."

I nodded. "I know."

"Thank God for Ford, that's all I can say. He always showed up," Porter said. "Every single game, no matter how far away. And he made his friends come, too."

"Jenny's brothers were like that," I said. "There were five Fife brothers and they used to hug her goodbye in the morning when they got to school. I wanted to be the second Fife sister more than anything in the world."

"My whole goal in life has been to make Ford proud and not end up some douchebag trust fund baby."

"I'm sure your brother is proud of you."

Porter shrugged. "I went off the rails a few times. But by the time Claire and The Colonel died, I was on my own and hadn't taken money from them in a long time."

He and Ford felt it was the highest level of irony that their grandparents, who could barely stand to be in each other's company, had died together, Porter said. Their 1969 Daimler Sovereign, which had purred along Virginia's leafy byways for nearly thirty-five years, rolled down an embankment one Sunday afternoon and deposited them in six feet of the James River. The policeman who came to the door told Porter's father it was likely they both could have survived, given that the indestructible Daimler was upright in its relatively shallow bath, but they appeared to have been drinking heavily, which compromised their ability to save themselves.

"See what I mean? Claire hated my dad for being a drunk, but where did she think he learned it?" Porter said. "Everyone acted like they were saints and it was so great that they died together, but hello? My grandmother had been having an affair for, like, sixty years."

"Seriously? Please tell me it was with a gardener or a pool boy?"

Porter shook his head. "No, no. She would never screw the help. It was a jowly old guy named Hampton Fitzhugh the Fourth. Or maybe the Fifth. I think he was at VMI while she was at Stuart Hall, and then he went off to war and got engaged to someone else and she met The Colonel at some dinner-dance in Washington when he was down from West Point."

"But they still loved each other all those years, Claire and Hampton? That's kind of sweet."

"He sat behind me at the funeral and cried so loud I couldn't even hear the priest. And the louder he cried, the louder the

West Point contingent got, coughing and clearing their throats to drown him out," Porter said. "Ford and I could barely keep it together, it was so absurd."

"They were expressing their expectorate disdain," I said.

Porter laughed. "Are you going to add that to our list?"

Somewhere in my dad's police academy trunk was a list of band names scribbled on a brown paper bag. Awesome names like *Rejected by Porpoises*, which we came up with after we tried to swim out to a pod of dolphins in Florida. *Creamy Bubbles*, from a sommelier's description of champagne that we overheard in a fancy restaurant. *Six Sigmas*, which was the number of fraternity brothers my friend Kick had once proudly boasted of bedding on Spring Break. I hadn't opened that trunk in years, but I was sure the list was still in there.

After his grandparents' funeral, Porter said, there was a reception at the Club and then the remaining Haven men returned to Monument Avenue to eat the ham and green beans and deviled eggs Delia laid out while the lawyer read the wills. Along with shares in IBM, Coca Cola, RJ Reynolds, and Boeing, plus enough Oriental carpets and furniture to fill multiple homes, Ford got Claire's diamond ring.

"It was massive. A cluster of white and yellow diamonds that looked like a bird shit on her finger, it was so big."

"Courtney must have been thrilled," I said.

"Ford didn't give it to her. He sold it."

"Because it was too big?"

Porter cleared his throat and grinned at me. "Well, that…and I may have wondered out loud how many times it had touched Hampton Fitzhugh's dick."

I started to laugh. Oliver looked up, startled by the unexpected noise, then put his head back on his folded paws.

"It was a legitimate concern," Porter said. "Ford had it cleaned, but he said he would never be able to see it on

Courtney's finger without seeing Hampton Fitzhugh's wrinkly old man dick, too. So he sold it."

"And to think you could have been the lucky recipient of Hampton Fitzhugh's dick ring, if only you'd been the older brother," I said.

"I know. That's the real tragedy, isn't it?" Porter nudged Oliver. "Come on, Ollie. Time for bed."

I took our wine glasses to the kitchen while Porter closed up the house. As we parted in the hallway upstairs, I put my hand on his arm and stopped him.

"That thing you said, about how your family never acknowledged what was really going on? That's why I need to go back to London," I said. "I can't just keep my head in the sand and hope that things are going to fix themselves."

Porter was quiet for a minute, then nodded. "If you really think it will help, then you have to go back," he said. Then he turned and went to his room.

Cinque

Ispent the morning cleaning my room and putting my few belongings in a duffle bag while Porter went to deliver wood to the old lady down the street. When he came back, Oliver pushed past him to get in the kitchen, where I was doing the dishes and wondering what to make for lunch.

"I'm kind of burnt out on working in the barn. Want to take another road trip?" Porter asked. "I'd like to talk to you about something before you leave, anyway."

"Sure," I said, swallowing down the lump of anxiety that rose in my throat. "Where should we go?"

"Florence? Or maybe somewhere more peaceful. How about La Verna? We can grab a pizza on the way back."

It started pouring on the way to La Verna and Porter's car, a black Fiat that whined at a high pitch when too much was asked of it, hydroplaned in and out of our lane and complained audibly on the switchbacks. Luckily the rain subsided to a light drizzle as we reached the top of the mountain, which is called either Monte Penna or Monte Alvernia, depending on who you ask.

Porter folded up the umbrella he'd brought from the car and tucked it under his arm as we passed under the arch that led inside the cluster of medieval stone buildings that make up La Verna. The whole sanctuary is perched on top of enormous gray boulders that are divided by deep clefts and covered in green moss, and it seems to be holding on by faith and willpower alone, forever in danger of toppling into the valley below.

"Can you imagine walking here from Assisi?" I said.

"No way. Especially not in sandals."

"Even riding a horse would be exhausting. How far do you think it is?"

"From Assisi?" Porter thought for a minute. "About seventy-five miles."

A count named Orlando Cattani originally owned the land where La Verna is, but one day, Cattani heard Saint Francis preach and was so inspired that he gave La Verna to Francis and his followers as a place of retreat. Francis made the trek from Assisi several times until 1224, when he arrived, ill and feverish, for the last time. During that final visit, he was praying at the foot of a cross when wounds spontaneously appeared on his hands and feet and torso, wounds that were in the same place as the ones Jesus received when he was nailed to the cross. These *stigmata* bled continuously for two years, until Francis died at the age of forty-four.

I did some reading about *stigmata* one afternoon and found out that Francis was the first to receive the wounds, but a few others got them later, like feisty Catherine of Siena, who chopped off her hair and went on a hunger strike so she wouldn't have to marry the widower of her sixteen-year-old sister who'd died in childbirth. Catherine also refused to become a nun, and was eventually allowed to do as she pleased, which was to minister to the sick and write prolifically about religious piety and be a sort of diplomat on behalf of the Pope.

After Catherine died, people wanted to bring her body back to Siena and put her on display for the faithful, but they knew the Roman guards they'd have to pass on the way out of town wouldn't allow it, so, being creative and resourceful fellows, they decided to chop off Catherine's head, which was much more portable, and just bring that back to Siena. When the Roman guards stopped them on the way out of town, the body snatchers said a quick prayer, and lo and behold, Catherine's head turned into rose petals. The petals eventually changed back, and Catherine's head, and her thumb, which someone must have pocketed during the whole head-removal effort, are on display in the church in Siena.

Saint Rita of Cascia, the patron saint of abused women, bad marriages, heartbreak, and the lonely, also received *stigmata*, but unlike Catherine's, which were in the form of pain that did not leave a permanent mark, Rita got a thorn in her forehead. Poor Rita was married off when she was not even a teenager, despite begging her parents to let her be a nun, and apparently her husband was a real prize pig, abusive in several different ways. But through her tender loving ministrations, Rita made him a better man. That's such an odious narrative, about the long-suffering woman who puts up with her brutish husband's temper tantrums and makes him a better person, but there you go. Rita probably stuck the thorn in her head herself, hoping to get away from him.

I meandered across the courtyard at La Verna while Porter took off to walk the path that winds through the forest around the sanctuary. I took a quick look at the murals about the life of Francis before moving on to the della Robbia ceramics, and then to the relics room.

Italy is full of relics, but one of the things at La Verna that you don't see everywhere is the *disciplina*, the whip of choice for fervent flagellators. Apparently in medieval times, the body, with all of its impulses and desires, was seen as something of a rogue outlaw that needed to be controlled, and flagellation was a means of atoning for the body's sins. I was standing in front of a *disciplina*, imaging what it must feel like, when Porter found me.

"Have you had enough of whips and finger bones?" he asked.

"I feel oddly at home here."

"Because you're a relic?"

"Yep," I said. "Just the thumb of my previous self."

Porter laughed and slung his arm around my neck and kissed the top of my head and I had to fight the urge to wrap my arms around him and hold on tight. When we were first dating, he'd told me that Delia was the only person who ever hugged him when he was a kid, that she used to wrap her arms around him and rock him from side to side and whisper *Everything's gonna be alright, little man* over and over before he left his grandparents' house, and he used to hug me all the time when he was my boyfriend. He never let go first.

"I'm starving," he said, letting go of me and putting his hands in his pockets. "You ready for pizza?"

I nodded and followed him outside and across the courtyard, pausing to look in the window of the small gift shop run by monks.

"Did you ever read anything about the mind-body connection, Porter?"

"I don't think so. But we did have someone come in once to teach the team how to meditate our way out of injuries. Is that what you mean?"

"Maybe. I was thinking about this experiment I read about once, with hypnotized patients. The psychologists told them they were going to be touched with something red-hot, but the patients got touched with a pencil instead. But some of them got blisters, anyway, as if they'd really been burned."

"Who volunteers to be burned?"

"That's a good question. But I was thinking, maybe that explains the *stigmata* Francis got. Maybe if you believe in something so much, you can manifest it physically."

Porter twisted his mouth. "Hmm. I don't know." He patted his stomach. "Did I mention I'm starving? We need to manifest a pizza before I get hangry."

We stopped at the small pizzeria at the base of the mountain and as soon as we'd shucked off our jackets and ordered, Porter cleared his throat.

"So," he said, "I've tried really hard not to pressure you. Not to ask what you plan to do."

"I know."

"I don't think going back to London is a good idea, but obviously it's your call," he said. "But I don't think you should stay too long."

"I really don't have a plan."

"Why give Crawford the chance to do more damage? You don't want to stay married to him, do you?"

"Even if I did, Porter, it's probably not an option. I left. I abandoned the marriage, or whatever you call it when you go to Italy for a week and stay for four months."

"But you said he was involved with someone else."

A lump rose in my throat. "Yeh. He is."

"So you didn't actually abandon anything. He did. And by the way, Beth, in case you don't realize it? You deserve better than that."

I didn't answer.

"Divorce his ass. Get a lawyer and take everything he's got."

"Even if I wanted to do that, I kind of doubt it's an option after I've been staying at my old boyfriend's house for four months."

"Does he know you're with me?"

I shrugged. "I don't know. And honestly, what difference does it make? I don't care about the money. He can have the house and all our stuff, too. None of it matters without my daughter."

"You feel like that now, but you won't always feel that way."

"Yes, I will," I snapped.

Porter reached across the table and squeezed my fingers. "I didn't mean—that didn't come out right." The waitress arrived with the pizzas and he passed me his napkin to dry my eyes and asked for another one.

I picked the grilled vegetables off the top of my pizza, then pushed the rest towards Porter. We didn't talk while he finished his food, and then mine, and then asked for the check.

"You okay?" he asked as we walked back to the car.

I nodded. "I'm sorry."

He waited for me to pull my coat inside the car before closing my door and walking around to the driver's side.

"You don't have to apologize, you know," he said, settling into the driver's seat. "Love means never having to say you're sorry."

I started to laugh and cry at the same time. "I hate that damn movie."

Porter looked over at me. "I know. That's why I said it."

"It reminds me of Kick."

"Now I'm going to cry."

"It's in her top three, I think," I said, pulling a ratty wad of Kleenex out of my pocket and blowing my nose. "She likes *Pretty Woman* more, though."

"Only because she's a hooker."

"Not a hooker. Just determined," I said, hiccupping loudly. "And I could name twenty of your friends who slept around way more than Kick did."

"Fair point. I still never liked her, though."

"Only because she didn't fall at your feet like every other girl," I said. "And that was only because she knew I'd kick her ass if she did."

"Somehow I missed all the girls falling at my feet," he said, putting the car in reverse and draping his arm over my seat while he backed out of the parking lot. "You should have pointed them out to me."

I thought about Kick as he drove us home. She'd plopped down next to me in Econ 10 the first day of spring semester freshman year, decked out head to toe in pink and green sorority duds, and until she wrote her name and phone number on the top of my notes in purple bubble letters, I thought her name was "Tick." When I got to know her, I found out that, as was the case with so many Southern girls, there was real substance and strength under the pastel candy-coating. She would occasionally interrupt her monologue of froth with a really insightful observation or something wickedly funny, and she was a whiz at math, which I found out when we had Statistics together sophomore year. That was also when Kick's father lost his job. She couldn't afford the dues anymore and had to go inactive with her sorority, so we started hanging out together socially, too, where my role was to play wingman to her mission to snare a boyfriend who played a televised sport so she could throw him in the face of the sorority sisters who'd forgotten their pledges of eternal sisterhood and discarded her like last season's dress.

"You're so lucky," Kick would sigh, steering with her knees so she could apply another layer of mascara in the rearview mirror. "You don't care about how you look. I wish I could be that way."

That wasn't really true. I'd just spent twelve years wearing a school uniform and, when I wasn't in a plaid kilt, jeans and a parka. One time I actually let Kick give me a makeover, but about two minutes into it, after fighting over the fact that I wouldn't let her thin my eyebrows, she grabbed a handful of my hair, heaved a huge sigh, and said, "I've never really thought about not being blonde," and that was the end of that.

But I enjoyed her company, and by senior year, Kick and I had a well-established Thursday night routine that included Kick detailing her future, including a plantation-style brick mansion, a country club membership, and a smoking-hot husband, as we got ready to go out. I once made the mistake of asking if there wasn't something more she should be aiming for.

"Like what, a career? Do you want me to be a math major and teach?" she asked, pausing from lining her lips to shudder as if the thought made her physically sick. "I'd rather die."

Despite our differences, there was something I found inspiring about Kick. Remember that Carly Simon song, "Boys in the Trees," about how stifling it is that girls are meant to wait to be noticed while the boys run wild? Kick was out there in the trees with the boys, hanging upside down with her panties showing. I admired that.

As Porter merged onto the four-lane road towards Umbria, I wondered what Kick would do in my current predicament. She would probably fly back to London, confront Crawford, then max out his credit cards on a manhunt in Monte Carlo.

"What do you think Kick would do in my place?" I asked Porter.

"*What would Kick do?* is not a question any sane person should ask."

"No, I'm serious. What do you think she'd do about Crawford?"

Porter glanced at me. "Get a lawyer. Leave him. Make a new life."

"I think you're saying what you think I should do."

"They're the same thing," he said. "Trust me, it will never happen again that my thoughts align with Kick's, but this time, they do."

I was quiet while Porter got the ticket from the toll booth and drove the deserted two-lane road home.

It wasn't until we turned onto the gravel road that led to the house that I said, "I hope you know that I will always be grateful to you for the last four months, Porter."

"That sounds like you're leaving for good."

"I don't know what I'm going to find when I get home. Maybe things will be different."

Porter laughed. "Sure. Maybe he'll apologize for cheating and abandoning you when you lost your daughter, and you'll take him back and live happily ever after."

"People do change, Porter."

"Not when they were pricks to start with," he said, turning into the driveway.

"You don't even know him. And Mia was his daughter, too."

"I know enough."

I turned towards the window and rolled my eyes. "Right."

The moon ducked in and out of view as we passed through the alley of cypress trees that lined the long driveway.

"You can let him walk all over you if that's what you want to do," Porter said. "But that's not the Beth I know."

"You knew me thirty years ago, Porter. I'm not the same person now."

"That must be true, because the Beth I knew would never go back to Crawford."

I threw open the door before the car was fully stopped, slammed it shut, walked right past Oliver, and went to bed.

Porter was waiting in the kitchen the next morning when I came downstairs, dragging my duffle bag behind me. He nodded in my direction and said, "There's coffee on the stove."

Oliver sat on my foot while I drank my coffee. I held my cup with one hand and scratched behind his ears with the other.

"We need to leave soon," Porter said. "Two hours to Rome, and that's if there's no problem on the way."

"I'm ready whenever you are."

"Oliver, you want to go for a ride?"

We didn't talk at all on the drive to Fiumicino. Porter turned on *Radio Subasio* and I occupied myself by staring out the window and trying to catch my tears in Kleenex before he could see them. Oliver stretched out on the backseat until we exited the highway for the airport, at which point he sat up and poked his face between the seats.

"Move, dammit. This is a merge lane, not a dead end," Porter said as we arrived at the bottom of the exit ramp and entered the roundabout. He downshifted so abruptly that Oliver's paws skittered against the console and he fell against the seat. I reached back and held his collar to steady him.

The car with Swiss plates in front of us braked again and Porter leaned on the horn.

"Go back to Zurich, you stupid fuck," he yelled, accelerating to swerve around the Mercedes and nearly broadsiding a truck.

"They're used to orderly traffic, I guess."

"Then they came to the wrong place," Porter said. "Look for British Airways. I think it's Terminal Three."

By the time we got to the terminal, Porter had sworn at several more people and nearly taken out an entire Indian family shuffling down the access road.

"Get out of the road," he yelled, gunning the engine and barely clearing the side of their overloaded luggage cart. "And get some real fucking shoes."

The short-term parking area was crowded, despite the signs reminding everyone that there was a fifteen-minute limit. Porter inched the Fiat along the row of parked cars and stopped behind one that was idling, with two people locked in a passionate embrace in the front seat.

"It's called *Kiss and Go*, assholes, not make a baby and stay for hours."

After Porter had hit the horn twice, the man in the passenger seat finally got out of the car, gave Porter the finger, took his time extracting his bag from the back seat, and headed into the terminal. His girlfriend took such a long time backing up that I thought Porter was going to get out and physically pull her car out of the space, but he managed to remain seated until she had barely cleared the parking spot, then he turned the Fiat into the space so sharply that my head smacked against the window and Oliver fell over again.

Porter snapped off the ignition, reached behind his seat to grab a leash, and clipped it onto Oliver's collar before getting out and opening the door so Oliver could jump down. By the time I was out of the car, Porter had released the trunk and was holding my duffle bag.

"I guess this is it," he said.

I nodded and knelt to bury my face in Oliver's fur. Oliver stood still for a moment, enduring the embrace, then stepped backwards and licked my face, his tail beating a rhythm against the back bumper. I wiped my eyes on the sleeve of my jacket and got to my feet.

"Thank you," I said. "For everything."

Porter's expression softened. He set the bag on the ground and held out his arms and I stepped into them and buried my face in his chest. We remained that way, locked together tightly, for several minutes until Porter pulled away, held me at arm's length, and said, "I hope you get what you want, Beth. But you're always welcome to come back."

I nodded mutely and made myself pick up my duffle bag, pat the pocket of my jacket where my passport and boarding pass were, hoist the bag onto my shoulder, and walk into the terminal without turning around. Like Lot's wife, I knew that if I looked back, I would turn to stone and never be able to leave.

While I was in the security line, my phone dinged. It was a photo of Oliver sitting next to a small, Formica-topped table.

Stopped for coffee. Can be back at airport in 30 min. Say the word.

The urge to ask him to come back was so strong that I had to turn the phone off.

I couldn't think about Porter anymore.

London was waiting.

Sei

It wasn't until I was on the subway from London Bridge to St. John's Wood that I started to panic. Part of me really hoped that I would open the door and walk in on an intimate scene that would make things crystal clear. I'd simply throw my clothes into a suitcase, call a taxi, and go to the nicest hotel I could think of, compliments of American Express. Or maybe I would try the door and find that the locks had been changed, and end up at the same hotel and send for my clothes later. Either way, I would know for sure that my suspicions had been founded and that my life with Crawford was over.

But no such luck. My key worked just fine. I dropped my bag in the entryway and went downstairs to the kitchen, which was spotless, before tiptoeing up the two flights of stairs to the master bedroom. The house was empty. I went back down to the kitchen and poured myself a glass of water and turned on my phone.

Let me know you made it safely.

I did, I wrote back. *Thank you for everything, Porter. I'll be in touch.*

Three dots appeared and then disappeared. I put the phone back in my pocket, drank the water in one gulp, and left the glass on the counter while I went up to your room.

A thousand times I'd come upstairs and found you curled up on this window seat, Mia, an array of books strewn on the wooden floor around you and your feet propped high against the wall. The wide wooden bench, with its thick orange cushion and pink and orange Indian print pillows, was your favorite perch as you typed on your laptop or texted on your phone.

I made a pile of pillows on one end and stretched out on the bench, leaning back into the soft cushions. The paint was marked in shadowy prints where your feet had rested on the wall, and I kicked off my shoes and placed my socked feet on top of yours and turned to watch the raindrops hit the windowpane and slide down the glass. The bare branches of the trees moved in the wind and scraped the window.

I inhaled deeply and caught the faintest whiff of you, the citrusy smell of the *Acqua di Parma Meditteraneo* that you and Devon both wore. The scent reminded me of Italy and my failed attempt to make the drizzle cake you and Salma loved so much with lemons from Porter's terrace.

"What's wrong?" Porter had asked, leaning against the doorjamb with his boot halfway off. "Are you okay?"

I shook my head.

"What's going on?"

"I just was making this cake and... I don't know. I don't know what's wrong with me, Porter. I just miss my daughter so much. I miss my life. I'm sure that sounds stupid—"

"It doesn't."

"—but how can I be fifty years old and not belong any place? I haven't worked in months. I don't know what I'm doing. I used to have an anchor. A home. And now I could disappear and it would be like I never existed."

Porter quickly pulled off his boot and gestured towards the table. "Sit down."

"No, it's okay. I need to finish the cake and make lunch."

"Lunch can wait. The cake can wait." He pulled out a chair and waited for me to sit down before lowering himself opposite me. "What happened?"

"I don't know. I was fine and then I just—it all hit me. That everything is gone."

"Mia, you mean?"

"Of course Mia. Everything is so pointless. I don't know why I get up in the morning. Why I'm still alive."

Porter sat silently, only getting up to grab a dish towel, which he handed to me to dry my face.

"I am not okay, Porter. You realize that, right? I've been wearing the same clothes for weeks. I can't sleep. I have no plan. I don't even recognize myself. And I'm dreading Christmas. I honestly don't think I'll survive it, I really don't."

He nodded. "I know. But listen, we can—"

"What's the best thing you've ever done?" I interrupted.

Porter started to answer and then hesitated. "I don't know. Maybe the—"

"See? It's such an easy question for me. The best thing I ever did was be her mother. And now she's gone. And I just don't see the point of carrying on, because for the rest of my life, nothing will ever mean anything again."

"I understand."

"No, you don't."

"You're right. I don't. I'm trying to, though."

I put my head down on the table. Porter scooted around next to me and put his hand on my back and rubbed gentle circles, but after a couple of minutes, I felt like there were ten pounds of pressure in my face and I lifted my head and took deep, open-mouthed breaths.

"You okay?"

"My sinuses. I can't breathe when I cry."

"I remember," Porter said. "Can I make you a cup of coffee? Or some lunch?"

I shook my head. "I think I'll just go upstairs and lie down. I'll finish the cake later, I promise." I pushed my chair back and started to rise but Porter put his hand on mine.

"You do have a home, you know. For what it's worth, you do have a home."

I pulled my hand away. "This is your home, Porter, not mine."

I never finished the cake.

I took my feet off the wall and curled on my side to look out at the rain and our tiny back garden and wondered what Porter was doing. If he was reading, his brow furrowed and his glasses perched on the end of his nose, with Oliver napping in front of the fire, his fur smelling of the rosemary and lavender bushes he liked to roll in. That life seemed a million miles away, like a fever dream that had finally abated, even though I'd been there only hours earlier.

I must have fallen asleep then, because the next thing I knew, the overhead light was on and Crawford was standing over me.

"Look what the cat dragged in."

"Hi," I said, struggling to sit up.

"To what do I owe this great surprise?"

"I should have let you know I was coming. I'm sorry."

"That definitely would have been appropriate."

"Okay, well, it's still my house, too, Crawford."

He laughed sharply. "We'll have to talk about that." He turned and started to walk away. "Are you coming downstairs?" he asked, pausing in the doorway.

I nodded.

"Fine," he said. "I could use a drink."

Porter hated vodka and said it made him mean, but it had always been Crawford's drink of choice and vodka tonics were the one cocktail I made well. I made two of them, heavy on the vodka, light on the tonic, with a squeeze of fresh lime juice and an expertly sliced twist of lemon hanging off the edge of the glass, while I browned grilled cheese sandwiches on the stove. When they were done, I took the drinks and sandwiches into the sitting room on a tray and put one of each down for Crawford, who was stoking the fire.

I curled my feet under me in the wingback chair, sipping my drink and looking at the Oriental carpet, the heavy drapes, and the expensive tapestry on the wall. This had always been my favorite room, cozy and close on a dreary day, but now I found it suffocating.

"What prompted you to come back?" Crawford asked, startling me out of my thoughts.

"I don't know," I said. "It was time, I guess."

"Time for what?"

I shrugged. "I don't know. To see how things are here."

"Porter tired of you?"

My stomach clenched. Of course he knew.

"We're just friends. He offered me a place to stay. He has a big house in the country."

"How convenient."

I studied Crawford closely, unsure if this was the parry before the thrust.

"It was good to get out of the city," I said.

Crawford raised his eyebrows and turned his attention to his sandwich. I took a bite of mine, too, but instantly regretted it as the cheese and bread stuck midway down my throat. I set the sandwich back on the tray.

"So how long are you staying?" Crawford asked, rattling the ice in his glass.

"What do you mean?"

"It's not a complicated question. I assume you're going back to Italy?"

My heart was beating out of my chest. "I wasn't planning on it."

Crawford cocked an eyebrow. "Really? So what do you plan to do?"

"Stay here? Get some new assignments and start working again?"

He didn't answer immediately. "Well, we'll have to discuss all of that, too," he said finally. "Graciela keeps the guest room made up. I'll see you in the morning."

I slept in your room, Mia, not the guest room, although I don't think any actual sleep was involved. I looked at the photos of you and your friends stuck to the walls, and at your bulletin board crammed with dried flowers and concert stubs and a Valentine's card from Devon, and at the books stacked everywhere. I pulled a copy of *Travels on My Elephant* off the shelf and tried to read, but gave up after a few pages and just lay there, letting the memories wash over me until the sun came up.

As soon as I heard the water running in the shower the next morning, I got up, pulled on my ratty cashmere sweater, and went downstairs to make coffee.

Crawford looked surprised to see me in the kitchen, as if he'd forgotten I was home.

"Do you want coffee?" I asked, but he shook his head.

"Early meeting," he said. "They always put out a good spread."

"Oh, okay. I was thinking maybe we could grab dinner tonight, if you want to?"

He cocked his head to the side and looked at me, like Oliver did when he wanted to be invited onto the couch.

"No, not tonight," he said. "I'll let you know if I can make something work this week."

I nodded. "Okay. Have a good day."

"You, too."

And then he was gone.

I took my coffee into the sitting room, but after a few seconds on the couch, I got up again and went back to the kitchen. I had no idea what to do with myself. I wasn't ready to call anybody, much less see any of the friends I'd ignored over the past seven months, and the house was so clean that I couldn't keep myself busy with mindless tasks.

I checked my watch. Porter would be out in the barn already, but I pulled out my phone and texted him anyway. *Buongiorno.*

Buongiorno, he wrote back immediately. *You ok?*

Yes. Just at loose ends.

Is he glad you're back?

I started to reply, then erased what I'd written and wrote, *About what I expected.*

There was a long pause before the next text.

Not sure what you expected, but hope all is well.

On your end, too, I wrote.

I took a bundle of clothes to the bathroom and turned on the hot water, thinking about when I met Crawford for the first time.

It was a week after I arrived in D.C. for grad school. I was missing Porter and my uncle David terribly, and I hated my little overpriced basement apartment in Foggy Bottom. One scorching hot afternoon, I had to go to the registrar's office to pay some fee and was standing in line, holding my shirt away from the pool of sweat between my breasts, eavesdropping on the guys in front of me, when one of them made a comment that made me laugh out loud. The three of them turned around and we started talking. They invited me to join them for lunch, and several hours later, worn out from laughing so hard and buzzed from too many beers, they walked me home.

I was gathering up my dirty clothes to haul to the laundromat the next evening when my buzzer rang. When I opened the door, there was Crawford, carrying three enormous pizza boxes with three six packs of beer balanced on top, followed by Hugh with a ficus tree so big he couldn't see around it. Mac was holding a box of cupcakes.

"We came to help you settle in," Crawford said.

"Apparently we think you need a tree," Hugh said, setting the pot on the floor with a thud.

"I brought patty cakes to distract you while I go through your panty drawer," Mac said.

We did everything together. Mac and Hugh and I were all in the same political rhetoric program and Crawford was in law school, and we spent endless hours together studying in Hugh's spacious, light-filled apartment in Adams Morgan, going out for pizza in Georgetown, brunching in Dupont Circle, and drinking all over the District.

"We've decided to keep you," Hugh announced one night about three weeks after we met. "We need some estrogen in the mix."

"As if you don't provide enough?" Crawford asked him.

"I'm only an X and a half."

"I don't know, mate," Mac said. "That jacket you're wearing is pretty girly."

Hugh looked down at his Army jacket, which was covered with embroidered peace signs and flowers.

"I found it in Mère's closet," he said. "A relic from her sordid past, before she drank the Kool Aid and voted Republican."

"It's very Haight-Ashbury," Crawford said.

Hugh turned back to me. "You can leave a toothbrush at my place."

"Everyone has a toothbrush at Hugh's," Crawford said. "We take oral hygiene very seriously."

I laughed. "Well, I'm flattered." I turned to look at Mac. "Are you good with this, too?"

He shrugged. "It will do until we get married and ditch these dags."

They were my family. But while I loved Mac and Hugh dearly, it was understood that Crawford and I had a special bond.

After graduation, I got a job on the House side of Capitol Hill. Crawford landed a position with a prestigious law firm on K Street, Hugh went to work in the Senate, and Mac went to work at the Australian embassy, although we were never quite sure what his duties were, besides getting loaded at receptions and watching videos of *Home and Away* that his mother sent from Melbourne. We got together as often as we could, usually to drink Bloody Marys over brunch at Annie's, where we tried to convince ourselves that we were working for a purpose and doing something with our lives beyond running up bar bills.

Crawford was a lot of fun back then. Spontaneous. On our way back from his swearing-in for the New York Bar in Albany, for instance, he detoured all the way to Metropolitan Avenue in Brooklyn just to get cannoli from his favorite bakery. It was the dawn of recordable CDs and I'd made a playlist for the trip, and we blasted the Beastie Boys "No Sleep 'til Brooklyn" on repeat as he sped like a madman across the city to get to the bakery before it closed. They were flipping the sign on the door as we rushed in and bought an entire box of cannoli and two large coffees, and by the time we hit D.C., we were out of our minds on sugar and caffeine and the inside of the car looked like a snowstorm.

Washington was a good place to be young then. The city was undergoing a sort of reverse-aging process, with the Old Guard of the Reagan/Bush era being replaced by a zillion bright-faced, earnest youngsters trailing the Clintons into town, and there was a new energy as the stuffy white tablecloth restaurants and evening gowns gave way to breweries and barbecue joints and scuffed up boots. Eastern Market on a Saturday morning was jammed with young families and twenty-somethings sipping lattes, and I even heard they did away with the pantyhose requirement for women in the White House, which, given what we found out about Bill Clinton, seems highly likely.

I probably would have stayed there forever if the perfect storm of bullshit hadn't unleashed in my life, a storm that began when Steve, our Chief of Staff, tried to die in the office on an otherwise normal November morning.

I was running Communications for Senator Michaels then, and was sitting at my desk, drinking a cup of the motor oil that masqueraded as coffee in our office, and thinking about an engagement party I'd recently attended. The bride-to-be had met her husband on a train when they were both returning to Paris after seeing the Dalai Lama in Rome.

When I'd told Crawford and Mac and Hugh that couple's engagement story, Mac said he could top it. He had a cousin in Sydney who made a totally offhand comment to his girlfriend at a bar one night, something meaningless like, "Yeh, if we got married and bought a house, I'd want to get a dog." His girlfriend squealed, "We're getting married?" and the bartender, overhearing everything as bartenders do, grabbed a bottle of champagne and toasted the happy couple. The entire bar joined in to celebrate the engagement, and Mac's cousin couldn't muster up the courage to correct everyone, especially as the free drinks kept coming.

"His girlfriend called her mom from the bar phone, and that was that," Mac said. "The water was chummed and the sharks were circling. Poor bastard didn't have a chance. They had a huge wedding and split a year later." Mac looked at each of us in turn, the way he always did when he was about to lay some deep Aussie philosophy on us. "Moral of the story," he said, "if you want a dog, get one and shut your hole about it, mate."

That's what I was thinking about that morning at my desk while I procrastinated starting yet another fourteen-hour day of crafting brilliant messaging that would be ripped to unrecognizable shreds before it left the office.

I'd just agreed to cover the phones so the intern could make a bagel run when one of our legislative assistants called to say that she wouldn't be in to work because "her head wasn't in it." I started to tell her how ridiculous that was—this was this United States Senate and no one's head was in it, only their ego—but as I opened my mouth to talk, I looked up and saw a bat tucked into the corner of my office where the wall met the ceiling.

I did what any rational person would do, which was drop the phone, scream, grab the trash can, dump its contents on the floor, and hold it over my head as a shield while I ran out the door, slamming it closed behind me.

The maintenance guy showed up about fifteen minutes later, wearing overalls and carrying a wooden box that looked like a tiny lobster trap, with a stick and net contraption propped against his shoulder. All that was missing was a piece of straw and a paintbrush to whitewash Aunt Becky's fence.

"We get these calls a lot," he said, opening the door to my office. "Bats and rats. Same tool for both of 'em." Then he told me about a rat who lived in the Rotunda and was thought to be the reincarnation of Thomas Jefferson, which explained why the entire Capitol was a no-kill zone. "We just trap 'em and set 'em free. That's the policy."

I started to say something about that being a perfect metaphor for Congress, where you never actually solve a problem but just move it down the line and hope it doesn't come back until after you're gone, but I thought better of it. Personally, I didn't care what happened to the bat, I just wanted it out of my office. So I affixed a polite smile to my face and inched past the rodent wrangler, citing a meeting I was going to be late for. Then I took a leisurely walk around the corridors of democracy, stopping to see if Hugh was available, which he wasn't, and chatting with a security guard before returning to the office a half hour later, holding my phone to my ear to prevent any further conversation. The maintenance guy was just leaving. He held the wooden box up as I approached, like I might want to bid my visitor adieu, but I pointed to the phone against my ear and shook my head.

Our Chief Counsel, who was the person I liked best in our office, popped his head in as I was settling back into my desk.

"Ah good, you're alive. I wasn't sure how big the beast was."

"Velociraptor size, but I fought it off."

"Impressive. Bagels are here. I waited for you."

We were leaning against the counter in the break room, which wasn't so much a room as an alcove crowded with boxes, while he told me that he'd put a contract on a house over the weekend when we heard an unholy noise from the front of the office. A yelp and then a thud, followed by high-pitched screaming.

We looked at each other for a split second, then dropped our bagels and raced towards the front of the office. Steve was lying on the floor with his hands wrapped around his throat and a bluish tint creeping up his face. The intern was standing behind her desk, screaming.

I dropped to my knees next to Steve's head, pushed two fingers into his mouth, and dragged a chunk of croissant out of the back of his throat. Then I grabbed his left arm and rolled Steve, who was built like Humpty Dumpty, onto his side so I could pound on his back. He made a horrible sound, somewhere between a cough and a gag, and I crawled back around to the front of him and used my fingers as a pincer to dislodge another piece of wet croissant.

At that point, I honestly thought the whole thing was over. I sat back on my heels and looked at Steve, who had returned to supine when I let go of him, expecting him to say something. Thanks, maybe. But instead of talking, he went very still, and the color drained out of his face. I bent over him and could feel his breath coming in short, shallow puffs that were way too far apart.

All of the CPR training I'd taken as a thirteen-year-old babysitter came roaring back. I put my lips on Steve's blue ones, pinched his nose shut, and breathed air into him. Then I pulled my face back and leaned on Steve's massive chest as hard as I could, four rapid pushes and a pause, and kept doing it until the medics rushed in and shoved me aside.

Senator Michaels called later from the field office.

"Beth? Can't thank you enough," he said. "You're a hero. Only seems right that you take over as Chief of Staff until Steve comes back. Shouldn't be more than a couple of weeks. Deeply appreciative of what you did today. Truly heroic. Ask Kimber to get you on my schedule for Wednesday. Great work. Transfer me to Keith, please. Thanks again."

When I hung up, I pulled out my Blackberry and texted Crawford, who was always the first person I told when anything happened.

He texted back right away: *Wow! I'll assemble the team.*

It's only because it's easier than finding someone competent, I wrote.

Don't be stupid. Dinner tomorrow @ 7 pm.

"There she is!" Mac bellowed as I approached the table the next night, almost an hour late after a horrible first day of trying to assume Steve's role and do my own job, too.

Hugh pulled me down to kiss my cheek as I passed his chair. "Everyone in Dirksen's talking about you," he said.

"I gave CPR to a bloke once when I was a lifeguard," Mac said as I dropped into the chair next to Crawford. "Disgusting. He gagged seawater right into my face."

"The whole idea is revolting," Hugh said, shuddering dramatically.

"Oh, please," Mac said. "You've done mouth-to-mouth on half of D.C."

"Only on the dance floor," Hugh said.

"Nice job on the promotion," Crawford said, patting my shoulder.

"It's just an interim gig."

"Doesn't matter. You'll do good work and people will notice."

"And if I fail miserably?"

"Not an option," Crawford said, shaking his head.

"Does anyone care that I don't actually want Steve's job?"

The only answer was the vibration of my Blackberry, which was sitting on the table in front of me. I glanced down, saw who was calling, and flipped it over.

"Anyway, her old man is huge, like a bear," Mac said.

Apparently we were done talking about me.

I sat back and took a huge swallow of the beer Mac had set in front of me and tried to pick up the thread of conversation.

"There was vodka everywhere," Mac said. "Frozen in ice with flowers and berries, all fancy like."

"Where was this?" I asked.

"A reception at the Russian Embassy," Hugh said.

"I met Anastasia's dad and he nearly crushed my hand with his giant bear paw." Mac held up his right hand as evidence. "Naturally I had to drink a lot because of the pain."

"Naturally," Hugh said, nodding agreeably.

"I was off my face by the end of the night," Mac said, shrugging.

"Because of your hand," Crawford said.

Mac nodded. "Right."

"Not because you're a raging alcoholic."

Mac nodded again. "Exactly."

"Obviously he was trying to hurt you. Blatant act of aggression," Hugh said, looking at Crawford for confirmation.

Crawford nodded solemnly. "Blatant."

"You can't trust the Ruskies," Hugh said. "Tricky bastards, all of them. I'd get myself a fur hat and try to blend in next time, if I were you. Or maybe find a girlfriend who's not from the Soviet Bloc. One who doesn't break the lamps."

"Wait, what about the lamps?" I asked. My phone was vibrating again and I slid it under the table and set it on my thigh.

Hugh grinned at me. "Turns out the lovely Anastasia is a destructive little minx."

"She tore up my apartment," Mac said, making a sad face. "Bouncing around like a crazed kanga, shouting at me in Russian."

Crawford started laughing. "Naturally, the only word Mac knows in Russian is *Da*," he said. "So while she's tearing things off the wall and breaking the lamps, Mac's just urging her on."

"*Da*, baby!" Hugh shouted, throwing his head back in ecstasy. "Smash that shit! Daddy never liked that lamp anyway!"

I laughed out loud. "Honestly, Mac. Have you ever considered dating anyone sane?"

"Water seeks its own level," Crawford said.

"Nobody said anything about water, mate. Although maybe a nice dip would calm her down," Mac said. "I once saw a cranky koala get dunked..."

Luckily the waitress came with our nachos before Mac could get his wildlife story off the ground. We ordered another pitcher of beer and some real food and Hugh launched into the latest about his parents, buttoned-up economists for the Federal Reserve who were shockingly avant-garde in their personal lives, constantly seeking enlightenment through things like Kabbalah and colonic cleansing.

"The Feds have covered the entire apartment in prayer flags," Hugh said. "They chant and ring little bells they wear on their fingers and the whole place reeks of incense. I went over for breakfast and Mère actually offered me yak butter tea. As if."

"That might be a first for the Watergate, finger bells and yak butter," I said.

"They're called tingsha bells," Mac said. His accent made it sound like he was saying *tincture.* "I dated a girl once who was into all that. She moved to Kathmandu when we broke up."

"Such is the power of the Man from Melbourne," Hugh said. "Take a bow, Mac. Poor girl had to go all the way to Nepal to recover from dating you."

"Is she still there or did she hurl herself off Everest?" I asked.

Mac shrugged. "What can I say? My love is atomic."

"Radioactive, you mean," Hugh said.

"Contagious," Crawford said. "How's the rash, by the way?"

"Are you going to answer that?" Mac asked. My phone had been buzzing nonstop against the bottom of the table.

I sighed. "I guess so."

I went outside the restaurant and stood on the sidewalk, shivering in the fall darkness, to return the call.

"Jesus Christ, Beth. How many times do I have to call before you answer?"

"Looks like nine. What can I do for you, Jude?"

"I'm doing you a favor. A heads-up about something coming down the pike."

That was when Jude, a reporter I'd dated a few years earlier, proceeded to inform me that news of an insider trading investigation was about to hit the press. Some kind of artificial blood product that could be worth billions of dollars, particularly to the Department of Defense, and guess who was at the center of the investigation? My boss, Senator Michaels.

"I want no part of this, Jude," I said. "Consider me the Apostle Peter. I don't know Jesus and I've never even been to Galilee."

"You don't remember the meetings?"

"Of course not! Until a day ago I was in Communications. We don't know anything until someone asks us to spin it."

"Well, you're going to know about it now. Is Steve available for a comment? He's not answering his phone."

"He had a heart attack."

"I heard he choked?"

"I can hear you taking notes, Jude. This entire conversation is off the record, let's be very clear about that. Steve choked because he had a heart attack. Or had a heart attack because he choked. What difference does it make? Leave the poor guy alone."

"Just getting the facts."

"Please don't involve me in this. I'm only filling in temporarily—"

"You're Chief of Staff now. You're going to be involved, Beth."

A wave of nausea rolled over me. "Tell me what to expect."

When Jude finished laying out the allegations of insider trading and information swapping, I hung up and went back inside.

"We thought you'd been kidnapped," Hugh said as I slid back into my seat.

I shook my head. "Work stuff. But thanks for looking for me."

As Mac and Hugh launched into a discussion of which one of them would actually be more useful in a kidnapping situation, Crawford leaned over and whispered, "Are you okay?"

I made a face and shook my head. "I don't want to be Chief of Staff."

"Are you serious? This is a fantastic opportunity for you to move up."

"To screw up? Yes, I agree."

"To *move* up."

"I don't want to do it. I didn't ask for it."

"Of course you didn't ask for it. That's why it's such a great stroke of luck." He shook his head. "What's with the crisis of confidence?"

I sighed. "I'm tired, I guess."

"So get some sleep. This is going to be great, Beth. You'll see."

"Did I tell you my building is going condo?"

Crawford shook his head. "Where are you moving?"

"I haven't found a place. I can't afford to stay, though, that's for sure. They sent out an information packet and it's ridiculous what they're asking for a one bedroom."

I didn't know it then, but that series of events—Steve's heart attack and Jude's investigation and my imminent homelessness—was the beginning of the end for me in D.C. And who had I leaned on during all of it? Crawford, the same man whose hatred for me now radiated off his body.

I shut off the shower and grabbed a towel off the rack, avoiding my reflection in the mirror. Once I was dressed, I went downstairs to the little office next to the sitting room. I hadn't opened my laptop since the day of the accident and chewed my thumbnail down to the skin while I waited for it to power on.

Nearly four thousand emails in my inbox, plus half as many in the Spam folder. It was going to be a long morning.

Sette

When it got late enough to call the U.S., I took a break from deleting emails and dialed David's office.

"I had a feeling I would hear from you today," he said by way of a greeting. "Are you okay? I've been very worried."

"I'm alright. I just got back to London."

"You've been in Italy this whole time?"

"Yes."

"Anything I should know about that?"

"Well, Crawford's not happy."

"I can imagine. But Crawford's not my concern, you are."

"I took a lot of walks. Tried to help out. Porter's place is beautiful. And he was really patient and considerate, right up until the end."

"What happened at the end?"

I thought of how to explain Porter's uncharacteristic behavior on the way to the airport.

"He just seemed angry that I was leaving, even though he said he understood."

"What do you think that was about?"

"I don't know." I sighed. "I guess he thinks I'm stupid for coming back."

"Well, the only way to know for sure what he thinks is to ask him."

"I don't have the capacity to deal with his feelings, David," I said. "I've got my own trainwreck unfolding here, and besides, what difference does it make? My life is here, in London."

"I understand. So how did you find things when you got back?"

I told David about the icy reception from Crawford and the feeling I couldn't shake that my return home had displaced someone.

"You think someone's been staying there?"

"I don't know. I didn't see any real evidence of it, but I just have this sense. And I found some things yesterday."

David was quiet, waiting for me to continue.

"Just...he's definitely with someone else, David. And I think it's been going on a long time."

I heard the voice of Margaret, the church secretary, in the background and David asked me to hang on.

Margaret was in her sixties, with two ne'er-do-well adult sons, an ex-husband high in the ranks at Fort Bragg, and a hairdo that hadn't changed since 1982. I didn't think David could function without her. She kept him on task and on schedule, fed and watered him during Christmas and Easter, and had an encyclopedic knowledge of his parishioners' lives. She knew who was in the hospital and who was expecting a baby, whose marriage was collapsing and whose family was calling hospice, and when Porter and I got engaged, Margaret was the first person to know that, too, before even David or Jenny. She'd come around the corner while I was waiting in the hall for David to get off the phone.

"Hello, Tigger," she said. "What's got you bouncing today? Tracking down something exciting for Professor Whatshisname?"

I was working as a Girl Friday for my Old Testament professor until grad school began, doing odd bits of research and running stacks of books back and forth to the library. I loved the scavenger hunts to find some obscure bit of *midrash*.

"You're just mad about midrash," Porter had said at dinner the night before, cutting into his New York strip while I explained the difference a single letter could make when it came to biblical Hebrew.

"No, but it's fascinating to look at how an oral tradition was put into writing, Porter. When you think that the first written texts didn't even have vowels until the Masoretes added them six or seven hundred years after Jesus lived, it's incredible. And one letter can make a difference. I mean, there is a ton of scholarship on the fact that God wasn't *jealous,* God was *zealous.* See?"

"That's two for the list. *Mad About Midrash* and *Zealous Not Jealous.* We really need to start a band."

"I'll add them. But think about it, Porter. It makes no sense that God would be jealous of anything the Israelites had or did, but it makes total sense that God would be zealous about bringing them back into right relationship when they start worshipping other gods and breaking the laws. Yet *jealous* is the translation that has persisted."

We were eating at The Angus Barn in Raleigh, a big splurge for us. Afterwards, we went back to Porter's house and were slapping at mosquitos on his back deck, listening to Carly Simon's *Live at Martha's Vineyard* and a chorus of cicadas, when Porter suddenly pulled a small black box out of his pocket and slid onto his knees in front of me.

I'd held my left hand out so Margaret could admire the ring in the hallway of the church.

"Oh, that's a beauty," she said, holding my hand close to her face.

"Porter said it's from the 1880s. Look at the filigree on the sides."

"That boy's got class." Margaret dropped my hand and gave me a hug. "Congratulations, honey. Just don't forget," she said, letting go of me, "men need constant training. Take your eyes off them for one second and they backslide. You won't believe the stupid stuff they say and do."

David came into the hall then and I held out my hand. He looked at the ring and then at me. "Well, well," he said. "I assume this came from Porter?"

"See what I mean?" Margaret said to me, rolling her eyes. "No, David, it's from the Easter Bunny. By the way, the guy's coming about the roof at eleven." She turned back to me. "Let me know when you're ready to start planning the ceremony. And congratulations again, sweetie."

"As always, my dear, your timing is impeccable," David had said, gesturing towards his office and following me inside. I flopped on the couch while he flipped through the tower of papers on his desk. "I just found something that I was planning to use for the couples in pre-marital counseling, and now you can be my guinea pig." He handed me a magazine. The pages were folded back to an interview with a priest named Henri Nouwen, a man with a long, kind face, thick eyebrows, and oversized wire-rimmed glasses.

"Read what's on the page," David said, pointing to a passage that was circled.

I read the passage quickly and looked up at my uncle.

"These questions are easy to answer, David. Porter is my source of affection. Porter makes me feel alive. Porter makes me feel like I can do a thousand things."

David nodded. "Good. I hope it's always that way."

Little had I known how quickly our engagement would end.

Listening to his conversation with Margaret across the Atlantic, I could so easily picture David in his office at the church, sitting at his desk in front of the wall covered in crosses he'd collected from all over the world. I'd spent hours in that church, studying on the couch and eating snacks left over from Sunday coffee hours and Wednesday Bible studies. I knew every nook and cranny, from which cabinet held the coffee filters to how many copies of the *Book of Common Prayer* were supposed to be stacked in the back of the sanctuary. It had been a second home to me, as comfortable as David's own house.

"Sorry about that," David said when he came back on the line. "Margaret sends her love."

"How is she?"

"Feisty as ever. She's on a dating app now and each date is more catastrophic than the last."

I had to laugh. "I can only imagine. She doesn't tolerate fools well."

"You two have that in common. So tell me, what kind of foolishness is it that you think's been going on?"

I didn't know how to answer that question.

There seemed to have been a thousand things I'd missed over the years, little bits and pieces that had clicked into horrifying place when I'd made a discovery the day before. Things that made sense in the most nonsensical, through-the-rabbit-hole kind of way.

I thought about how to explain to David how I felt, and flashed back to one of the most disorienting experiences of my life, a Philosophy of Ethics class I took as an undergrad. It was taught by an associate professor in her early thirties who looked like she got dressed in Stevie Nicks' closet. The material was boring, all that Hobbesian stuff about is it ethically okay to steal an apple if you are starving, but the professor had two obsessions that made the class feel like a drug trip: isometric exercise and Greek deities. She would stand in the front of the small classroom in floor-sweeping skirts and flowing cloaks, droning on about social contracts and collective security and Locke's rights of the individual, and the whole time she was talking she'd be doing deep knee bends and lunges and curling invisible barbells.

But just when you'd relaxed into this bizarre rhythm of her stretching and bending while discussing the right to homestead private property, she'd become intensely animated and start shrieking about the Pythia at Delphi and Apollo raping Daphne. Crazy battle cries would emerge from her swirl of scarves—*Be like Athena and strive for justice and fairness in this patriarchal world! Be like Aphrodite and own your sexuality!*—that stunned us all and left us looking at each other like, *Did I just miss something? Some connection between Locke's social contract and tricep curls and Aphrodite's sex life?*

It was a feeling I'd had before, of course. One minute my dad and Kirk were telling me they were going to bring me back a moose from Canada, and the next minute, they were markers in the ground. One night I loaned my mom a pair of earrings to wear to a wedding, and the next morning I signed paperwork to take possession of her purse from a morgue attendant. What happened on the way from Point A to Point B could never make sense.

"Well," I told David, "I told you I thought Crawford's been seeing someone."

"You did, yes."

"So what I know now is that the person he's been seeing is a man. A junior partner at his firm," I said, and burst into tears.

David was quiet for a long minute.

"Oh, my dear," he said finally. "I am sorry."

We talked for another half hour; or rather, he talked and I cried, and then we hung up. I was totally exhausted and wanted nothing more than to crawl back into bed, but I needed to get in touch with Jenny, whose emails had become increasingly frantic over the months I was in Italy. I hated that I'd made her worry, and started composing an email to my oldest friend about the disaster my life had turned out to be.

Dear Jen, I wrote. *I've been in Italy this whole time, at Porter's house, and have just come back to London. A lot has happened...*

That was the understatement of the century.

Otto

Jenny and I had such an ordinary childhood, Mia. Very different from yours. No trips to the Victoria & Albert, no picnics in Hampstead Heath, no holiday house in the south of France. Just a normal American childhood. Your grandfather was a cop, your grandmother worked at the church, and until my dad's death, our lives were your standard suburban upstate New York existence. Scooby Doo and Schoolhouse Rock and tube socks, and three channels on the television that all went off the air at eleven.

My parents never took vacations, so the trip my father and Kirk took to the Northwest Territories was a very big deal. When it was finally time for them to pack, I sat on a cooler in the garage, twisting the mood ring on my finger and watching them take apart rods and reels, until I got too cold and went inside. My mom and Aunt Celia were sitting at the kitchen table drinking coffee.

"Mom?" I said. "Who's Dolly Varden?"

My mom's brow furrowed. "I don't know, sweetie. Why?"

"Dad and Uncle Kirk are going to try to catch her with a spoon," I said, "and I'm just wondering what you put on the spoon?"

"Chocolate," Celia said. "Or a dollar bill."

"A nice pair of pantyhose," my mom said.

As I went down the hall to my room, Celia said something to my mom and the two of them howled with laughter. Maybe you know that Dolly Varden is a type of fish and a spoon is a type of lure, but I had no idea.

My dad and Kirk had only been gone two days when the expedition company called to say that their plane had disappeared on the way to the fishing camp. The search team had already been out for hours, so the first thing we heard was "missing and presumed dead," which was painfully final and impossibly open-ended at the same time. I remember Celia, white as a sheet, kneading her hands while my mom begged the voice on the other end of the line to keep looking.

The air felt strange, crackling and tense, and time seemed slippery. Our house filled up quickly. Two police officers from my dad's precinct came and sat at the kitchen table, followed a few minutes later by Kirk's boss, the Fire Chief, and Father Patrick, and our neighbors, the Morgans. The phone rang constantly and every time it did, everyone in the kitchen held their breath, but it was only another neighbor, another friend who'd just heard the news, and my mother hung up as quickly as she could to keep the line open while Celia lit another cigarette with shaking hands.

A girl I knew from church came over, but while her mother fussed around the kitchen, putting a fresh pot of coffee on the stove and refilling the sugar bowl, she just stood in the doorway clutching her stupid Holly Hobbie doll and staring at me like having a missing dad was contagious. At some point, her mother suggested that we go to my room and play. I shook my head no, but my mom suddenly noticed I was there and said, "Go, Bits," so I dragged myself off the chair.

"This is my room," I said, gesturing with the enthusiasm of a prison inmate.

She sat on the bed while I looked at my bookshelves, hoping to find something I hadn't already read several times.

"Do you have any dolls?" she said.

"No."

"Not even Barbie?"

"No."

She was quiet for a minute. "Your dad is missing."

"Duh."

"So's your uncle."

"Duh."

"They're probably dead."

"I hear your mom calling," I said, applying a layer of strawberry Bonne Bell Lip Smacker to my mouth. "You better go."

I kicked the door closed and lay on my bed rereading *Blubber* until I heard Jenny come in the house. She'd been visiting her grandparents in Rochester, but Mrs. Fife drove up and got her as soon as she heard the news. We curled up on the couch together and Mrs. Fife brought us ham sandwiches and potato chips and peach Hi-C, our favorite, and Jenny and I watched *CHiPs* and then *The Love Boat* and *Fantasy Island*, which we were ordinarily forbidden to watch, and then went to my room and gave my Barbie dolls wedge haircuts like Dorothy Hamill.

Most of the time after that is a blur, but a few memories stand out. One of those is an argument between my mother and Father Patrick, who was her boss as well as our priest. I was doing homework under the dining room table, which was my spot for keeping an eye on my mom since I lacked the dumbwaiter of *Harriet the Spy*, and the icy tone of her voice made me sit up straight and bang my head.

"How can you tell me not to hope?" she was saying to Father Patrick. "What if they're out there freezing? What if they're waiting for me to *do* something? You want me to give up on my husband and my brother? I won't, Patrick. Absolutely not."

"Eleanor, it's highly unlikely they could have survived this long. The temperatures alone..."

"I can tell you some other things that are highly unlikely, too, Patrick. An empty tomb comes to mind. But aren't we supposed to have faith?"

"Don't say things you're going to regret, Eleanor."

"The only thing I'm going to regret is calling off the search."

"It's not your decision to make."

At that, my mother suggested that Father Patrick show himself out.

When I got up every morning, she was already at the kitchen table, working the phones. Had the rescue team checked here? What about there? Had they scoured every inlet and outpost of the coastline? I can't imagine how much all those long-distance calls cost.

Badgering the Canadian authorities took all of her energy. She didn't notice that my uniform needed to be ironed or that we were out of peanut butter and milk and bread, or that a tremendous knot had formed in the curls at the nape of my neck. I dragged the ironing board out of the closet and pressed the collars of my uniform so I wouldn't get sent to the office, made my lunches out of whatever I could find in the refrigerator, and stole her sewing scissors so Jenny could hack the knot out of my hair during recess. One day, after I brought yet another unidentifiable blob of casserole for lunch, Jenny showed up with her Wonder Woman lunchbox packed with two sandwiches, two baggies of cut up carrots, two cookies, and an extra quarter for milk.

"Here," she said, unfolding a napkin and laying the food out on the table in front of me. "I'm going to go get milk. Should we get chocolate?"

"It's not Friday. Won't your mom be mad?"

Jenny shrugged. "I think it's fine. Would your mom be mad?"

I shrugged. "She won't even know."

"Then let's get chocolate."

I don't know what made my mom finally agree to have the funeral, but it was the last time either of us ever set foot in Saint Barnabas. To be honest, I never gave much thought to what it cost her to lose her husband, her brother, her job, and her church all in one fell swoop, and we certainly never talked about it. The prevailing wisdom then was that if there was food on the table and a roof over your head, you were doing alright, and whatever feelings I had about my father's and uncle's deaths, I kept them to myself, and so did she.

My mom took a job as a receptionist in a doctor's office, Celia ate dinner with us every night, and I was allowed to stay over at Jenny's most every weekend, where the happy bedlam of the Fife's house provided a welcome respite from the suffocating silence of my own home. Life went on. I got good grades and won some writing awards and had crushes on boys and froze on the sidelines in a polyester uniform cheering for the football team.

But then, when I was seventeen, everything changed again.

I was spending the night at Jenny's and we'd snuck out, taking the screen off her bedroom window to climb down the trellis and go to a party in someone's basement. We were staggering home several hours later when Jenny suddenly grabbed my arm.

"Again?" I said, reaching for her mane of red-gold hair.

She retched and vomited into the bushes. "Why did I drink so much?"

"It's just what we do," I said, laying my free hand on her back and waiting for her to stop heaving. "We're dumbass teenagers, remember?"

Jenny moaned and wiped her mouth on her sleeve. "How am I going to get up the wall?"

"I'll push you. Just don't smash the roses again. Poor Roscoe got blamed last time."

We were weaving down the sidewalk on the final stretch towards home when I noticed a police car pulled up along the curb in front of the Fife's house. For a brief second, I thought my dad had come to pick me up like he used to. Jenny was leaning heavily on my right side and stumbled when I stopped walking.

"There's a cop at your house," I said.

"Oh my God! Why would my parents call the cops on us?"

I had a sudden insight. "They must think we were kidnapped."

Jenny clapped her hands to her cheeks. "Sweet Mary and Joseph. I won't be allowed out again until I'm eighty."

"What should we do?"

"Run away?"

I nodded. "I think we have to."

"Okay, but I want to say goodbye to Roscoe first."

"Me, too."

"We should give him a couple Milk Bones," Jenny said. "So he knows we love him."

Roscoe's bed and Milk Bones were in the laundry room, so our plan was to go around to the back of the house, where I would push Jenny through the doggy flap so she could unlock the door. But as soon as we got to the edge of Jenny's yard, her oldest brother, Colin, who was home from the Marines, materialized on the stoop.

"Get inside now," he barked.

We scurried across the lawn. Colin held the door open with his foot and put a hand on each of our backs as we entered the house, propelling us into the kitchen where both of Jenny's parents and two police officers were standing.

But the cops weren't there because Jenny and I snuck out.

They were there to tell me that my mom, a woman who'd never had a drink or smoked a cigarette in her life and couldn't even bring herself to say *dammit*, was driving home from her cousin's wedding on a two-lane road when an oncoming car drifted across the center line and hit her head on. Celia, who was in the passenger seat, had been pinned in the car for over an hour before the EMTs were able to free her with the Jaws of Life.

"She's got numerous broken bones," one of the policemen said, consulting the small notebook in his hand. "Braced herself against the dashboard. Both of her feet and hands. One of her legs. Cracked pelvis. Several broken ribs."

"Where is she?" I asked him, instantly sober.

"Trauma ICU."

I looked at Jenny's mom. "Can you take me? I don't want my mom to have to wait by herself."

Mrs. Fife shot a look at her husband. "Your mom got hurt, too, honey," she said, and glanced at Jenny, who was standing by the kitchen sink looking like she might throw up again. "Let's make some coffee and sit down for a minute."

"I'm sorry everybody is awake," I told her. I looked at the officers. "Maybe it would be easier if one of you could take me. You can do that, right? I can just stay in the waiting room until visiting hours."

One of the officers started to speak but seemed to think better of it.

Jenny's mother glanced at her husband again. He nodded slightly.

"Oh, honey," Mrs. Fife said, and started crying. "Your mom's not in the hospital. Not where you can see her."

It was Colin who finally made me understand that my mom was in the morgue.

Over the next few days, we learned a lot about the other driver. She was in her early twenties, with two little kids, and this was her second injury-causing DUI. She'd been lucky in the first one and had only totaled someone's car and broken her own leg, but her blood alcohol level this time, when the doctors took it against her will in the emergency room a couple hours after the wreck, was three times over the legal limit for the state of New York. The cops told me she had actually passed out behind the wheel, which is why she was uninjured; her body had been as limp as a rag doll when the crash happened.

Mrs. Fife said I didn't have to go back to school until I was ready, but after three days watching game shows and soap operas on the couch with Jenny and Roscoe, I couldn't take it anymore. Celia was pinned back together with steel parts, and my mother was on a cold slab in a refrigerator locker, and I just wanted to hunt that driver down and make her suffer. I was furious. My skin felt like it was on fire, and I needed to stay in motion or I'd burn up.

David flew in from North Carolina and sat next to me at the funeral, and Jenny and her family sat in the row behind us, and I shook hands and accepted people's kind words without ever actually hearing a word that was said. When it was over, David and I drove back to my house. He adjusted the thermostat, emptied the refrigerator, closed the shutters, and sorted through the mail while I packed a couple of suitcases, then we locked the doors and David drove me to Jenny's and flew back to North Carolina. I spent the rest of that day and night lying on the twin bed in Jenny's room that had been designated for me all my life, dangling one arm over the bed to pet Roscoe while Jenny unpacked my clothes and made room for my school uniforms in her closet.

I didn't make it easy for Jenny to remain my friend over the next few months.

"Beth?" she said one morning a couple weeks after the accident. She was bent over about two inches from my face and shaking my shoulder. "You have to get up."

"Leave me alone, Jen."

She straightened up and looked down at me. "We're going to be late. You need to get in the shower."

"You go. I'll take the city bus."

"Beth...."

"Just go, Jenny. I'm getting up." I pushed myself up on one elbow. "See? I'm getting up."

Jenny sighed and turned away, hoisting her backpack onto her shoulder and easing the door closed behind her. I flopped back onto the pillow and groaned. My mouth tasted like an ashtray and every part of me hurt, and I was afraid that I was going to throw up the half-bottle of Southern Comfort I'd drunk the night before.

When I finally made it to school nearly two hours later, Jenny caught up with me in the hall before AP English.

"I'm glad you made it," she said, glancing at her Swatch.

"O'Shaughnessy busted me coming in and I already got reamed by Sister Agnes, so please spare me your lecture."

She made a face. "This is like your tenth time being late. What did you expect?"

"What are they going to do? Call my parents?"

Jenny looked like I'd slapped her. She opened her mouth to speak and closed it without saying a word.

I nudged her with my elbow. "I'm sorry. What did I miss?"

"Useless announcements. Prom committee. A quiz in History."

"I'll see you at lunch, okay?"

I hadn't done my homework and didn't even bother to get my books. I just walked into my next class, dropped my backpack on the ground, put my head down on the desk and took a nap. The teacher ignored me. When the bell rang, I yawned and joined the stampede to the lockers to grab a hoodie before heading to the lunchroom, which, in our antiquated school, hovered somewhere around freezing all year long.

My locker was smack in the middle of senior hall, a coveted top spot, and like all the lockers, had to remain unlocked and accessible to the administration. That meant it could have been anyone who had used a black Sharpie to scrawl the word "WHORE" inside, maybe not even the same person who'd written something similar the week before.

I grabbed my hoodie, slammed the door closed, and went to the lunchroom where I slid into the seat Jenny had saved for me.

"Aren't you eating?" Jenny said.

I shook my head. "I'm not hungry."

"I think we're having pot roast for dinner. My mom was putting it in the Crock Pot this morning."

"There are some people going to Bond's Lake tonight."

"Who?"

"Some guys I know from work. Public school guys."

Jenny made a face.

"Do you know who wrote in my locker?"

"Wrote what?"

"Whore."

She closed her eyes and exhaled loudly. "No, I don't," she said, opening her eyes and regarding me tenderly. "But it's not— it could have been anyone. People are talking, Beth."

"What a shock. The gossipers are gossiping."

"Darren is really upset."

Darren was a guy who'd been in love with me since he and Jenny and I were all in kindergarten together. A nice enough guy, but I was never interested in him as a boyfriend. Two weeks earlier, though, I'd had way too much to drink after school and accidentally had sex for the first time in the basement of someone I didn't even know. After about forty-five seconds of panting on top of me, Darren had grunted "I love you, Beth" and then collapsed. I hadn't even responded, just pushed him away and rolled off the couch.

Jenny pushed her apple across the table towards me and bit into her sandwich. "Do you like Darren at all? As a boyfriend?"

I shook my head and pushed the apple back across the table.

"Eat something," she said through a mouthful of bread and turkey.

"I said I'm not hungry." I pushed myself up from the table. "I'm going to go to the nurse's office to take a nap."

I don't know what would have become of me if Jenny hadn't ratted me out to David. He called the Fife's house one evening when I was supposed to be at work but was drunk at Bond's Lake again, and Jenny dragged the Fife's old rotary phone down the hall and into her closet, which was the only way she could have privacy, and gave him a tear-filled account of all the idiotic stuff I was doing. The next morning, she dragged the phone back to her room and knocked the receiver against my shoulder until I opened my eyes.

"Wake up," she said. "I'm going to school and you're talking to your uncle."

David didn't hold back. He gave me an earful before softening his tone and telling me that he understood how I felt, but it was time for the self-destruction to stop.

Five weeks later, after I'd apologized to Father O'Shaughnessy and Sister Agnes and rewritten several essays and retaken a bunch of tests, David listened to me practice my speech over the phone. I'd been on track to be valedictorian for four years but had screwed things up too badly for the school to allow that to happen and had to settle for being salutatorian while Erin O'Ryan, who was an insufferable bitch, took my spot.

David flew up for the ceremony and manned the grill alongside Jenny's dad in the Fife's back yard, and the next morning, waited in the car while I hugged Jenny's parents and brothers goodbye. Then it was just me and Jenny left in the kitchen.

"I can't believe I'm not going to see you every day anymore," I said, crying into her hair. "I know I've been a huge asshole. I'm so sorry, Jen."

"Love means never having to say you're sorry," she said.

"I hate that movie so much," I said, laughing through my tears.

"I know, Bits," she said. "I know."

I moved in with David in Chapel Hill for the summer. He bought me a bike as a graduation present, mint green with wide handlebars and fat tires, and I rode it to my job at the bookstore every day before hauling my stuff to the dorm for freshman orientation. Jenny and I didn't have the money for long distance calls, so we wrote each other every week, long letters so full of detail that when I finally went back to Syracuse for a visit, I felt like I already knew all of her college friends.

Jenny had always been my touchstone. Always there, willing to listen and talk through whatever I was feeling, without my ever having to provide context or the backstory. She knew me better than anyone. She would know how devastated I felt about Crawford, which made telling her that much harder.

I fixed myself another cup of tea and spent an hour on the computer pricing flights from London to Syracuse, imagining how reassuring it would be to sit in her kitchen and have Jenny tell me that everything would be okay. I was about to get up and find my wallet so I could input my credit card information when a thought hit me.

Jenny was my best friend. I couldn't drag my disaster into the middle of her happy life.

I closed my laptop and dropped my head into my hands.

Nove

It was still pouring outside when I finally got up from the desk.
I went to the coat closet and added a fleece jacket to the layers
of shirts I was already wearing and pulled on my waterproof
walking boots and wool-lined raincoat and hat.

I left the house and headed for Regent's Park, thinking
about my conversation with David. The rain was coming down
sideways and it was cold in the way that reaches right down
into your bones.

"He's seeing a man," David had repeated when I told him,
and then exhaled audibly. "Okay. I know what you're thinking,
but is there another explanation? Could they just be friends?"

"I don't think so," I said. "And honestly, it explains so
much."

"Like what?"

"His lack of affection. This feeling I've had since we got married that he'd just checked a box somewhere and stopped caring. And why he was never home."

"I always thought you and Crawford were the greatest of friends."

I stifled a sob. "I thought so, too. But I also always felt like he was disappointed in me."

"Disappointed? Really?"

"Disappointed, disgusted," I said. "Honestly, David, I don't think he valued anything I did. Raising our child. All the socializing and holidays and trying to make a nice home... None of it mattered."

"I cannot imagine that he didn't value that, no matter what might be happening now."

"I just feel so stupid. I've spent all these years trying to get his attention and his approval, jumping up and down like *Notice me! Love me!*" I said, unable to staunch the tears that were pooling between my face and the telephone. "What a waste of my time. What a waste of my life."

"Beth," David said. "I want you to take a minute and calm down, and then I want you to listen to me."

I clawed at the tissue box on the desk and extracted a handful of Kleenex and then held the phone away from my face while I blew my nose.

"Okay," I said finally.

"I want you to hear what I'm going to say. It might not mean much to you in this moment, but I want you to remember it."

"Okay," I sniffled.

"There is nothing about your life that has been wasted. You've been a good friend to many, many people, and a good wife to your husband. Most of all, you were a great mother to your daughter."

I started sobbing again.

"I know you're in pain. I know you feel betrayed. But you have a choice to make. Are you going to let yourself be crushed by someone else's actions? Or are you going to pull yourself together and be the person you were created to be?" David let me cry for a minute or two more, then said, "You and I have so much in common, Beth. A lot of loss. Loved ones gone way too soon. And in no way do I want to suggest that those losses were any part of God's plans."

I nodded, even though he couldn't see me. "I know, I know. The chaos," I said, blowing my nose.

"Right. The chaos. But when it hits, we have to deal with it, and try to respond in faith and remember that God is with us."

I was quiet.

"You haven't told me much over the years about your relationship with Crawford," he said, "but I'm not blind. I thought you had a great friendship, but I also noticed the lack of physical affection. And I've seen the way you make yourself smaller in his presence."

I reached for more tissues and pulled the last one out of the box.

"I want you to think about this, Beth. What's happening now, as painful as it is, is happening *for* you, not *to* you."

"What does that even mean?"

"That you are not a victim. That you will not only survive, but thrive, because whether you can see it or not, things are falling into place for you. You're being set free from something you didn't have the strength to leave."

"It doesn't feel that way."

"I understand that. But falling apart is the first step to rebuilding. When painful things happen, you have to ask yourself, 'How will I craft my future, despite the pain I feel now? What do I need to let go of so I can move on?' It's a grieving process, and grieving has its own agenda. I'm not saying it's going to be easy or straightforward, but it has to be done, and ultimately, it will be what defines your life."

"I just can't believe how much this hurts."

"I know," David said. "There's something about a breakup and the primal need we all have to be loved and held close. That's why people stay in bad marriages."

"I didn't even know it was that bad. Our marriage, I mean."

There was a long pause before David said, "Oh, I think on some level you did. But for several reasons, you tried very hard not to know it."

I was thinking about this as I crossed the park and showed my patron pass to the ticket taker and entered the London Zoo. The rain was still coming down in sheets and the zoo was deserted except for a large group of tourists in bright yellow ponchos. I threaded my way through them and headed for the Rainforest Exhibit, where the steamy heat hit me like a wet blanket as soon as I opened the door.

I shook out my raincoat and my hat and draped my coat over my arm before stepping onto the walkway that wound through the leafy treetops. A pair of monkeys shrieked and swung on a thick vine to my right and a bird with vivid blue and green feathers flew directly across my path as I walked to the end of the Treetop Trail and downstairs to the Night Zone, where I tucked myself into a corner on a bench near the badgers to think.

David had said that I made myself smaller in Crawford's presence. Was he right? Had I really diminished myself to let Crawford shine? Yes, I'd moved to London with him and left my job, but I'd wanted a family, and wanted to be married, and Crawford seemed like the right person to do that with. He was reasonable. Solid. Dependable. So when I got pregnant the very first time we were together, an event that occurred after several margaritas and surprised both of us, it seemed like the universe was green-lighting the whole plan.

My mind scrolled back to the weeks after Steve had collapsed and I'd been promoted to Chief of Staff. Every day I'd woken up nauseous, wondering when Jude's newspaper would put the artificial blood product investigation out into the world, and I'd monitored Steve's recovery as closely as his cardiologist. One day, after weeks of working late nights and early mornings, I met Crawford for lunch at Old Ebbitt Grill. As soon as we'd ordered and the waiter was out of earshot, I looked around to make sure no one I recognized was in the room and leaned across the table.

"I absolutely do not want to work in the Senate anymore, Crawford."

"Don't be silly. Steve will be back in a few weeks and you can go back to Communications."

"And it will still suck," I said. I picked up the breadbasket and started pawing through it. "Nothing goes out the door the way I write it. Why do I even bother? I'm totally invisible until someone needs my help, and then I have a target on my back."

"Are you having some sort of early midlife crisis?" Crawford said, holding out his hand for the breadbasket. "I was glad to hear you cut Niall loose, by the way. You've got to stop wasting time with losers." He took the basket and put a brown roll on my bread plate, then selected one for himself.

"I went to a therapist," I said.

Crawford's eyebrows shot up. "Really?"

I understood his surprise. Therapy was something neurotic people in Manhattan did. We Washingtonians were too important to be introspective.

I nodded. "Last Friday. Birthday present to myself."

"And?"

"Every corner of her office was overrun with ferns. I felt like I was in the Hanging Gardens of Babylon."

"That's weird. What did she say?"

I reached across the table and plucked the lemon wedge off the rim of his tea glass, squeezed it, and dropped it next to the one that was already floating in my iced tea.

"She thinks I'm still mourning my parents, and that grieving them was keeping me from connecting with Niall."

"Somehow I'm missing the logic in that statement."

I shrugged. "It's therapy theoretics," I said, and immediately thought of Porter. *Band name!* "Logic isn't required."

"The fact that he's an insufferable snob kept you from connecting with Niall."

"I've been thinking I should get out of D.C. for a while," I said, affecting a lighthearted tone as the waiter set our food down and left. "Maybe go back to North Carolina and see what's happening there. At least I can afford to live there."

Moving back to North Carolina was an idea that had hit me like a freight train in the therapist's office. I was sitting across from her in a pink overstuffed chair, trying to explain why I felt so trapped by my life, when I had a Eureka! moment. *I don't have to be here.* I didn't have to be in the therapist's office, and I didn't have to be in Washington. I'd been happy in North Carolina, and David was there. Maybe I could be happy again there. It was worth a shot, at least.

"North Carolina? Do you honestly think you'd enjoy going from one of the most powerful offices in the Senate to some backwater state party?" Crawford said. "What are you going to do, write press releases about pig pickings? That's absurd."

When I didn't answer, he leaned back in his chair and threw his hands in the air.

"What the hell. They've even got cell service in West Virginia now. If North Carolina doesn't work out, you can always go there and learn how to strip mine." He laughed. "Why not? That ought to be just as rewarding as Ways and Means."

"I just think there are other things to care about, besides my career. Like some sort of work-life balance. Happiness.

Personal satisfaction." I jabbed my fork into one of my crab cakes, breaking the crust and revealing steaming lumps of crab meat inside. "And I would never characterize Ways and Means as rewarding, by the way. Exasperating and soul-crushing, yes." I shoved a chunk of crab in my mouth. "Rewarding, no."

"A state party would be a huge step backwards, no matter how you cut it," Crawford said, expertly excising a chunk of salmon and dragging it through dill sauce. "Frankly, I think you're being completely irrational."

"Maybe I am," I said, shrugging. "But rationality isn't everything. What about happiness?"

"Rationality is what separates us from animals and amoeba and psychopaths, but you're right, it's highly overrated. Why be rational?" He shrugged. "Be happy, instead."

"Jesus, Crawford. You sound like Niall! He said Americans are the only people on the planet who actually expect to be happy."

Crawford rolled his eyes. "Spare me. What else did the therapist say?"

"She said that when you go through some sort of trauma, the pathways in your brain are disrupted and disordered and you have to create new positive pathways, to overcome the negative ones. Neurogenesis, she called it."

"How do you do that?"

"Well, that's the tricky part. You have to figure out what's good for you, and what will make you happy, and what's not working. And then you do the positive things and find strategies to eliminate the negatives. Simple, huh?"

Crawford was quiet for a minute, then put his fork down and wiped his mouth with his napkin.

"What am I missing here, Beth? You are a Senate Chief of Staff. Temporarily, sure, but it won't go unnoticed that you were the one tapped to fill in. You have friends who love you. You—"

"I don't have any agency in my own life, Crawford. My entire life is about what the Senator wants, and what Steve and his clogged arteries need, and what fresh hell Jude and his exposé are about to unleash." I sighed. "I can't even find an apartment I can afford."

"So move in with me," he said, twisting in his chair to find the waiter. "Do you want coffee?"

"No thanks," I said. "I mean, this can't be real life, just ping-ponging around, reacting to whatever bullshit the day serves up."

"I think that's exactly what life is."

"Then I'd like to opt out. There's got to be something more."

"So your plan is to go to North Carolina to find the meaning of life? Most people with existential angst go to India or Machu Picchu, but you do you."

"I'm talking about going to a different state, not a fucking ashram, Crawford."

"You're talking about running away."

"It scared me, what happened to Steve. He nearly died two feet from me," I said.

"And he's alive because of you. His kids have a father because you knew what to do and you did it."

I didn't respond. I was thinking how much I envied Steve, getting to lie in bed all day.

"If you want to make changes, fine. Leave politics. Take up yoga and get a dog. Go back to the therapist and figure out the workarounds. But don't run away from your life, Beth."

I was quiet for a minute, waiting until the waiter had placed a cup of coffee and the bill in front of Crawford.

"You know, when I was walking out of the therapist's office, it was all I could do not to grab as many ferns as I possibly could and rip them to shreds in the parking lot."

Crawford laughed. "You have issues. Did you ask her why she had so many ferns?"

"I did, actually. She said 'Did you know that ferns grow without seeds or flowers? They're unique in that way. And they have adapted to thrive in the most unlikely places. Trunks of trees, crevices of rocks, salt marshes. They flourish where nothing else can grow. We should all be so resilient.'"

"She has a point. Resilience is the fundamental difference between failure and success."

I rolled my eyes. "When did you start speaking in poster slogans?"

"Was that verbatim, about the ferns?"

"Probably," I said, nodding.

He smiled and shook his head. "You're a lawyer's dream witness."

"I can't find my keys nine days out of ten. It's not exactly a useful talent."

"You know what I want for you?" Crawford said, leaning back in his chair and folding his arms over his chest. "I want you to look in the mirror and see the same person I see. Capable and strong. Special."

"Oh, I know how special I am," I said, fishing a piece of ice out of my water glass with my fingers. I shoved it in my mouth and crunched loudly. "I'm a goddamn miracle."

Crawford laughed. "Be serious for a second. Running away isn't going to solve anything. You just need a plan. First, stop picking the wrong guys."

"You make it sound like I've been hooking down at the bus station."

"Jude," he said, holding up one finger. "Total user." He extended a second finger. "Niall. Pompous asshole. Three, the surgeon who was never going to leave his wife, no matter what bullshit line he was feeding you."

"They were separated."

"Uh huh. By a pillow. And the advertising guy, what was his name? The guy from Belgium?"

"Fabien."

"Complete tool." He looked at the fingers he was holding up and then at me. "Do you see a pattern here?"

"Then you agree that I need to change my life."

Crawford looked away for an uncomfortably long time. When he finally looked back at me, he said, "I'm not going to pretend to be happy about this, Beth. I don't understand what you're looking for."

"I just need something different, Crawford. I need control over what happens in my own life."

He made a face and opened the black folder containing our bill. "You know, you can't go home again. It never works."

"Thank you, Thomas Wolfe. But my home is in New York, just like yours." I looked at him for a minute before reaching across the table to squeeze his hand. "You know that the thought of leaving you kills me, right?"

"If that were true, you wouldn't do it," he said. He scrawled his name and flipped the bill folder closed. "Ready to go?"

I tugged on my raincoat as I walked towards the door of the Rainforest exhibit and stepped out into the zoo. The rain changed to little pellets of stinging ice as I walked home through the deserted park, thinking about what David had said, that things were happening for me, not to me. Maybe he was right, and Crawford's betrayal was setting me free.

But somehow that didn't change the fact that I still felt like I was dying.

Dieci

Crawford didn't come home until almost eleven last night. I was reading on the window seat and didn't get up when I heard him drop his briefcase and stomp up the stairs. He turned on the hall light, walked into the master bedroom, and closed the door with a bang, leaving the hall light on. I sighed, flipped the covers back, got up and turned off the light, then crawled back into bed.

This morning, I waited for him to leave before I got dressed and went down to the kitchen. I was drinking coffee when Graciela came in. Her face when she saw me looked like Munch's *The Scream*.

"Hola," I said, dropping two pieces of bread into the toaster.

"You come back," she said.

"Yep."

"For how long?"

"As long as I want, seeing as how it's my home."

She ducked out of the kitchen.

I considered the day stretching out in front of me. The very last thing I wanted to do was have a conversation with Crawford, but I knew I wouldn't be able to tolerate this silent stand-off for long, and David had made me promise that I would do everything I could to initiate some sort of dialogue. "Some things resolve with inaction," he'd said, "but I highly doubt this is one of them."

I texted Crawford's phone. *Any chance we can have dinner and talk tonight?*

He answered a couple of hours later, when I was on the phone with my assignment editor, doing what I could to repair that relationship and simultaneously convince myself that I was ready to work again. She was explaining a travel assignment in Athens she wanted me to consider, profiling a couple of old men who still made sandals by hand, and I was thinking how desperately I wanted to get out of London and the house and was about to say *yes, I'll go tomorrow* when Crawford's text came through.

I put her on speaker and glanced at the screen.

That's fine. 8pm at Royal Orchid.

"I've got something I've got to wrap up in London first," I told her. "Can I let you know tomorrow?"

"You can," she said. "But another writer also wants this assignment. If she answers first, I've got to give it to her."

After we hung up, I had several hours to kill before dinner and went for a walk. I swear I'd never noticed how many Italian places there were in our neighborhood, but every other storefront was flying the red, white, and green *tricolore*. I thought about calling Porter, but what was I going to say? *I think my husband of two decades is having an affair with a man, and I have no idea what to do, so I thought I'd call you, my ex-fiancé of almost thirty years, for some advice?* Even I could appreciate the level of absurdity in that scenario.

Instead, I shoved my phone deeper into my pocket and thought about how much I wished I could turn back time. Go back to a simpler era, when you couldn't accidentally discover that your whole adult life had been a lie, or Google an old love and discover the heaping pile of crap their life had become. A time when meeting people only happened by chance, or fate, or the hand of God.

Porter and I had met by chance, but it had always felt like something more than that. Destiny. It was a particularly warm fall, our senior year of college, and I had a Foreign Policy class with a professor I adored, a two-hour seminar full of serious, intelligent people, with one exception: the guy who sat behind me. He was cocky and obnoxious, with his long legs sprawling into the aisle and his entitlement sucking the air from the room on the rare occasions he deigned to show up. His only saving grace was his chiseled body and bone structure. I'd started calling him the Idiot Adonis in my mind in the first week of class.

We were talking about Germany's mobilization into the Sudetenland one day when he tapped my shoulder and asked to borrow my notes. When I turned around to tell him there wasn't a chance in hell I was going to let him take my notebook, he held up the syllabus and pointed to Friday's lecture on the rise of fascism.

"I heard he really has it in for Italians," he said, nodding toward the professor, "so I need to lay low until we're a few chapters ahead." He looked me up and down, like he was considering a purchase but thinking he could probably find the same thing cheaper somewhere else. "You're not worried about that?"

"I'm not Italian," I said, and turned back around.

"Really?" he said, tipping forward in his desk until his breath scorched my ear. "Well, if you'd like to have some Italian in you, I'm happy to help."

I turned back to look at him. "Does that line actually work for you?"

"All the time," he said and let his desk fall backwards. "By the way, my fraternity brothers said all you have to do for the section on Fascism is write about a guy from the reading, Mussolini's boy Johnny something, and it's an instant A."

"Giovanni Gentile?"

"Yeh. Dude's apparently obsessed with him," he said, jerking his chin in the direction of the professor.

That was the end of my interaction with the Idiot Adonis, or so I thought. But the following night, he was at the second bar Kick and I went to.

"I'm off to do recon," Kick said, pinching my arm as we stepped inside. "Tonight's my night, I can feel it."

"You say that every Thursday, Kick."

"Yeh, but tonight I mean it. There's bound to be a few basketball players here."

I was minding my own business in the beer line when the Idiot Adonis spotted me and slithered over, wrapping his arm around my torso just under my bra and asphyxiating me in his toxic cloud of Wild Turkey, Polo cologne, and Marlboro fumes. When Kick returned to report on her findings, she saw him, stopped dead in her tracks, and began to purr. The Idiot let go of me to greet her and I race-walked to the bathroom in the back of the bar. When I came out, throwing my shoulder against the perpetually sticky door, Porter was there.

There's a scene in *The Godfather* when Michael Corleone is out walking with his bodyguards in Sicily and he sees Apollonia for the first time. He stops in his tracks, and the bodyguards laugh and say that Michael has been struck by the lightning bolt of love at first sight, *il colpo di fulmine*. That's exactly how it was when I met Porter. A lightning bolt that rewired my body and brain.

"Do you want to escape your admirer?" he asked when I emerged, wiping my hands down the sides of my jeans. "I'm Porter Haven, by the way."

I shook the hand he extended and tried not to swoon. "Beth Steeler. I'm not sure the window in the bathroom opens, if that was the escape route you were considering."

"Hmmm," he said. "I hadn't factored that in. Why don't we dance until we figure out a Plan B?"

Porter led me to the tiny area of the bar without tables. He was such a good dancer, muscular and lithe, and he smelled like the woods and tobacco and beer and something deliciously smoky and spicy that I couldn't identify. One of the buttons on his chambray shirt was hanging by a thread and there was a spray of freckles across his slightly sunburnt nose and his eyes were the purest green I'd ever seen.

He was singing in my ear as we danced when the Idiot Adonis suddenly walked up and punched him in the back.

"Oh, look who it is," Porter said, letting go of me to loop his arm around my waist. "Beth, do you know Vinnie Pellati? Pellati, have you met my cousin Beth?"

A look of confusion crossed the Idiot's face and I could actually hear his brain cells battling to decide if he was being made fun of or not.

"Unfortunately we don't take baths together as much as we used to, but you know how it is down here in the Dirty South," Porter said, tightening his grip so that our hips pressed together. "We like to keep it all in the family."

Vinnie stood there for a minute, obviously confused, before walking away.

When he was out of earshot, I burst out laughing.

"Just so you know, I'm from central New York," I told Porter. "We don't bathe with our cousins there. At least not as adults."

"Then let me be your guide to our Southern ways," Porter said, grinning at me.

"Is he a friend of yours?"

"Teammate. Great midfielder but a total jackass."

"He's in my Foreign Policy class."

"I'm sure he adds a lot to the intellectual discourse."

"He's convinced that Professor Wolf hates Italians and has it in for him, but is also secretly in love with one of the architects of Italian fascism. Who's long dead, by the way."

Porter laughed and held out his arms. We danced for a ridiculously long time after that, talking nonstop, until Kick suddenly materialized next to me.

"We have to go," she slurred, digging her fingers into the flesh of my upper arm. "Right now. I saw a spider."

That was our code word. It usually meant that some guy Kick had slept with, who'd never called again, was at the bar.

"Sorry," I told Porter. "She's my ride."

"I can take you home," he said.

"I'm pretty sure I need to drive."

"Can I have your number?" He dug into his pocket and unearthed a matchbook. "Hang on, I'll grab a pen from the bar."

When I handed the matchbook back to him, Porter said, "Hey Beth Steeler, a quick question before you go. How do you feel about Ajax?"

"The cleaning product or the Greek warrior?" I said. "Or the soccer team?"

Porter's face lit up. "My housemates and I are huge Ajax fans," he said, pronouncing it the Dutch way, *eye-axe*. "You're the first girl who's ever known what I meant," he said, and looked at me like he'd won a prize.

Porter and I understood each other on a molecular level, and I don't think it ever occurred to either of us to pretend otherwise. Even though we had wildly different interests, his enthusiasm for the things he loved, sports and food and movies and music, was contagious, and he once told me that listening to me talk about something I found fascinating was when he loved me best.

"You light up," he said. "Like a firefly."

"I don't think I've ever been compared to a bug before," I said. We were eating breakfast at Breadmen's and I was stabbing home fries with my fork. "But listen, Porter, this is funny. Remember when the Israelites were wandering in the desert and flakes of food started falling from the sky?"

"The manna from heaven, right?"

"Exactly. Here's the funny part: *Manna*, in Hebrew, means 'what is it?' So the story is saying that this unexpected food, literally the *what is it?* kept raining down every morning."

Porter reached for a piece of green pepper on my plate. "I love the obscure shit you know. Can I have this?"

I nodded. "Of course. But do you get it? The name never got corrected! No one ever knew what it actually was, so they just kept *what is it?* as the name, and that's what's been handed down. There's no way to translate that word without making up what it was. But it's not like you can get a side dish of *manna* in a Jerusalem diner." I forked potatoes into my mouth and shrugged. "Funny."

"I would read the Bible if it explained stuff like that," Porter said.

That was later, of course, after we were a couple. First, though, I left the bar with Kick and went across the street to get a chicken biscuit at Time Out, the traditional consolation prize after running into a spider, and then drove her home. Porter called the next morning, and from then on, we were together as much as our schedules would allow. I used to tell Porter that he was a human narcotic, because as soon as he took my hand, or wrapped his arm around me, I felt a deep sense of peace.

I could use some of that peace now, I thought, checking my watch as I turned the corner and our house came into view. It was almost six. I was so tempted to call Porter and tell him what I'd found and let him send a car for me. I could be sitting in front of the fire with him and Oliver by midnight.

But I didn't. Instead I went home, to get cleaned up before meeting Crawford for dinner.

Undici

Dear Jenny,

I got your email and I promise, I'm okay. Or rather, I'm alive. Gutted, but alive. I promised I'd let you know how dinner went, so here goes...

I feel like an idiot writing this, but I had really high hopes. I thought maybe Crawford was going to explain, and I'd see that I'd been ridiculously mistaken about him, and he'd apologize and we'd go home and watch the news together like we used to and peace would return to the kingdom. I mean, he chose Royal Thai, where we've been going for twenty years, right? It was our place. Mia loved it there, even as a little kid. She'd sit in her highchair with a big plate of pineapple fried rice in front of her, carefully picking out the cashews and handing them to Crawford before scattering rice everywhere on the way to

111

her mouth, and at the end of the meal, when they brought her fortune cookie, she'd crack it in half and solemnly hand me the slip of paper. I'd make something up, like Mia is a good girl with new pink sneakers, and her eyes would get as wide as a dinner plate.

"But how'd dat cookie know dat?" she'd say.

"Magic," I'd tell her.

So I interpreted the fact that Crawford suggested Royal Thai as a good sign.

I was so wrong.

Crawford showed up half an hour late, which he blamed on traffic, but it was obvious he'd had a couple of drinks, and I suppose some Dutch courage is in order when you're about to ruin your wife's life—or try to persuade her she's crazy, both of which he actively did.

We made small talk at first. Crawford was bristly and I was trying not to cry, which is not a productive conversational mix, and I finally just asked him straight up whether he was happy that I was home.

"Sure," he said. "I'd love to hear how you and Porter Haven finally got back together. People's love stories are always so fun."

"It's not a love story," I said. "He read about the accident on the internet and invited me to visit. I was barely functioning, and he thought a change of scenery would help. So I went."

"I guess certain parts of you were functioning, though, huh?"

I shook my head. "We are friends, and that's all."

"Sure."

"Why do you even care? It's not like you're interested."

He took a sip of his vodka tonic. "I'm just trying to figure out why you came back."

"Because this is my home. And you're my husband."

"In name only. You made that point."

"How?"

"By leaving. By not telling me where you were going, or with whom."

"I told you I was going to Italy."

"Umm hmm. That's what we call a lie by omission," he said.

I wanted to kick the smirk off his face.

"What are you doing, Crawford?" I asked.

"Having dinner with the prodigal wife."

I started to respond, but Malee came over and set a plate of spring rolls on the table between us.

"Long time I don't see you!" she said, beaming at me.

"She's been visiting an old friend," Crawford said, nodding in my direction.

"Yes, I just got back," I said. "It's good to see you, Malee."

"Where baby?"

Jen, my first thought was that I had been wrong about Crawford. That he had a mistress, not a boyfriend, and had been stupid enough to bring his side piece and bastard offspring to the Thai restaurant we'd been eating at for twenty years.

But then it hit me.

She meant Mia.

"She is traveling," Crawford said. "Taking a gap year."

"Ah," Malee said. "She pretty girl, like her mommy. She come home with boyfriend, daddy angry!"

"You're right, Malee," Crawford said, and laughed a big, honking laugh like a braying donkey. "I wouldn't like that! Not at all."

He ordered for both of us and Malee went away. I just stared at him, my mouth hanging open. Honestly, Jen, I felt like I'd slipped into some sort of altered state, like the time we smoked that horrible pot and couldn't feel our legs and were so scared. Meanwhile, Crawford was dunking spring rolls into peanut sauce like it was just another Tuesday night.

We didn't speak again until after the entrees had arrived.

"So just to be clear," Crawford said, vigorously mixing the rest of the peanut sauce into a bowl of noodles, "Your expectation is that I am going to sit tight until you decide what to do?"

"What to do about what?"

"About your boyfriend."

"Isn't that exactly what you're expecting me to do?"

He shot me a look, his eyes narrowed. "What is that supposed to mean?"

"It means I know about your lie by omission, Crawford. I know you've been supporting Trevor Kent for almost two years. The same Trevor Kent who is a junior partner in your firm and has been to our house a million times."

For a brief second, Crawford looked like I'd hit him. But he recovered quickly and said, "I'm helping a friend."

I nodded. "Sure. And Porter was helping me."

"I don't know what you're insinuating, Beth, but I suggest you think carefully about what you say next. You're not on very solid footing here."

"Solid enough that I can finally see what's been going on right under my nose. All the secrets, all the late nights," I said, my voice cracking. "The hours and hours spent everywhere but home."

"The demands of my career, you mean? The same career that pays for a house in London and school fees and a house in France and skiing holidays?"

I reached into my purse. "Speaking of the house in France, how did he like it?" I asked, tossing two photos onto the table. "He looks pretty happy sitting by my pool. Or did he like Mykonos better? Nice Speedo, by the way. You've managed to carve out a lot of vacation time for someone who can never be away from the office."

"My daughter died. I needed some time away to grieve, just like you."

"I thought she was taking a gap year?"

Crawford rolled his eyes at me. "There's no need to broadcast our lives to people who don't need to know our business."

"Like the waitress who knew Mia her whole life?"

Crawford nodded. "Precisely. We are customers in a restaurant, not personal friends."

I shook my head, as if it might be possible to clear away the shock I felt.

"But Trevor helped you grieve?" I said, as Crawford pocketed the photos. "And you're helping with his bills?"

"So you came back to snoop?"

"No, Crawford. I came back to see whether there was anything left of our marriage. And shockingly, it all gave me a massive headache that required paracetamol. And guess where we keep that? Next to your box of souvenirs."

"You're pathetic," he said. "And it was Santorini, not Mykonos."

"You know what? You've done everything you could to make sure I knew you weren't interested in me. That you couldn't stand to be in my company," I said, hot, furious tears rolling down my face. "But I could never put the pieces together. I could never solve the mystery of why you were always so disappointed in me. It never dawned on me that you'd been lying to me since the day we met. But I get it now."

Crawford glared at me. "You've lost it completely."

"Do you think that has anything to do with my husband pushing me away for twenty years?" I was shaking and my knee knocked against the bottom of the table. "Do you know what that feels like, to be rejected every single day by the person you're supposed to be closest to?"

Crawford laughed. "Yes, I can see why having a beautiful home and all of your needs met would feel like rejection."

"*The thing I needed most was for my husband to love me, Crawford. For my husband to want to spend time with me. For my husband to value me and treat me like an equal partner. Not to live in a gilded cage with some never-ending mystery about what I'd done to piss you off every day. I always told myself that it's because you had such a shitty example from your parents, that's why you couldn't be affectionate, but...*" I had to stop and collect myself for a minute before I could continue. "*But it's not like I didn't feel it, Crawford. You did everything you could not to be around me. Why didn't you just tell me? Wasn't I worth the truth?*"

"*Tell you what? That you're a miserable person and I have tried everything I can but it's impossible to make you happy?*" he said. "*I just told you. You're welcome.*"

"*I wasn't always miserable, Crawford. Jesus! You can't ignore someone for years and pretend the person who shares your life doesn't exist. Do you have any idea the toll that takes on someone? Do you have any idea what that feels like, not to have a voice in your own home?*"

"*Keep your voice down,*" he hissed.

"*Fuck you.*"

"*Classy.*" He tilted his glass in my direction. "*Hard to imagine why I don't like you.*"

"*Who knows about this? Who knows you've been lying to me? Does Mac know? Does Hugh?*" A thought struck me and I gasped. "*Oh my God. Were you and Hugh an item? Has this all just been a giant mind-game for thirty years?*"

"*You're insane.*"

"*Right. I'm the problem.*" I pushed my chair back and stood up. "*I'm not the one who's been hiding. I'm not the one who's been lying. Go to your boyfriend's house, Crawford. Go convince him that your daughter is traveling and your wife is a miserable bitch who can't be happy.*" I picked up my dinner napkin, *smashed it into a ball, and threw it at his chest. "Everything is my fault and you're completely innocent, as usual. The perpetual victim. See if your boyfriend will buy that."*

"I'll be going back to my own house, thank you very much. But you're welcome to go back to your boyfriend. I hear Italy is lovely for the holidays."

"I'm done."

He lowered his voice to just above a whisper and smiled at me. "Get a lawyer, Beth," he said. "This is going to be fun."

So that's how dinner went. I'm currently holed up in Mia's room with my laptop and Joan Baez singing "Diamonds and Rust" on an endless loop in my earphones. She's talking about Bob Dylan, of course, but she might as well be talking about Crawford.

He's in our bedroom with MSNBC blaring, and I feel like whatever was left of my heart has been smashed to pieces under his feet. How is this the man I married and had a child with?

I'm weighing my options. So far what I've come up with are: (1) Pack a suitcase and get on a plane to David before Crawford cuts off the credit cards, or (2) Throw myself off London Bridge.

I'd be lying if I said I wasn't leaning towards the latter.

Beth

Dodici

Yesterday was my birthday. I spent the whole day in bed watching Netflix, knowing that if I went out I wouldn't be able to resist stepping in front of a train. Graciela knocked on the door and brought me a plate of enchiladas and a Coke, and returned a couple hours later to take it all back to the kitchen, and after midnight, when the wretched day was over, I listened to the birthday messages from Jenny and David and Porter and then went right back to bed.

This morning I made myself take a shower and get dressed, and I went to a cafe around the corner for coffee and a piece of Victoria sponge with strawberry jam. I would have preferred carrot cake.

Carrot cake was my dad's favorite, too. The last birthday I had with him, my mom made a huge carrot cake with cream cheese icing. We had a party at our house, with school friends and Snoopy plates and tons of balloons, and my parents gave me a record player. It came inside a big square box with a metal latch and weighed about five pounds, which was considered a portable device at the time, and Jenny gave me my first record, a 45 of "Don't Go Breakin' My Heart" by Elton John and Kiki Dee, along with three of the yellow plastic inserts that allowed you to listen to a 45 on a record player meant for 33s. After my party, I went to Jenny's for a sleepover and took it with me so we could choreograph a dance in her bedroom.

"You know, there's another song on the other side," Colin said, sticking his head in Jenny's room without knocking.

But whoever listened to the B side? And if you didn't interrupt it, the record player's arm would simply reset and play the same song again, which is exactly what was happening until Jenny's brother Patrick stormed in and lifted the needle and threatened to snap the record in half if we didn't listen to something else. He then went to his room and brought back a milk crate of albums, and a couple hours later, all five of the Fife brothers and their beanbag chairs and Doritos and cream sodas were packed into Jenny's room so they could school us on the musical superiority of Led Zeppelin, Cream, and the Rolling Stones.

After dinner with Crawford at Royal Thai, my brain was just like that record player. The arm went back to the beginning and played the same song on an endless loop: *I don't have to be here. I don't have to be here.*

The same realization I'd had in D.C. all those years ago.

Crawford had wanted me to believe I was crazy then, too. Crazy to leave my job in the Senate, crazy to leave D.C., crazy to walk away from my career. But when Steve finally announced that he would be coming back to resume his post as Chief of Staff, I knew that it was time for me to go. I considered warning him that he was walking into a buzzsaw of insider-trading allegations, but

I didn't want him to reconsider his return, so I kept my mouth shut and started looking in earnest for another job and let Steve deal with Jude and the other bottom-feeders.

Finally, I got the call I'd been hoping for. I took a personal day, got up in pre-dawn darkness, made a mad dash to Raleigh to meet with the Governor's Chief of Staff, and accepted the job they offered me via car phone while doing eighty-five miles an hour on the highway back to D.C. When I got back to my apartment that evening, I threw back a glass of wine, took a deep breath, and pushed Send on the email I'd drafted to the Senator giving notice, then forced myself up and out of my chair and down to the lobby, where I put the letter for my landlord in the outgoing mail, then came back upstairs, texted Crawford that I'd found a job and was moving, and turned off my phone.

On my last Saturday in town, Crawford came over early to go with me to rent the U-Haul truck and drive it back to my street. He managed to wedge it into a space in front of my building in a remarkable feat of parallel parking, and then we started loading. Mac and Hugh showed up around noon to help, and when we finished, we sat on the floor and took turns passing around the bottle of champagne that was the last thing left in my refrigerator.

Hugh and Mac went back to Hugh's to get cleaned up and I gave Crawford a towel and cleaned the counters and window ledges while he showered and dressed. When he walked out of the bathroom smelling like soap, he stretched out on his back on the floor with his hands folded over his chest.

"I think I pulled something carrying the sofa," he said.

"I'm sorry, old man. Have I told you how much I appreciate your help?"

"You have. I just need to stretch out here for a minute."

"You look like a monk," I said.

"Mmm hmm. *Labora et ora*. Work is over, now I pray."

"Such a good little Papist." It was always a joke between us, that we were both Catholic, yet neither of us had been in a Catholic church in years.

"Go take a shower, Beth. I'm starving."

Crawford grabbed my hand as we stepped onto the street less than an hour later. We had been habitual hand holders for years, ever since the night a few weeks after we met when I dashed across Constitution Avenue trying to keep up with his ridiculously long legs and got hit by a car. I bounced off the bumper as the car skidded to a stop on the rain-slicked pavement, not really damaged but for an enormous bruise that turned purple and green over the next few weeks, but from that evening on, Crawford always held my hand, as if dragging me alongside his double-time gait would keep me from harm. Once when I was dating Fabien, the three of us were walking to a restaurant on M Street and Crawford and I were so absorbed in our own conversation that we didn't notice that Fabien was no longer rattling away *en français* on his phone behind us until he cleared his throat and suggested that perhaps handholding was a privilege that should be reserved for the boyfriend. Crawford dropped my hand like it was on fire, but a few weeks later, Fabien was the butt of our jokes and Crawford and I were back to our old habits.

"Are you going to be okay driving that truck?" he asked as we walked to dinner. "The brakes are pretty loose. Make sure you leave plenty of room to stop, especially now that it's loaded. You've got a crew lined up on the other end, right?"

"I do." I squeezed his fingers as we turned onto Wisconsin Avenue. "I have to do this, Crawford. I know you don't understand, but I have to."

"You keep saying that. Are you trying to convince me, or yourself?"

I was starting to answer when a shout turned both of our heads.

"Oi! Lovebirds!"

Mac was wearing a ridiculous yellow ski hat with a red pompom on top and waving frantically from the other side of the road, where Hugh was leaning inside the passenger window of a cab. When the cab pulled away, the two of them bounded across the street, causing horns to blare as they dodged traffic.

Mac grabbed me and kissed the side of my face like a slobbery dog, as if we hadn't been together all day. "You taste like roses," he said.

"Hey, Steeler, check out my shirt," Hugh said, unzipping his parka to show me the t-shirt clinging to his flat stomach. "It's an homage."

Hugh's shirt was from our grad school study group, The Thousand Yard Stares. We'd chosen the name to honor the vacant look shared by shell-shocked veterans and people forced to sit through endless political speeches, and we wore them every time we competed in Trivia Night at Ed's Bar, where we'd been reigning champs for two years.

"I love it, Hugh. Mine has bleach on it."

"Campbell, you're looking dead serious, old man. What did we interrupt?" Mac said.

"He was getting ready to tell me that I'm being irrational," I said, and nudged Crawford with my elbow. "For the hundredth time."

"Well, you are a girl," Hugh said, shrugging. "Hormones and whatnot."

"You're more of a girl than I am," I said, swatting at his midsection. Hugh squealed and jumped out of my reach.

"I wasn't going to say anything about being irrational," Crawford said. "Although now that you've brought it up, I'll go on record that I think this is a case of negligent entrustment."

"English, mate," Mac said, making a face. "How many times do I have to tell you we don't speak your poncy solicitor lingo?"

"Let's say you have a friend with a history of multiple wrecks, yet you still lend him your car, and he gets in another wreck," Crawford said. "You're guilty of negligent entrustment, because you put your car in his possession knowing he was a danger to other drivers."

"Can we walk and talk?" I asked. "I'm freezing."

"I hope he's not referring to Mac taking my car next weekend." Hugh tightened his arm around my neck and made our hips bump as we walked. "He's got a driver's license, I swear. It's just printed upside down."

"No, he thinks I have a secret reason for moving away," I said.

"I'm suggesting that you're going back to North Carolina to entrust your emotional well-being to someone who has established, via precedent, that he is an unworthy trustee," Crawford said from behind us. "You say you're leaving because you want to be happy, but you're going back to find someone who has historically made you very unhappy."

"Wait...who are you looking for in North Carolina?" Hugh asked.

"That fuckwit who broke her heart," Mac said.

"This is all in Crawford's head. Can we change the subject?"

"You are breaking up the team, though, Steeler," Hugh said.

"I know. I've been getting your texts. And Mac's, too."

"I think you're going because you want a bloke with a wheelie house," Mac said from behind me, where he was walking next to Crawford.

It took me a second to figure out what he was talking about.

"That's it exactly, Mac," I said, laughing. "My dream is to find a man with a double-wide."

Mac's conception of the American South was based completely on reruns of *The Dukes of Hazzard*. He thought everyone below the Beltway owned muscle cars and routinely outran the cops. I stopped on the sidewalk and tried to explain to him that Raleigh was a city, smaller than Washington, but with buildings and businesses and universities, but he wasn't buying it.

"Hold up," he said. "You're saying there's not even one bridge out of order there?"

"I doubt it. Even if I had the General Lee, I wouldn't have anywhere to jump it."

Mac thought for a moment. "But you'll still wear the short shorts and tie up your flanno?"

I shook my head. "The dress code's a little more relaxed, but you're still supposed to wear actual clothes. Sorry."

Mac sighed loudly. "Well, there goes that fantasy. You might as well stay here and marry this ugly bastard," he said, pointing at Crawford.

"I can't do that," I said. "It would ruin our beautiful friendship." Crawford shot me a look that I couldn't interpret, but before he could say anything, Hugh launched into the latest about his parents, who had abandoned the tingsha bells in favor of the teachings of Sri Ramakrishna and were now intent on finding evidence of the workings of God in everyone and everything, including their fellow economists and their only son. We started walking again and I dropped back and changed places with Mac, sliding my gloved hand into Crawford's.

"I'm worried," he said, looking down at me.

"What about?"

"That the torch you carry for Porter Haven is going to burn you."

"You know this is something you've made up, right?" I looked up at him and squeezed his hand. "Pretty much the only thing I have going for me right now is that you're my best friend," I said. "I mean that. But I have to do this, Crawford. And it has nothing to do with Porter. I haven't seen him in years and I don't have any plans to see him."

We stopped on the sidewalk in front of Vito's Pizza and let Mac and Hugh go in before us.

"I was there, you know, when your relationship with him crashed and burned," Crawford said. "I saw what it did to you."

"I know. But this has nothing to do with him."

"Promise me that if it doesn't work out, you'll come back," he said.

I nodded.

"Will you call me at Christmas and distract me from Blythe and Number Three?"

"Of course."

"Are you sure you don't need any money?"

I couldn't answer because of the lump in my throat and simply nodded.

He reached over my head and pulled the door open. "Let me know if you change your mind. About any of it."

Our Last Supper, as Mac kept calling it, was pretty standard fare. The guys drank several pitchers of beer and ordered too much pizza, we made fun of everyone we knew and each other, and Crawford badgered Hugh, who was working on a piece of legislation about grazing rights in Colorado, about going to law school.

"For the last time, I don't need another degree," Hugh said. "I'm smart enough. Look at me, man! I radiate intelligence."

"You have tomato sauce on your face," Crawford said. "Besides, law school isn't about being a lawyer. It's about learning how to think."

"You actually could use some help in that department, Hugh," Mac said. He was refilling our beer glasses, a process that he took very seriously.

"You suck, Mac," I said, pointing to the foam that was rising in my glass. "My dog doesn't even wear a collar that big."

"Get stuffed, Steeler. That's a perfect pour. And you don't have a dog."

"You should consider it," Crawford said, turning back to Hugh. "You can go at night and keep your job. I'm sure the Feds would spring for it. Tell them it's what Sri Ramawhatever would want."

"I agree, Hugh," Mac said, setting the pitcher down. "You're my best mate and I'd take a bullet for you, but your thinking's right dodgy. Bit more school, she'll be alright."

"It's not gonna happen," Hugh said, waving his hand to dismiss Crawford. "Let's move on. Someone ask Mac about his new girlfriend."

"Who is the latest fly in your web, Mac?" I asked.

"I have a couple of tasty flies in my sights, darling, unless you're finally ready to give ol' Mac a go?"

"She's not, I can assure you," Crawford said. "She's leaving to exhume an old lover, remember?"

"She'll be back," Hugh said.

"No one can resist me forever," Mac agreed. "I give you two weeks before you fold and come back to Mac. And I'll be waiting."

"That's fine. Just don't hold your breath."

When it was time to go, I hugged Mac and Hugh goodbye and Crawford and I left the restaurant together. I was supposed to retrieve my overnight bag and spend the night on his couch so I could leave for Raleigh early in the morning.

"You didn't eat again," he said, after we'd walked a few blocks in silence.

"I did. I had some pizza."

"Picking the cheese off and tearing up the crust doesn't count as eating."

"Nerves, I guess. I'll have a big breakfast, I promise."

I could see the white bulk of the U-Haul halfway down the block when Crawford, apropos of absolutely nothing, said, "I've been thinking about what Niall said the last time you saw him."

"Why? You can't stand Niall."

"I think maybe he had a point."

I mentally ran through the list of hurtful things Niall had said the last time I saw him and couldn't imagine which one Crawford agreed with.

"About what?"

"About needing to be in control. That you'd rather limit your options than tolerate uncertainty."

"Look who's talking! You're the king of control, Crawford."

"It's my job to mitigate uncertainty, Beth. It's not what I do in my personal life. But you are running away. Niall was right. And all the things you're so worried about, your job and the apartment, they're temporary. If you had the strength to wait it out, you could. Easily."

I stopped in mid-stride and stared at Crawford with my mouth hanging open for what felt like ten minutes, fury boiling up inside me. Then I started walking towards my building, fast.

Crawford caught up with me and grabbed my elbow.

"Thank you for making it easier for me to leave," I said, wrenching my arm free. "And that will be the last time I tell you anything personal."

"Beth, come on." He reached out and grabbed my arm again. "I just meant—well, never mind what I meant. Let's get your bag. My bed's all made for you and I'm looking forward to the couch."

I was shaking mad. Crawford had already told me I was crazy and misguided more times than I could count. That I was committing career suicide. That I had to be doing this because of Porter. He knew that I was scared witless and that saying goodbye to him and Mac and Hugh was breaking my heart, and yet he still chose to kick me when I was down.

"Let go of me, Crawford."

"Come on. Let's go to my place."

I shook my head. "I'm going to get on the road. Less traffic."

"You've been drinking."

"No, I haven't. And the fact that you have does not excuse the fact that you're being an unbelievable asshole right now."

I turned away and let myself into the lobby of my building. But as I jabbed the call button for the elevator, the finality of the situation hit me. I was about to be miles away, without much of a chance to repair things, and as furious as I was, I couldn't imagine my life without Crawford.

So when the elevator thunked into position and the doors creaked open, instead of getting in, I turned and ran to the door of the lobby, intending to call Crawford back so we could smooth things over.

But when I stepped outside, he was already halfway down the block.

I stood in the doorway, shivering in the night air, marveling at how fast he could move when he wasn't pulling me along with him.

Then I went upstairs and got my bag, closed the door of my empty apartment, and left Washington, blasting the heater in that loose-braked U-Haul, with the record player arm resetting again and again to the same tune: *I don't have to be here.*

Tredici

In a city like London, there are a thousand ways to occupy your time so that you never have to go home, and I did them all in the days following the disastrous dinner with Crawford. I went to Wimbledon and walked through the Commons and the gardens of Cannizaro House. I sat in posh tearooms in Richmond and working-class pubs in Tottenham and Hackney. I explored the artists' lofts of Shoreditch and the new construction of Canary Wharf. I took the train to Bath one day and to Canterbury the next. But no matter how I tried to distract myself from the funeral pyre of my marriage, the smoke clung to my body and followed me wherever I went.

I envy Crawford, I texted Jenny. *He just files this away as a legal and financial problem to be dealt with and carries on with his life. But I feel like I'm drowning 24/7. This hurts so unbelievably bad....and just when I was starting to get back on my feet.*

I know, Bits.

If it wasn't for you and David, I would take a bottle of pills. Not having to know any of this, not having to feel it, seems like bliss...

Please don't say that. You have so much to live for.

I understand now how I've failed my friends who've gone through divorces. How totally inadequate my "support" has been. It's one of those things, like becoming a parent, that you can't understand until you experience it yourself. And I totally get it now why most people don't leave until they have someone else. This would be so much easier if there was someone in my corner, telling me how great I am and what an asshole he is. Reassuring me that there's something about me that's worthy of love. Because that's so, so hard to believe.

There is, but I know what you mean. If Scott and I ever split up, I'm sure I'd run straight into the arms of the first man who'd have me. I think that's the whole reason for dating apps, huh?

I want to be numb, Jen. Everything hurts. There's no protective covering anymore. No harbor, no safety net. I don't do drugs, I can't drink enough to forget. I'm just out here, feeling all the feelings. And all of the pain of losing Mia has come roaring back to dance some sort of death tango with losing Crawford, and I can't handle it. I just want to sleep.

Have you given any more thought to coming back to the US? Scott and I would love to have you and we've got plenty of room. And if you don't want to stay with us, what about David?

I've thought about it, I wrote. *I'm still thinking about it. I'm just terrified to do anything at all. I can barely dress myself in the morning.*

Have you heard from Porter?

He texts every couple of days. There is so much between me and Porter that has gone unsaid, so much I don't understand, and I don't have the energy. Talking with him is just trading one tar pit for another...

I was tempted, though. Every time I saw Porter's name in my Inbox, I had to fight the urge to toss my clothes into a bag and get on the first flight to Rome, to go back to his house and climb into bed with Oliver and wait for spring. But I couldn't let myself do it. I couldn't take the coward's way out and hide away from my life, no matter how much I wanted to do exactly that.

Plus, I'd been so blind to the truth of Crawford, the person I lived with and had a child with, that I couldn't possibly trust Porter. If Crawford wasn't the person I'd thought he was, when I'd lived under the same roof with him for decades, how could I be sure that Porter's intentions were pure, when I'd only recently met again after thirty years? So I didn't call, and when he texted, I kept my answers short and noncommittal.

David checked in every couple of days, too. He urged me to pray, not only for myself, but also for Crawford and for peace between us.

"Peace would be a nice change. Right now it's like a standoff at the OK Corral in our house," I said. "We avoid each other, but on the rare occasions we come face to face, we both have our guns drawn and are just waiting to see who will fire first."

"How's that feel?" he asked.

"Like death row. I know I'm about to get killed, emotionally, but I'm holding out hope for clemency."

"What would clemency look like, though?" David asked. "You can't un-know what you know."

"It would look like the old Crawford," I said. "The guy who didn't resent the fact that I was born."

David was quiet for a minute. "You know," he said finally, "maybe it's possible to find that person you used to know, or maybe he's gone forever. But either way, you've got to take action. You can't just exist in a stalemate. It's not good for either of you."

"I know. But I'm paralyzed, David. I'm terrified to do anything, because I know that whatever I do, it will be wrong."

He was so quiet that I thought the call had dropped. I was about to hang up and redial when suddenly he said, "Did I ever tell you where I went after college?"

I sat down on a park bench and held the phone between my ear and shoulder so I could dig my gloves out of my coat pocket. "Seminary?"

"No, not right away," he said. "First I hitchhiked out to Malibu and lived in the back of a Volkswagen van. My hair was as long as yours and I waxed surfboards on the beach for food money." He chuckled. "Your father never understood why I loved surfing so much. Remember how in Genesis the first thing God does is calm the sea, because the ocean is the terrifying chaos of *Tiamat*? That was your father's thinking, too," David said. "But surfing requires you to welcome the chaos. It's the turmoil that makes the experience meaningful! That's true of life, too."

"Then my life is meaningful as shit," I said.

David was quiet.

"Sorry."

"No need to apologize. All I'm saying if that if you don't have the chaos, you can't appreciate the calm. And if you wait for the perfect wave, you end up stuck on the beach and never surfing. And that goes for the perfect person and the perfect opportunity, too. Better just to accept that we're not in control and things will never be perfect and keep moving forward."

"I definitely know I'm not in control of anything," I said. "My life is just a shit show that's happening to me."

"*For* you."

"Trust me, it doesn't feel like that."

"Not that you can see at the moment, no. But have faith."

I was about to reply that on the spectrum of things I had, ranging from a solid marriage to chronic hives, faith was down there by marriage, but I decided I'd rather change the subject.

"Tell me more about Malibu," I said.

"Malibu changed my life."

"Because you fell in love with surfing?"

"That," David said, "but everything started for me on the day I heard a conversation that deeply affected me. I was in the water, and there were two guys nearby. One of them was Miki Dora, the king of the Malibu surfing scene. The other guy asked Miki about me, probably because he was trying to decide whether he needed to run me off their turf, and Miki said something profound."

"Which was?"

"'Don't worry about him. He's just decorating the shallows.'"

I thought about that for a minute as I watched two little kids fight over a red plastic ball.

"What does that mean," I said, "decorating the shallows?"

"That was what they called it when the girls sat near the shore in bright bikinis, hoping to catch some surfer's eye. Just being decorative, taking up space and air, waiting to be noticed, never riding a wave or paddling out beyond the break. Basically," David said, "he was calling me a poser."

I started to respond, but before I could, David said, "You know, Beth, when your dad died, I was a wreck. I was getting divorced, and I didn't have the best relationship with my bishop, and I asked God a million times why a good man like my brother would be taken so young." He exhaled audibly. "I was the pesky kid brother, but he and your mom used to take me with them everywhere. And Kirk was my idol. A lefty like Sandy Koufax, with an arm that just wouldn't quit. I used to hang on the fence and watch him pitch. Losing them ... well, there went my whole childhood," David said. "Yours, too, of course."

"That's exactly what it feels like," I said. "My childhood disappeared. And then Mia's did. And now Crawford has erased several more decades, because apparently everything he ever said to me was a lie." I lifted my shoulder to hold the phone against my chin again and dug in my coat pocket for a tissue. "I was someone's kid and someone's mom and someone's wife.... and now I'm just.... nothing. I wish someone would tell me what I did to deserve this."

"You didn't do anything at all. No one knows why bad things happen to good people," David said. "Augustine and Leibniz and Weber and all the great minds have tried to answer this question, but you know what?"

"What?"

"They've all reached the same conclusion. We don't know. We can't know. The only thing we can do is accept the chaos and continue to do our best for each other."

"So I just need to accept that Crawford's been lying to me and move on?"

"In a nutshell, yes. Because whatever has been happening with Crawford, whatever internal battle he's been fighting, it's not about you. You can't change it. All you can do is try to find some peace and rebuild your life."

"I have no idea how to do that."

"Get back on the board and start paddling, kiddo."

After we hung up, I walked across the park towards home. A memory had been nibbling at the corner of my brain for a couple of days, an experience I'd had in D.C. that had left me shaken, and I wasn't sure why.

I was leaving for Capitol Hill one morning just after the whole Steve choking incident when my neighbor Samantha stopped me in the lobby. She was just back from a workout and looked like Lululemon Barbie.

"Did you see this?" she said, waving a sheet of paper in my face. "It came in the mail yesterday."

"I haven't checked the mail in days. What's it about?"

"The accelerated construction timeline."

"Wait—what? I thought we had until January 20th?"

Sam shook her head and jabbed at the paper with a manicured index finger. "December 30th."

"Can they do that? Just move up the date that we all have to get out?"

"I doubt it. I'm meeting with Max from the fourth floor, he's a real estate attorney. I don't know how this is legal." She pushed a strand of expertly highlighted hair out of her face. "I'll call you after I talk to Max. We're going to need everyone involved to fight this."

"Jeez, Samantha..."

She narrowed her eyes. "Are you really going to just sit back and get steamrolled?"

I sighed. "Okay. Count me in." I checked my watch. "Listen, I'm late already."

"Go, go. But I'm counting on you."

As I went out the door, I collided with Ben, Samantha's brother, who was staying with her temporarily. I'd been introduced to him at a cocktail party on the roof and had seen him a few times in the building.

"Ben, make yourself useful and give Beth a ride to work," Samantha barked at her brother.

"It's okay, I'll grab a cab," I said.

"Don't be stupid," Samantha said. "He doesn't have anything else to do."

Ben handed Samantha the pharmacy bag he was carrying and looked at me. "She's right," he said. "I don't have anything else to do."

As soon as we pulled out of the parking garage, Ben started talking as if he'd just been waiting for the chance to dump his story in my lap. He told me that five months earlier, he'd purchased a car in Atlanta, where he and Samantha were from, and had driven it to their brother's house in Memphis the same day. It was late at night when he arrived, but he wanted to show off his new car, so Ben cajoled his brother, Adam, and Adam's girlfriend and her visiting cousin, to go for a ride.

"I got that car up to a hundred and fifteen miles an hour," Ben told me as we joined the traffic jam on the Memorial Bridge.

"What the hell for?"

He shrugged. "I just wanted to see what it could do."

So Ben went speeding down a two-lane road, music blaring, windows open, showing off. When a deer leapt into the road, he swerved and lost control of the car, which flew into the woods, flipping over and over before becoming wedged on its side between two trees. Ben was pinned in by the steering wheel, but Adam was able to kick out the windshield and drag himself to the road for help.

"His girlfriend's cousin was in the back seat, screaming so loud," Ben told me. "But his girlfriend was really quiet. And then everybody was quiet."

"Please tell me you were wearing seatbelts?"

He shook his head. "I was nearly cut in half from the impact," he said. "I lost half my stomach and nine feet of intestines. I was in the hospital for four weeks."

"Jesus," I said. "What about your brother?"

"Really banged up. Lots of broken bones, lots of rehab, but he'll be okay."

"Thank God."

"But his girlfriend is paralyzed from the waist down."

"Oh no."

"And her cousin is dead."

"Oh, Ben."

He didn't respond, but there was obviously more.

"And...?"

"And I'm adopted. After the accident, my parents—well, Samantha and Adam's parents—they didn't want me living with them anymore. Adam is there now and they have to take care of him, and I'm not even allowed to call the house. I wrote him a letter to tell him I'm sorry, but I don't know if they gave it to him or not. And when Samantha said I could stay with her, our parents stopped speaking to her, too." He glanced at me. "Adam's girlfriend's parents came to the hospital to try to kill me. They had to put a cop in front of the door."

I turned in my seat to face him. He looked haunted.

"Listen, Ben, I don't really know you, but you seem like a good guy. But honestly, I would have wanted to kill you, too," I said. "I'm sorry, but that's the truth. Their daughter's paralyzed and their niece is dead. I've been on the other side of that equation. And trust me, I wanted to kill the driver, too."

He nodded. "Yeah. I get it. It's unforgivable, what I did. I know that. It's just...what am I supposed to do now? I can't take it back."

"How old are you?"

"Twenty-two."

"Things will get better. It won't always be this way."

He didn't answer. I stared out the window for the rest of the ride, and as soon as we got near the Capitol and stopped at a red light, I said, "It will be easier if I jump out here, okay? You can take a left up there and head back."

As I reached for my briefcase, Ben put his hand on my arm.

"I want to take it back more than anything, but I can't. It's impossible to undo things, ya know?"

As I waited in the London drizzle for the light to change on Carlton Hill, I was thinking about the haunted look on Ben's face. I wasn't married and I wasn't a mother when he told me his story, but even then it had been unconscionable to me that his own parents, biological or not, could simply turn their backs on him. Maybe they had their hands full looking after Adam and were furious at Ben's foolishness, but to reject him outright? To stop speaking to Samantha because she was letting him sleep on her couch? Ben was physically battered and broken, but more than that, he was despondent. All he wanted to do was change one fundamental thing in his life, but he was powerless to do that, and the guilt was killing him. Surely they could see that? I remembered wanting to reach across the emergency brake and give him a hug, but I hadn't. In fact, I hadn't even seen him again, because I'd left D.C. a few weeks later.

I turned this story over and over in my mind as I walked home. I couldn't imagine turning my back on my own child for any reason, but plenty of parents did it every day, and after thirty years of knowing Blythe and Number Three, I wondered if Crawford had always feared the kind of rejection Ben experienced?

Maybe David was right. Maybe at the heart of it, this situation with Crawford wasn't about me at all. Yes, it upended my life and hurt me deeply, more deeply than I thought anything would ever hurt me again after losing my daughter. And yes, I felt like the world's biggest fool, used for decades and then thrown away when something better came along and I wasn't needed anymore. But like Ben said, none of us can undo what's already been done.

The trick, as David so often said, was to find a path forward, out of the pain.

I can do that, I thought, squaring my shoulders and stepping off the curb.

A horn blared and I jumped back on the sidewalk.

Quattordici

B,

Sei viva? It's been a few days since you've written back and I just want to know you're alive. Things here are fine. Patrizio and Alberto send their love and want to know when you're coming back. Oliver sleeps on your bed as often as I let him. I'm thinking of heading to the Dolomites for Christmas. I found a nice little cabin that's available for two weeks—lots of hiking and fun in the snow and, of course, Scarlett and Rhett on Christmas Eve. Interested?

P

P,

Thanks for the invite, but I don't plan on celebrating Christmas, or New Year's, or anything else, for that matter, this year. Give

Oliver a treat for me, please, and for what it's worth, I never minded if he slept on the bed. Gone with the Wind—I'd almost forgotten your bizarre family tradition.

B

I always loved Christmas. The Fifes went all out with decorations and food, and after my dad died, they always invited my mom and Celia and me every year. When I moved to Chapel Hill, I spent every Christmas with David. I'd move into my room at his house as soon as I finished my exams and we'd put a tree in front of his big bay window, and Margaret would send a Tupperware of treats from the parish hall home with him every couple of days. I'd make soups and stews and casseroles, and we'd eat just enough of them to justify having cookies and champagne every night.

My first year of grad school, I rented a car and drove to Chapel Hill from D.C. for Christmas, feeling happier than I could ever remember feeling. The antique diamond on my left hand caught the winter sun and projected rainbows onto the windshield, and when I got to Porter's house, I dropped my duffel bag and catapulted into his arms. We dragged a giant tree into David's living room, and on Christmas Eve, Porter and I went to church at midnight, then drank champagne and ate cookies with David after the service before going back to Porter's house to watch *Gone with the Wind* and wait for Christmas morning.

"I have no idea why Claire insisted we watch this on Christmas Eve," Porter said, sliding the tape into the VCR.

"Why on earth did she think *Gone with the Wind* was a Christmas movie?"

"Maybe she thought Robert E. Lee and Jesus were equals and should be celebrated together," Porter said.

"Tell me," I said, snuggling into his side as Mammy cinched Scarlett into her corset. "How much of this movie was like your life?"

"Other than growing up on a plantation and fighting in the Civil War? None of it."

"Did you go for Scarlett or Melanie?"

"Melanie isn't my type. Too soft. I like a woman who knows how to run a lumber mill and kill carpetbaggers."

"Good luck finding that."

"And who will tolerate the fact that my friends and I play Rollerblade hockey in the house."

"Total football, baby," I said. "If it's good enough for Johann Cruijff and Team Ajax, it's good enough for me. Hopefully the tracks will buff out so you can get your security deposit back."

"See?" he said. "Who needs a Scarlett or a Melanie? I just want my own little Yankee."

I loved Porter desperately and never would have believed then that our time together as a couple would be so short. But after that Christmas, in the spring semester of my first year of grad school, things started to change. There was a string of unreturned phone calls, a couple of unanswered letters, and then Porter stopped communicating altogether. The silence was absolutely deafening. I had no idea what was happening, but I imagined all sorts of scenarios, most of them centered on Porter having met someone he liked better than me.

Finally, I couldn't take it anymore and borrowed Hugh's car and skipped class and drove to Chapel Hill. Porter usually slept until lunchtime if he'd worked the night before, but when I got to his house around ten in the morning, his Jeep wasn't there. I had a key, but I couldn't bring myself to be the psycho girlfriend who'd driven four and a half hours to invade his privacy, so instead I drove to a few places I thought he might go and checked back at his house three or four times, but Porter never turned up. Around four in the afternoon, when I'd exhausted all other possibilities, I went to the restaurant where he worked and pulled into the employee parking lot in the back, my hands shaking against the steering wheel.

Porter's Jeep wasn't there, but Porter was. He was standing outside the back door in his apron, talking to a group of guys and smoking a cigarette. His back was to me, but as I walked toward them, one of the guys jerked his head in my direction, and Porter turned around.

"What are you doing here?" he said.

"Can we talk?"

Porter glanced at his coworkers, one of whom said something in Spanish that made them all laugh, then looked at his watch. "I've only got five minutes."

We walked a few feet away from the group.

"Why haven't you returned my calls?"

Porter dropped his cigarette and ground it under his shoe. "I've been busy."

"Too busy to make a phone call?"

"You know what my hours are like."

I wanted to believe this, probably more than I'd ever wanted to believe anything at that point, but I knew he wasn't telling the truth.

"Are you—did you meet someone else? Are you with someone else?"

Porter's eyes narrowed. "Why would you go there?" he said. "I wouldn't do that to you."

"How am I supposed to know that when you're not talking to me?"

"I'm not seeing anyone else," he said, glancing back at his coworkers, who were still huddled by the door. "I promise."

"You're just all of a sudden so busy that you can't make a phone call?"

"I'm not going to fight with you here, Beth."

"Then just admit that you met someone else."

"I didn't."

"Liar," I hissed through my clenched jaw.

"What's gotten into you?" he said. "That's not the way it works. You don't just love someone one day and stop loving them the next." He shook his head and smiled thinly. "You're being crazy."

"That's exactly what happens," I said. "It happens all the time."

"Well, not to me. Nothing's changed except I'm busy."

"You're not telling me the truth, Porter, and I know it."

He shook his head and started to say something, then seemed to think better of it and looked at his watch. He sighed heavily. "Can we talk about this later? I have to get back inside."

"I drove all the way down here."

"I know. And I'm really happy to see you." He glanced back toward the kitchen door. Only one of his coworkers was still standing there, finishing a cigarette. "But I have to get back inside. I need to keep my job."

"I've been looking for you all day."

"You should have let me know you were coming."

"So you could come home from wherever you spent the night?"

Porter glared at me for a second, and then his face softened. "It's not what you think," he said, shaking his head. "Listen, I'll explain later, ok? I should have called, I know."

"You definitely should have."

"Will you go to the house and we can talk about it later? I'll try to get home early. Hopefully by midnight."

"That's a lot of effort for someone who can't even pick up the phone. Don't bother."

I turned to leave, but Porter grabbed my hand.

"Are you going to the house?"

"I'm going back to Washington," I said, pulling free from his grasp. "There's obviously no reason for me to stay here."

"Other than I want to explain?"

"You've had weeks to explain!"

A guy in a stained apron stuck his head out the back door and yelled something in Spanish.

Porter waved him off and turned back to me. "I have to go. Please just go to my house."

"No thanks."

Porter threw his hands up in the air. "Okay. Do what you want," he said, and turned and walked back inside the restaurant.

It took me three tries to start Hugh's car and put it in reverse. I actually did go to Porter's house, despite what I'd said. I let myself in, walked straight into the kitchen, left the diamond ring he'd given me on the table, then walked right back out, locking the front door and pushing the key through the mail slot. Afterwards I drove to a McDonald's and sat in the parking lot, howling like an animal, until I calmed down enough to get a Coke at the drive-through and drive back to D.C.

On the way home I made a resolution. I would never, ever let myself be hurt like that again.

Thirty years later, I still didn't understand how Porter and I had gone from engaged to broken up in the span of a five-minute conversation, but I'd stopped thinking about it during the decades we were out of touch. And now I had no energy, and very little interest, in unearthing the past, which is why there was no way I would be going to the Dolomites for Christmas.

Graciela was cleaning the stairs when I started lugging suitcases up from the storage closet.

"I help?" she said, pressing herself against the wall so I could pass.

I shook my head. "No, thanks."

I laid the suitcases out on the floor of the guest room and started gathering my clothes from the drawers and closets around the house and dumping them in huge piles on the bed. My bleach-stained Thousand Yard Stares t-shirt was on top of the pile.

"Do you think the fact that we keep winning makes us trivial people?" Hugh asked when we won Trivia Night for the fifth or sixth time.

"Speak for yourself, mate. I'm as serious as they come," Mac said, preparing to pour the free pitcher of beer we'd won.

"You're about as serious as a coloring book," Crawford said.

"Actually," I said, "I'm very impressed with you, Mac. Who knew you're such a fierce competitor?"

He paused, the pitcher of beer and a glass suspended in mid-air. "I came here to win, Steeler, not fuck spiders."

I brought the t-shirt to my face, inhaling deeply, then set it aside to get rid of. Now that I knew it had all been a lie, that chapter of my life was another one I wanted to forget.

I began sorting through the jumble of clothes on the bed, making piles for things I wanted to keep, things I would donate, and things I was on the fence about. The trouble was, since I had no idea where I was going, it was hard to anticipate what sort of clothes I would need. I was pretty sure that I would end up going to David's for a while, but after that? Maybe I'd go to Greece, find a little place by the sea and huddle down, live on the cheap for a couple months while I formulated a plan. Or maybe Scotland, to a little cottage in the Orkneys, in which case I'd need every warm item of clothing I owned. Or maybe San Miguel de Allende, Mexico, a place I'd read about and always wanted to visit.

I had never felt so untethered in my life.

I made a pile of t-shirts to add to Graciela's rag bag and started a donation pile with some skirts I hadn't worn in years. Then I picked up a vintage black A-line dress that I'd bought in D.C. at a time when cocktail parties were a regular part of my life. Hugh and Mac and I used to go to all sorts of political events just to get free food and drinks, and I was always Crawford's date for functions at his law firm. That little black dress had seen some things.

I pulled the dress on over my jeans and fleece and looked in the mirror, remembering a cocktail party I went to with Crawford when he was just a baby lawyer. The managing partner of the firm had told a story about when he was starting his career in Louisiana. His wife was out of town, so he was charged with taking his daughter to dance class. When they got to the studio, the mother of another student asked if he would mind bringing her daughter home after class, the way his wife often did.

Not a problem, the lawyer said. When dance class was over, he loaded both little girls in his car, consulted the directions the girl's mom had given him, and went to drop off his daughter's friend.

"It was one of those big ol' bayou spreads, with a veranda running around the whole place," he told the group of us gathered around him at the party. "I'm walking this little girl up to her door when I happen to glance over and see something moving where the porch wraps around the corner of the house. I stand there looking for a minute, thinking my eyes are playing tricks on me, and then I realize, *Damned if there's not a horse on the porch!*"

"A horse?" one of the women listening asked. "An actual horse?"

"An actual horse," the lawyer said. "Right up there on the veranda. Now that's not something you see every day, so it kinda' took me by surprise. I'm thinking he's escaped from the barn or somebody left a gate open, right? So I knock on the screen door and I let this little girl in and I holler, 'Hey, Darla! We're here! And do you know there's a horse on the porch?"

He paused and we all waited for the punchline.

"She hollers back, 'Yeh, I know. He's afraid of the gator in the yard.' Let me tell you, folks, I closed that screen door and hightailed it back to the car!"

Everyone laughed at this, at the lawyer's animated telling of the story, at the absurdity of a horse on the porch and a gator in the yard, at the sheer incomprehensibility of life outside the Beltway. But the thing that struck me was that this was so normal for Darla that she hadn't felt it worth mentioning. Why? Because normal is what we are acclimated to, and acclimation happens in baby steps. The horse didn't materialize out of thin air; he was tempted onto the porch for whatever reason—an abandoned apple, a decorative bale of hay, a thunderstorm. The gator crawled up out of the bayou, maybe lured by the way the afternoon sun warmed the grass, and Darla created a connection between the two events that made sense to her and voilà: a new normal.

I thought about how I'd rationalized Crawford's indifference for years. He had emotionally stunted parents. He was stressed from work. I'd made him angry. Every day I'd created a new justification that allowed me to feel like what was happening around me shouldn't be questioned. Every day I'd invented a new normal.

I heard the front door slam and Crawford's briefcase hit the floor. I pulled off the dress and added it to the donation pile, and stayed upstairs sorting clothes for another hour or so, then went down to the kitchen to make myself a cup of tea. Crawford was nowhere to be seen, so I decided to check my email. There was a message from David.

Dear Beth,

I wanted to follow up on something we touched on the other day when we spoke, which is the power of forgiveness.

In the Old Testament, as I'm sure you remember, God makes a covenant with the chosen people, brings them out of bondage in Egypt, and promises them land and descendants. All God asks in return is that these polytheistic people make God their primary god, but the Israelites' faith is fickle, and whenever things don't go their way, they look to other gods for better outcomes. God gets angry, but nevertheless, renews the covenant and never loses 'chesed' – compassionate and loyal and steadfast love – for them, and eventually, the Israelites learn to put God first. Despite the violence and drama it contains, the Old Testament is in many ways a story of forgiveness that is recurring and renewable and relentless.

In the New Testament, our understanding of forgiveness comes from the life and teachings of Jesus, who forgives those who doubt, forgives those who actively work against his ministry, forgives those who undermine his efforts, forgives the one who betrays him, and even forgives those who bring about his death. Why? Because his faith in God is so strong that Jesus understands forgiveness as his duty.

I've always thought of forgiveness as the cross representing The Great Commandment, to love God and love our neighbors. The vertical beam of the cross is the first part of the Commandment, us looking upward to love God, who acts in our lives to forgive us in return for a penitent heart and a commitment to try to do better. But the second part, the horizontal beam of the cross, is trickier. That's us looking to the left and to the right, to our neighbors who are just as broken and flawed and prone to err as we are, and learning to forgive them, and be forgiven by them, so that we can live in community. If we want to fulfill The Great Commandment, both beams are necessary to keep the cross of forgiveness upright.

So, even though we may long for vengeance and justice and people getting what we think they deserve, the Bible teaches us that those things are not ours to wish for. "An eye for an eye," after all, is a caution against seeking revenge, not a formula for how to do it. It's a ceiling, not a floor—a reminder that justice is up to God, and our job is to forgive.

I understand how hurt you are, Beth. I know that you feel broken. And I wish more than anything that I could restore to you what you've lost. But if you were offered the choice, would you choose to have never loved Crawford? To have never had Mia? We both know the answer to those questions. Only by loving others do we experience the revelation of God in our lives—and that experience, that revelation, is something we have to be profoundly grateful for, no matter how things ultimately work out.

I will just say this, and then I'll close: I urge you to reach out to Crawford in peace, with forgiveness, as the father of your child and a man you once loved deeply. Do it for yourself, to rid yourself of the poison of anger and to free yourself to create a better tomorrow. Remember what Desmond Tutu said, kiddo: without forgiveness, there is no tomorrow. And you deserve a tomorrow.

So I urge you to set your heart and mind on forgiveness, and then walk away, physically and mentally. The stasis you're in isn't healthy. You need to turn your focus and your energy to the future and rebuilding your life. Whatever reconciliation will happen between you and Crawford in the future will come about because God is working in your midst, and all you need to do is let it happen in its own time.

Lastly, I will just remind you that I am here, and that I am your friend, as well as your favorite uncle.

With love,

David

When I finished reading, I closed the lid of my laptop, retrieved my phone from the kitchen counter, and texted Crawford. *Drinks and grilled cheese, part 2?*

Three dots appeared, then vanished, and my stomach sank. But a few seconds later, his reply appeared. *Sounds great. I'll come down and make a fire.*

Quindici

Crawford was kneeling in front of the fire, stabbing it with the heavy black fireplace poker we'd bought in Wales, when I walked in with the drinks and set them on the table in the sitting room. He got to his feet, leaned the poker against the wall, rubbed the palms of his hands together, and looked at me. In one step, his arms were around me and we were both weeping.

"I'm so sorry," he said.

"I'm sorry, too."

The familiar scent of him, the way I fit so perfectly into his embrace, brought a thousand memories flooding back. These were the shoulders, after all, that had supported my head on countless airplane rides. The hands I held when we said our vows, the same hands that had mopped my brow bringing you into this world and gently cradled your head to lift you onto his shoulder. This was the chest I'd collapsed against when you walked onstage to sing and I was totally undone with pride, and these were the hands I'd held for three decades of walks and weddings and funerals and scary movies. How could I hate him when we'd been through so much together? He was the only person in the world who loved you as much as I did.

David was right. I needed to forgive him.

The smoke alarm in the kitchen started shrieking.

"Oh shit," I said, wiping my eyes with the sleeves of my sweater and letting go of him. "The sandwiches."

Crawford opened the door to the garden and flapped a kitchen towel in front of the smoke alarm on the ceiling while I pitched the charred remains of our sandwiches in the trash.

"I'm sorry," I said. "I'll make new ones. There's plenty of cheese."

"I can help."

He buttered four pieces of bread while I cleaned the burned bits of cheese out of the pan and sliced white cheddar.

"There's a tomato," Crawford said, pulling his head out from behind the refrigerator door to look at me. "Want a slice of tomato?"

"Sure."

When the sandwiches were done, we carried our plates into the sitting room. I curled up in the wingback chair, tucking my feet underneath me. The fire was roaring and for a brief second I wondered where Oliver was, why he wasn't stretched out in front of it.

"The tomato was a good idea," I said.

"Adds a little something."

"I think I made the drinks too strong, though."

Crawford shook his head. "Nah, they're perfect."

"You know what I was craving earlier? Vito's Pizza. How many hundreds of slices do you think we ate at that place?"

He smiled. "It probably went under when we stopped going."

"Remember the last time?"

"How could I forget?"

Crawford and I had met Hugh and Mac at Vito's Pizza to tell them our news. I'd been living in Raleigh for nearly four years at that point, and when we walked in the door of Vito's, Mac jumped up and hugged me so hard that I honestly thought he might have cracked my ribs. Hugh pulled his chair as close to mine as he could at the table and slung his arm around my shoulders.

"I can't believe they still use these napkins," I said, holding one in the air. The napkins were the waxy white ones that every pizza place in the universe uses, totally ineffective against tomato sauce or any other liquid, emblazoned with the words *Vito's Pizza: Get some Italian in you!* which always made me think of the Idiot Adonis from my foreign policy class. "You would think political correctness would have made them rethink the slogan."

"I like it," Hugh said, laying his head on my shoulder. "Reminds me of someone I once knew..."

"Who was that?" Mac asked.

"Giuseppe from Genoa. Remember him?"

"Oof. I hated that bastard," Mac said.

"You were jealous of his body," Hugh said.

"You hate every guy Hugh dates," Crawford told Mac. "If I didn't know better, I'd think you want him for yourself."

"I'd marry him in a second if I was into blokes," Mac said sweetly. "He's my best mate."

"Speaking of," Crawford said, nodding in my direction. "Beth's getting married."

Mac clutched his chest.

Hugh lifted his head and looked at me. "How come we don't know about this? Who is he? Is it the fuckwit in North Carolina?"

"You found a bloke with a wheelie house?" Mac asked.

"It's actually someone you know," I said.

"Not that pommy bastard Niall?" Mac asked, crossing his arms over his chest.

Hugh shook his head and said, as if I wasn't sitting two inches from him, "No, she wouldn't do that to us. She knows we hate him."

"Not Niall," I said.

"Not that frog Fabrice?" Hugh said. "We hate him, too."

"I don't *hate* Fabrice, mate," Mac told Hugh. "That's a bit strong. I just thought he talked weird. Smelled a bit, too."

"His name was Fabien and he was from Belgium, but no, it's not him," I said.

Hugh inhaled sharply. "Oh my God. The vile reporter." He turned to Mac. "Remember his hideous shoes?"

"Only because you wouldn't shut up about them."

"Hush Puppies," Hugh said. "On a grown man. Wear a diaper, too, why don't you?"

I laughed and shook my head. "It's not Jude."

"I know!" Mac yelled. "It's the bloke whose life you saved. The one who bit you."

"Steve? God, no, Mac. What made you think of him?"

He shrugged. "I had a croissant the other day."

"Well, who then?" Hugh said.

"It's me," Crawford said, grinning like a little kid. "We're engaged."

"Are you kidding?" Mac slammed his fist down on the table, making all of our beer mugs jump. "Absolutely not," he said, shaking his head. "No. No. No. You haven't even given me a chance!"

Hugh nodded. "I agree. Mac deserves a chance. Put the old boy at bat," he said. "If he can't deliver a touchdown, game over."

"If we ever needed evidence that you don't know shit about sports, there it is," Crawford said.

"Put me in, coach," Mac said, raising his hand.

"She's pregnant," Crawford said.

Mac made a choking sound. "You must be kidding." He turned to Hugh. "I blame you for letting this happen."

"What did I do, steal her pills?"

"You were always saying nice things about Crawford. You know she listens to you. *He's so smart, such a good lawyer, what a nice guy.*"

"You know I'm sitting right here, right?"

"What about me, Hugh? Did you ever think to say something nice about me? I thought we were best mates."

"I'd say I was sorry," Hugh said, blowing Mac a kiss. "But you know, love means never having to say you're sorry."

The memory of that night made me smile, despite the pain that welled up in my chest.

I reached for my vodka tonic and asked Crawford, "What are Mac and Hugh up to these days?"

He shrugged. "The usual. Mac's still a serial dater, but his moving company is doing really well. Dumbass is some kind of logistics genius. And Hugh's got an exploratory committee going. I won't be surprised if he runs for office."

"He's in such a conservative district, though. Do you think he's got a chance?"

"I don't think he actually expects to win. He's just setting the stage for another run a couple of years from now. Testing the waters, getting organized. You ready for a refill?"

"I'll do it. Want another sandwich?"

As the butter melted in the pan, I closed the back door and turned off the fan over the stove and thought about the trip Crawford and I had taken right after the dinner with Mac and

Hugh. I really wanted to see Jenny before we moved to London, and we needed to tell his parents our news, so Crawford and I drove up to New York. Or rather, Crawford drove, and I napped in the passenger seat.

We got to Jenny's house in time for lunch. Crawford and Jenny's husband Scott stood around the grill while Jenny and I made a salad, seamlessly picking up the conversation we'd been carrying on since preschool. Scott was a blue-collar guy who'd gone straight to work from high school, and I'd been concerned that he and Crawford wouldn't have anything in common, but they got along surprisingly well.

After lunch we cleared the table and put on a pot of coffee and Jenny lugged out a stack of yearbooks and photo albums.

"I don't know if you want this one," Jenny said, handing me a scrapbook. "My mom asked me to see if you want it..."

Crawford peered over my shoulder as I flipped the book open and unfolded a newspaper clipping.

"What's that?" he said.

"It's the letter Beth wrote to the court about her mom's accident," Jenny said. "They printed it on the front page of the paper."

There were more articles about my mom's death in the scrapbook, as well as clippings about my dad and Kirk's plane crash. I turned the pages quickly, then shut the book.

"Will you hang on to this for me?" I asked Jenny. She nodded and set the scrapbook on the kitchen counter behind her.

"Check this out," she said, passing me a Polaroid.

Jenny and my dad and I were sitting on the front stoop, our mouths stained purple by the popsicles we were eating. My dad was wearing his police uniform, and Jenny and I had on roller skates and matching red and blue striped t-shirts and red yarn bows in our pigtails.

"Wow," I said, inspecting the Polaroid. "My mom must have taken this?"

Jenny nodded. "We had new skates. See? The stoppers aren't even used yet."

That cracked us both up. Jenny could bend one leg and pivot in a graceful circle on the rubber stopper of her right skate, but I would just fly into whatever I could use to stop myself—the garage, the bushes, my father's car—and as a result had scraped knees for about eight years straight.

"Those were our Bicentennial outfits," Jenny told Scott and Crawford. "We wore them basically every day that summer."

"Very cute," Crawford said. He pointed to a yearbook photo of me and Jenny at the Erie Canal Museum. "I'm a huge fan of those white sunglasses. The kilts, too."

I took the yearbook from his hand. "Sadly Britney Spears didn't make those uniforms cool until we were already gone."

"Those sunglasses were the envy of all the other girls, though," Jenny said.

"Crawford's eighth grade photo looks exactly like James Spader in *Pretty in Pink*. How many Polos were you wearing?" I teased.

"A few."

Scott laughed. "My friends and I would probably have beaten you up, man."

We took 17 out of Rochester, rather than I-90. Crawford said it would take the same amount of time, but I sensed he was in no hurry to get to Blythe and Number Three, and I wasn't, either. I'd met the Campbells years earlier, when they'd posted up in a suite at The Willard in D.C., and I'd found them entirely intimidating. Crawford treated them with tolerant amusement.

"They're like characters in a badly-written play," he said. "I'm sure they have interior lives, but I've never seen much evidence of it."

Crawford always referred to his father as Number Three, or, if he was being particularly sarcastic, *Crawford William Campbell the Third, Lion of Wall Street*, and I was always terrified I'd slip up and call him Number Three to his face, but it was Blythe, who was about as warm as a cobra, who really made me nervous. As far as I was concerned, we could detour to Florida on the way to Bedford Hills, as long as Crawford didn't mind driving.

By the time we finally got on the Sawmill Parkway, it was getting dark. The houses got larger, and the road narrower, the closer we got to Crawford's childhood home, and I kept yanking my leg away from the door, thinking we were going to scrape the low stone wall that bordered the road. Crawford laughed and assured me he could have blinders on and still navigate safely.

Finally, he slowed and turned into a driveway, the headlights illuminating a massive iron gate set into ivy-covered walls. He rolled down the window and punched in a code and turned to smile at me as the gates creaked open to reveal the largest house I'd ever seen.

"Welcome to The Shack, as Mac calls it," he said. "You'd think my parents had a lot of kids."

"It's enormous."

"Obscenely so."

"How many bedrooms is it?"

Crawford did a quick calculation. "Seven. No, eight. Nine if you count the maid's room, which of course you don't."

"Of course not."

"Just wait. There's more out back."

The house was immaculate, a stone Tudor castle with polished wood floors and sleek marble countertops. Every table was laden with silver candlesticks, photos in silver frames, and elaborate arrangements of fresh flowers. I bent down to look at a photo of Crawford in tennis whites as he got us drinks.

"How old were you here?" I asked.

He handed me a bottle of water and picked up the photo. "Ten, maybe? Possibly eleven. Club champion." He set the picture back on the table.

"I love the sweatbands," I said. "Very patriotic."

"McEnroe wore them," he said. "They would have gone nicely with your skating outfit." He bent down and picked up our bag. "Come on, we're staying in the guest house."

"Because otherwise we'd be on the pullout in the den?"

"My request."

The guest house was the size of my childhood home, with three bedrooms off a center living room and a full-sized kitchen. The walls around the stone fireplace were covered with old hockey and lacrosse sticks and tennis rackets in wood frames, and the shelves of the built-in bookcases were stacked high with board games and trophies.

Crawford watched me take it all in.

"I played baseball for sixteen years," he said, "but you'd never know it, huh?"

"Not from this," I said, inspecting the contents of one of the shelves. "But I see that your father was club champion in both singles and doubles."

"He's a beast on the tennis court."

"And Blythe holds her own."

"She's played golf with the same women every week for as long as I can remember."

"Where's all your baseball stuff? Or did you not win any trophies?"

"I won tons of them," he said. "I don't know where they are. Probably in boxes somewhere, or thrown away." He shrugged. "When I went to Georgetown, they remodeled the second floor of the house and I think Blythe used that as an opportunity to purge. Plus they didn't exactly approve of baseball. My dad's firm did sponsor us every year, though, so we always had the best gear in the league."

"What's wrong with baseball?"

Crawford smiled. "They don't play it at the Club. Speaking of, you ready to go to dinner?"

The Club turned out to be another ivy-covered behemoth. Number Three greeted us in the lobby wearing a pair of pressed khakis and a crisp blue Oxford under a navy cashmere sweater vest, obviously already well-lubricated. Blythe was coiled up at a table inside, sipping a glass of white wine and looking immaculate in a navy dress and pearls and her hair in a French twist.

Number Three had two more Glenfiddich in quick succession while we made small talk about the drive in and I fidgeted, sweaty and itchy in my vintage cocktail dress, and then he raised his drink in the air, tipped it in my direction, and said to Crawford, "Well I suppose congratulations are in order, Skipper. You sure took your time."

Crawford turned beet red and I couldn't help it, I started laughing.

Blythe looked at her son. "You certainly had us worried."

"Your mother's already spoken to the club about the wedding," Number Three boomed at Crawford. Then he turned to me. "You're not to worry about the cost of anything, young lady. Skipper's told us you're an orphan. My wife will arrange everything," he said, gesturing with his highball towards Blythe, "and I'm sure the two of you will be thick as thieves."

I sincerely doubted that.

"Actually," Crawford said, "we don't want a big wedding."

"Don't be ridiculous," Blythe said. "Our friends expect it. Planning it will be a snap."

"They're waiting for me in London, and neither of us cares about a big wedding."

A look of hurt crossed Blythe's face before she composed herself. "Then we'll plan a London wedding," she said, looking at her husband. "I'll take a suite at the Savoy and organize everything. Gayle Hartridge's daughter was married in London, remember? I'll ask her who she used."

"We want to get married right away," Crawford said. "Without any fuss."

"I'm sure we can arrange something within the year," Blythe said. "The months will fly by, with so much to plan."

"Beth is pregnant."

Blythe's mouth froze.

Number Three laughed. "Well, son," he said, holding up his drink. "You're full of surprises. I think that calls for another."

You can imagine how the rest of the evening went. Blythe couldn't bring herself to look at me, and Crawford and his father defaulted to talking about the stock market while I moved filet mignon around my plate and tried to stay awake while hoping a meteor would strike the country club and put us all out of our misery.

I replayed that conversation in my head as I sliced limes for Crawford's vodka tonic on the kitchen counter and listened to the rain pelt the window. The Campbells' reaction to our news had struck me as odd back then, but I'd assumed that Crawford being unmarried in his early thirties simply hadn't aligned with the schedule his parents had expected him to adhere to. But now, in hindsight, I wondered if they'd suspected that their precious only child was gay. Was that what Blythe had meant when she said they'd worried?

We'd come into the main house the next morning to find Number Three in the kitchen reading the *Wall Street Journal*. He put the paper down and handed me a rectangular box.

"Blythe wanted you to have these," he said. "Unfortunately, she had an early tee time this morning."

He gave me a quick hug, shook Crawford's hand, and we went back to D.C. Total time in Bedford Hills? Twelve hours.

Our wedding was a quiet affair in the chambers of the judge Crawford had clerked for, just me and Crawford, plus Mac and Hugh as witnesses. Then we were on a plane, and unpacking in London, and it seemed like we blinked and you arrived, my auburn-haired baby in a plush pink blanket. Whatever annoyance Blythe had felt about being deprived of a five-star wedding disappeared the instant she walked into David's church three months later and laid eyes on you. You were completely out of sorts from the flight and the time change from London, but your baptism was a wonderful weekend. Mac and Hugh were so proud to be your godfathers, although Hugh did insist on being referred to as your Fairy Godmother, and Blythe ordered so many flowers for the church that it looked like a garden inside. Jenny took all the stress off me about having Aunt Celia there by flying down and back with her and even taking an adjoining hotel room so that I wouldn't need to worry, and Margaret organized the service and reception afterwards. All we had to do was show up.

One of the funniest things about that weekend was that Mac, not finding any single women to amuse himself with, doted on Celia and spent most of his time wheeling her from place to place, bringing her food, refreshing her drinks, and chatting up a storm. When we were leaving to go back to the hotel after the luncheon on Sunday, Celia clutched my arm, pointed at Mac, and asked me who the foreign boy was.

"That's Mac, Aunt Celia. One of Crawford's best friends from college. You've been talking to him all weekend."

"He's a doll to look at," she said. "But I can't understand a word he says."

When I shared that story later, Hugh laughed for about five minutes, and said that Celia had cracked the code. "Mac is charming only because he's totally incomprehensible. If anyone could understand him, they'd know he's a complete degenerate."

I put the fresh drinks on a tray and balanced Crawford's second grilled cheese on top of the glasses and went back into the sitting room.

"Crawford," I said, handing the plate to him. "I want you to know that I don't hate you. Whatever has been going on, I don't hate you."

He looked up at me. "I don't hate you, either."

"I understand that we have to split up. It's not what I wanted," I said. "Not at all." My voice got caught on the lump in my throat. "It's just—can we do this as nicely as possible?"

"We can," he said, "but you should know that I'm not just going to fork over everything I've worked for. If you're reasonable, it will all be fine."

I nodded. "Just be fair with me, okay?"

"Obviously."

We sipped our drinks in silence for a few minutes.

"I'm terrified, Crawford," I said finally, looking up at him.

He met my eyes and held them for a minute before nodding. "I know you are. But you're going to be okay. Trust me."

Sedici

Maybe grilled cheese sandwiches are the key to world peace, because after that night, Crawford and I seemed to reach a detente in our Cold War.

Which is not to say that it was easy.

I was a ball of anxiety, unable to sleep more than an hour or two at a time, and I still had to jolly myself into getting up every morning. The only way I could do that was to promise myself that if I could just make it through the next twenty-four hours, I would give myself the option of jumping off a bridge. *After all, tomorrow is another day,* I'd think, like some kind of suicidal Scarlett O'Hara. I would have suggested it as a band name if Porter and I had been talking.

I'm sure that neither Crawford nor I completely trusted the other, but we held to the agreement we'd made about being as respectful as possible when it came to separating our lives, and bizarrely, when the pressure of unfulfilled expectations and hurt feelings and kept secrets had been lessened, we spent more time together than we had in years. We had drinks in the evening, ate meals in front of the fire, and even went on a day trip to Kent, just to get away from London. But while the togetherness was a balm to the loneliness and heartbreak I felt, it also came with frequent stabs of crippling pain. There were so many times when Crawford made me laugh, or said something kind, and I saw a glimpse of the man I'd married and felt a surge of love for him that quickly morphed into heartache when I remembered that he was only biding his time, waiting to get away from me and start his real life. It occurred to me often how much easier the whole process would be if I hated Crawford, or if I, too, was anxious to be free and join someone else. But I didn't hate him, and there was no one. I just ached.

David and Jenny checked in regularly, but Porter faded away completely after I told him that Crawford and I had gone on a road trip together.

Are you reconciling? he wrote.

Not the way you mean. We're just trying to be decent about the split, I wrote. *And we wanted to get away from the city for a day.*

I guess it's one of those "You had to be there" situations. Well, good luck.

I was relieved when Porter stopped texting, to be honest. I was over-capacity, emotionally, and just didn't have the bandwidth to deal with anything else.

The financial part of untangling our lives was a nightmare. I'd never given much thought to our finances once Crawford and I got married, and I'd always trusted him to make good decisions and handle everything, so separating our assets and taking control of that aspect of my life absolutely paralyzed me with fear. I felt nauseous anytime I thought of it.

We had a meeting with the lawyers yesterday, I wrote David, *and there was a big argument about the financial piece. It was the most degrading, humiliating thing I've ever experienced. I felt like a child no one wanted, as if my existence had never contributed anything to the marriage or the life we had together. And yet I've depended on Crawford for so long that I have to trust him now, too, because while I know I have to deal with the personal betrayal, if I can't trust him about the impersonal stuff.... well, it's just too much to think about.*

I am a firm believer that people are complex, and never wholly one way or the other, David wrote back. *We can be deeply flawed in one area of our lives, but does that mean we're horrible people? I don't think so. It means we have work to do. So I understand your need to trust him. My recommendation is trust but verify. Ask your lawyer for guidance. How's the rest of the legal stuff going?*

It's horrible, David. We're doing everything through a mediator, but it's still horrible. To be honest, I think Crawford and I are the only ones not profiting from this mess. And even worse, Crawford is the person I want to talk to the most. Anything that happens during the mediations, I instantly think, "I wonder what Crawford will say about that?"—as if he's not on the other side of the table. He's always my first thought, David. What does Crawford want for dinner? When will Crawford be home? Would Crawford agree with me? I want to tell Crawford what I saw on my walk...I never realized how much space he occupied, and without him and Mia, I'm not sure I actually know who I am.

I think anyone who's been through it will agree that the only people who profit are the lawyers. Everyone else just tries to minimize the damage and get out alive. And you've had years of thinking about Crawford, and maybe that's been part of the problem—you let him have the top spot in your mind. If you've both been putting you second, whose priority have you been, Beth? It's a habit that you'll need to unlearn, and that's going to take some effort, but right now it's time to think about you— what you want, what you think, what's right for you. Hang in there, kiddo. I know it's hard. I'm here for you. xo David

One evening in early December, as we were finishing bowls of beef stew in the sitting room, Crawford offered to buy me a ticket to David's for Christmas.

"I've been trying to pretend that Christmas isn't happening," I said.

"I know. It's going to be hard. I think you need a plan to get through it."

"You already have plans, huh?"

He looked sheepish for a brief second. "I'm going skiing in Chamonix."

I was quiet for a minute, trying not to let him see how hurt I was. "Okay. Yes, please. I'll call David today."

Two days before I left for the U.S., I booked a taxi and loaded it with all the clothes I'd bagged up, plus all the books and personal items I no longer wanted. When the taxi left for the charity shop, where the owner was eagerly awaiting the remnants of my life, I packed the last of my belongings. I was dropping my duffel bag next to the front door when Crawford came home.

"I'm going to leave three suitcases and a couple of boxes in the guest room," I said. "I'll have to let you know what I need you to do with them once I have a plan."

"That sounds like you're not coming back?"

I shook my head. "I can't. This is too hard, Crawford. It's like death by a thousand paper cuts, being in this house. I keep thinking I'll be okay, and then it hits me that it's over. That you don't want me, and that you never actually—"

"Hey, hey. Don't cry. It's going to be alright."

"No," I said, wiping my nose with a ball of Kleenex from my pocket. "It's not."

"I know it doesn't feel like it now, but I promise, it will be alright. For both of us."

"I'm just glad Mia doesn't have to see this," I said, sinking to the floor. "That's the only good thing about her being gone, Crawford, that she doesn't have to see what's happening to her parents."

Crawford dropped to his knees and knelt next to me, wrapping his arms around my shoulders. I buried my head in his chest, breathing in the familiar scent of him, and cried like I'd never cried before.

"I'm so sorry," Crawford said.

And maybe I was a fool, but I chose to believe him.

Christmas with David meant multiple church services, of course, and I sat in the back row for each one, wrapped in an oversized sweater and wearing the Jackie O sunglasses Margaret pulled out of her desk drawer as soon as she saw me.

"Here you go, Tigger," she said, coming around her desk with the glasses in her hand. "You won't be the first woman who's needed a little disguise in here."

"Thank you," I said, stepping into her embrace. "I know I look awful. I need to find a heavy-duty concealer."

"There's no concealer for a broken heart, sweetie," she said. "But you do look a little bit like a panda bear." She let go of me, gave me the glasses, and brushed my hair back from my face. "Just put those on and try to remember that it's not always going to be like this."

"Do you promise?"

She nodded. "I promise. Now come on. Grab that box of tissues and bring it with you. Let's go move the flowers around and see which member of the Altar Guild freaks out first."

I tried to make myself useful at David's house. It felt good to cook for him, and I loaded his freezer with containers of soup and marinara and stew until there wasn't room for anything else. Then I washed the blankets and dusted every surface and organized the closets and took long walks around the campus, marveling at all the ways things had changed since I'd left.

A few days into January, we were making breakfast when David asked if I intended to see anyone while I was in town. I told him absolutely not. The idea was overwhelming.

"Not even the Governor?" he asked, lifting the lid of the waffle iron. "You still like them crispy?"

"Yes, thanks. And no. I haven't talked to him in years."

"He called you after the accident."

"He did?" I shook my head. "I have no memory of that."

"I spoke to him. Lovely guy. Probably the most apolitical politician I've ever met. Can you grab the syrup off the stove?"

I nodded and pushed myself up from the kitchen table. "I loved working for him. I should never have left."

David shook his head. "Don't do that, Beth. Don't look back and regret your choices."

"Even though they were totally misguided and ill-informed?" I said, pouring the warm syrup from the sauce pot into a small pitcher.

"Were they?"

I laughed and put the pot in the sink. "Given what we know now, I'd say yes, David. Everything was a lie." I set the pitcher on the table and slid back into my seat.

"People change, kiddo," he said, forking a waffle onto my plate. "They evolve and grow. And sometimes that means realizing the truth about themselves."

"Remember when I first started working for Governor Brewer?" I asked, deliberately changing the subject. "One of the first things I wrote for him had a line in it like, 'There's no evidence to support that proposal,' and he crossed it out and replaced it with 'That dog just don't hunt.'"

David smiled. "He kept you hopping, going off-script."

"How about the Foreign Trade dinner, when he told everyone that he'd lost weight on his trip to Shanghai because no one ever taught the Chinese how to fry a chicken and all they'd served was peckers and lips?"

David laughed out loud.

"I loved working for him. If he was still Governor, I'd ask for my job back."

The transition from the Senate to working for Governor Brewer in Raleigh had been surprisingly smooth, mostly because of David's presence less than an hour away. David being so close by gave me a place to go, somewhere I could be utterly at ease.

It was still hard for me to imagine that there had ever been a time when my uncle wasn't a huge part of my life, but the truth was, I hadn't really known him until I was a teenager. My dad used to talk to him once a week, but I was never part of those calls, and the first conversation I had with David myself was when I was thirteen and my mother walked into my room carrying the phone, trailing the cord behind her, and interrupted my algebra homework.

"Dad's brother David," was all she said.

That first conversation was awkward. An adolescent girl and a grown man, we didn't have much in common. But at the end of the call, David cleared his throat and said, "So hey, I know I'm a poor substitute for your dad, and I'm really sorry it took me so long to call, but I was hoping we could be friends?"

"Sure," I said. "Okay."

"I live pretty far away, but if you ever need me, if there's ever any, I don't know, father—daughter stuff where I could be useful, you can call me collect and I promise I'll do my best to be there. And we'll stay in touch in the meantime."

David had been as good as his word. He called every Tuesday night and asked about my schoolwork and social life and how I felt about things going on in the world, and I started paying attention to the news so I'd be able to talk to him about current events. I read everything he recommended, from Evelyn Waugh to *East of Eden*, and we exchanged long letters about books. He told me funny stories about his parish church on the edge of the university's campus, and serious stuff, too, like why he'd left the Catholic Church to become an Episcopalian. Despite the fact that my mother found his religious defection absolutely heretical, she didn't say no when David sent a plane ticket for me to visit him in Chapel Hill my junior year of high school.

I left Syracuse under a blanket of snow clouds and walked out of the Raleigh airport into a glorious blue sky and thought I'd landed in Eden. When I saw David standing on the curb, with the same barrel chest and lopsided smile and wavy auburn hair my father had, I felt an instant connection to my uncle that went far beyond phone calls and books.

His sprawling, music-filled home in Chapel Hill was the antithesis of our brick rowhouse in Syracuse. Only a few blocks off campus, it was wood-sided and painted yellow, with a huge columned porch, four white rocking chairs, and a yard full of flowers. Books and plants filled every available space inside, and light poured in the windows, reflecting the diamond pattern of the transom onto the hardwood floors. Every breeze carried the scent of jasmine.

When I got the fat acceptance packet from UNC in the mail in early spring of my senior year of high school, it was David I called first, even before I told my mom.

"I woke up this morning and there was a bright red cardinal sitting on the branch outside the kitchen window," David said. "I had a feeling today was going to be a great day!"

Jenny put a good face on it, but she was crushed. She really wanted us to room together at Syracuse and I hated more than anything to hurt her feelings, but I didn't want to stay one more month in central New York and sent the forms to enroll at Carolina right away. Despite her disappointment, when my mom was killed less two months later, it was Jenny who kept reminding me that I would be leaving Syracuse soon, and that I had a whole new life waiting for me.

When I moved in with him the summer before my freshman year of college, David designated a bedroom permanently mine and we painted it a beautiful pale leafy green, and for four years, I had as many clothes there as I did in my dorm closet. We did Saturday projects together most every weekend, sanding and staining the floorboards of the porch and building flowerboxes and laying down plastic piping to guide rainwater away from the house, and we never stopped talking about religion and literature and the classes I was taking and life in general. I'd spent hundreds of hours in the same chair I was sitting in now, contributing my own marks to the battle-scarred farm table in the middle of his spacious kitchen.

As I spooned fruit onto my waffle, I remembered a conversation David and I had when I first arrived in Raleigh after leaving D.C. I'd asked my uncle if he thought what I'd done, walking away from my life in Washington, was foolish.

"That's not for me to say, Beth. I'm not on your journey."

"But you have an opinion, right? I mean, it was probably pretty stupid. I had a good job. Friends."

"So why did you leave?"

"Because ... because it just didn't feel right. None of it felt right."

"Then how could staying have been the right thing to do? You need to learn to trust yourself, kiddo. And have some faith that things are unfolding the way they should."

And now here I was, all these years later, back in my uncle's kitchen and still trying to answer the same question. Why doesn't my life feel right, and how badly have I screwed up?

"So why don't you give Governor Brewer a call?" David was saying. "They live in Southern Pines. You're welcome to use my car."

I shook my head. "I'm too embarrassed to see the Governor. Maybe when I have a plan."

"Okay," David said. "That's reasonable. But tell me, when do you think you'll have your plan in place?"

I thought about that for a minute. About how scared I was to spend money and how hard it was to make a decision, even about inconsequential things like what clothes to put on in the morning.

"Conservatively speaking?" I said. "The fifth of never."

Diciassette

I stayed at David's house for nine months. It wasn't my intention to stay that long, but then, nothing was what I'd intended, and the time just slipped by. David told me regularly that he was glad for my company, but I know he also worried about my lack of interest in my life.

Crawford and I, after several unbearable video conferences with the mediators, finally reached a financial settlement, and by that point, I was so far worn down that I didn't even care anymore. The whole process was so excruciating that starving to death under an overpass seemed like a fairly good option, if it meant we could stop talking about it.

"You can't take it personally," David said several times. "It's a negotiating tactic. Remember, he does this every day. This is a game for him, in some ways."

"But I'm his wife, not a client!"

"Trust me, Beth, he's not thinking that way. Remember, this is a man who has denied the truth about himself for a long time. There's an amazing amount of cognitive dissonance at work here."

"What am I supposed to do to survive? Where am I supposed to live? I feel like this would all go much better if I just disappeared."

"Unfortunately, you're going to have to see the process through to get those answers. And trust that it will work out. I know it sounds as if I'm being flippant when I say this, but you have to try not to take any of this personally. You have to remove yourself from the equation, just like he is doing."

"How am I not supposed to take it personally when we're talking about my life?"

"I understand how you feel. But you're wearing yourself out, internalizing all of this, and you have to focus your energies on rebuilding."

"Rebuilding with what? A couple of suitcases and a handshake? This is exactly what I feared, David. I knew something was wrong. I knew he kept a wall up between us. And now it's here. It's happening. And I really don't think I'm going to survive."

"Ultimately, this will all be liberating. Trust me. You will survive this, I promise, and then you will soar."

I wanted to believe David, but soaring seemed about as likely as walking on the moon. But Crawford and I did finally work out an agreement and put the house in France up for sale. Jenny flew down for a visit, and I started working again, writing the occasional article and proofreading course materials for a couple of political science professors.

As the fall semester got underway, David and I decided to retile the bathroom that had always been mine. We chose a blue and white tile that looked antique and hauled boxes of tile and spacers and a couple bags of thinset mortar into the bathroom. David's job was to mix and spread the thinset on the backboard, and mine was to place the tiles and spacers.

"Are you sure you want me to do this?" I asked. "I don't really know what I'm doing."

"I have full faith and confidence," David said.

"Oh God."

"And I also have an extra box of tile and a tool to pry up any mistakes."

At first we listened to Radiolab and didn't talk much, but after we'd eaten the peanut butter and jelly sandwiches I made for lunch and were settling back into the rhythm of the work, David said, "You know you can stay here as long as you want, whether that's a few more weeks or a few more years or forever, but have you given any thought to where you might actually *want* to live?"

I was trying to shake loose a tile spacer that was stuck to my hand and didn't answer immediately.

"I appreciate that more than you know," I said. "I know I need to have a plan, but honestly, I just don't feel ready to make a decision yet."

"Fair enough."

"I did get an email from my editor yesterday. An assignment she wants me to consider. It's a big partnership project with a tourism group."

"Oh?"

"Can you push the box that's by your right leg over here?"

David slid the box of tile across the floor.

"It's in Italy. Mainly Assisi, but a few other areas in Umbria, too."

David's eyebrows zoomed up his forehead. "Really? Back to Italy, huh?"

I nodded. "They'll pay for an Airbnb and give me a small per diem. Apparently this group has come up with a big new tourism plan for Assisi. A show about the life of Saint Francis and some exhibitions and partnerships with various Franciscan organizations around the world, that's where the funding is coming from. The main piece they want is a kind of long-form advertorial, a behind the scenes look at the plan coming together and how it can revitalize Assisi without destroying the authenticity of the town."

"Sounds interesting."

"Then there are about twenty smaller pieces to spin off. She's got contacts lined up already, so most of the grunt work is done, and plus, if I find anything juicy to write about, I can work up a piece for my own portfolio."

"It sounds amazing. Are you going to take it?"

"I feel like I need to," I said. "But I just don't trust myself. I don't trust my own instincts."

"I've heard you say that several times, but I don't know why that is, Beth. You're an extremely capable individual."

"But I was so wrong about Crawford, David. What if I'm wrong about everything else, too?"

"I wouldn't say you were *wrong* about Crawford."

"I would."

David set his trowel on the floor and rested his hands on his knees, then twisted his torso to the left and then the right. "Have you ever heard of anchoring bias?"

I shook my head and concentrated on positioning the piece of tile I was setting next to the base of the pedestal sink. We'd rented a small wet saw to cut angled pieces and I had cracked four tiles before finally getting one right.

"Anchoring bias is the tendency to look at everything through the lens of the first information we receive."

"Okay."

"So if I tell you that someone you're about to meet is a good person and you trust my opinion, you're more likely to excuse bad behavior from that person later, because you're anchored in the idea that he or she is a good person."

"Okay."

"What was the first information you had about Crawford?"

"I don't remember."

"I'm not trying to push you, Beth," David said gently. "I just want you to see that trusting him wasn't a character flaw."

I let go of the edge of the tile and pushed it into the thinset with my fingers, then rocked back on my heels, too.

"That he was a good guy."

"How so?"

"Responsible. Smart. Kind."

"Heterosexual?"

I nodded. "Mac and Hugh always joked that Crawford would never find a woman who lived up to his expectations."

"So when he eventually picked you..."

"I felt chosen. Approved of."

David nodded. "And you excused his inability to connect emotionally because..."

"He had horrible role models."

"And you didn't see him as secretive because...."

"He was just private, in the way that people with money are. The way lawyers are."

"And not particularly engaged at home because..."

"He was concerned with his career. Driven. And under a lot of pressure to be successful."

"Interesting."

"I see what you're doing, David. I get your point. But don't you think that after all those years of being married, I should have known something was off?"

"Not if he was working hard to keep that part of himself hidden. Or denying it altogether."

We sat in silence for a minute, and then David pushed the roll of paper towels towards me. "I didn't mean to make you cry, kiddo."

I nodded. "I know. I just spent so many years wondering what was wrong with me. Why I was so unlovable, so undesirable, that he didn't want me."

David sighed. "That's the part I hate most in all of this. Tell me more about this assignment."

"It's a gift that's fallen into my lap. And she's really going out of her way to make it easy for me."

"When does it start?"

"Couple of weeks."

David looked around the bathroom. "Great. Let me think of a couple more projects we can knock out before you go."

"Maybe I'll leave sooner," I said, wiping my eyes.

He laughed. "If you go, are you going to tell Porter?"

I shrugged. "I don't think so. I'm not ready for that."

"Do you feel like he wants more from you than you're ready to give?"

"It's not that. It's just..."

How could I explain how I felt about Porter's reappearance in my life after three decades? On one hand, it felt like a miracle, and on the other hand, it felt like a cosmic joke. Why would Porter show up when I was broken and totally incapable of trusting anyone? When the person he'd once known had been replaced with the damaged shell of who I used to be? I had never once run into him when I was living in Raleigh, single and gainfully employed and still optimistic about the future, so the only explanation I could come up with about why Porter was back in my life when I was at my lowest was that the universe was setting me up for another fall.

"I always liked Porter," David said, flinging a blob of thinset down and smoothing it with his trowel. "He's one of those people who occupies space in your life as soon as you meet him."

"What do you mean?"

"He felt like family right away. The kind of person who makes the label 'friend' seem inadequate. Although in my experience most labels are inadequate."

"Except for *most highly favored niece.*"

"That one is almost adequate."

"I think it helps that I'm your only niece," I said. "The lack of competition works in my favor."

"And you're a whiz at tiling. That's the most important thing."

We both laughed and then fell silent. The only sound was the scraping of David's trowel.

"Did I ever tell you about going to *La Foce?*" I said after a few minutes. "The house and garden in Tuscany?"

La Foce was one of the first places Porter had taken me when I arrived in Italy. We'd walked through the garden for well over an hour while Porter told me the story of Iris Origo, the woman who'd once owned the house.

"The garden was full of pomegranate trees," I told David. "Porter said it was because of me that he knew Eve gave Adam a pomegranate, not an apple."

"Did you give him your whole *Eve was framed* speech while you were there?"

I smiled. "Nah. Poor guy. If he remembers anything from our time together, it's that Eve wasn't created when Adam got the order not to eat the fruit."

I'd written my research thesis on the creation stories in Genesis while Porter and I were dating, and how the story of the Fall, which contained nothing seductive or sexual in the original text, had been perverted in translation. Poor Porter had been subjected to more feminist theology than he'd ever imagined possible.

I leaned forward to carefully place two more tile spacers. "I was pretty much a zombie back then. But I remember being really surprised that he remembered that, about the pomegranates. It made me think that Porter had always been listening to me, even when he wasn't particularly interested in the subject matter."

"He was interested in you, and that was enough for him. Porter once told me that he'd never been anywhere with you that you weren't the most interesting person in the room."

I looked at my uncle. "Really?"

"Yep." David set the trowel on the floor and pushed himself to his feet. "Oof," he said, putting his hands in the small of his back and arching backwards. "Want some iced tea?"

As David stepped around me towards the door, I caught sight of the small wave tattoo above his ankle. Even after all these years, it still surprised me every time I saw it, that youthful impulse permanently inked on his skin.

"What if you took the assignment and did tell Porter?" he said, returning to the bathroom with two glasses of iced tea. "I think more than anything he wants to be your friend. Maybe that's worth some effort, huh?"

"Thanks," I said, reaching for the glass he was holding out. "I don't know. I'm not sure I think there really is a future for me and Porter, friends or otherwise."

"You may be right. But you won't know unless you make space for the possibility. Sometimes the best thing you can do for yourself is get out of your own way."

"Just be totally passive?"

"Accepting that we are not in control isn't the same thing as being passive, kiddo. It's simply conceding that while we do our best, there are elements beyond our grasp. And those elements include other people, and how they feel and act at any given time."

"There's so much between me and Porter that still needs answers. Stuff I just don't have the energy for."

"And maybe that's how it's going to stay. But maybe not." David set his tea glass on the windowsill and gripped the edge of the sink to ease himself onto the floor. "I think you need to take as much time as you need to heal. But eventually, you may want to clear some of those things up. Say what you need to say to Porter, as long as it comes from a place of love and compassion, so you can move on. Same with Crawford."

"Porter seemed so annoyed that Crawford and I weren't at each other's throats when I was in London," I said. "He told me I let Crawford walk all over me."

"It's hard to see someone you care about being hurt."

"I was just trying to survive, David. I still am. And I can't handle Porter's anger on top of everything else." I finished my tea and shook an ice cube into my mouth. "And I don't want to fight with Crawford, I really don't. I never have. It's too much for me."

"Then tell Porter that."

"I tried. But it's like he thinks I should just erase that part of my life and never speak to Crawford again."

David nodded and stirred the tub of thinset before scooping a ball of it onto his trowel and expertly flipping it onto the cement backing board.

"How much does he know?" he asked, spreading it like icing.

"Porter? Not everything. Just that Crawford's with someone else."

"Is there a reason why you didn't tell him the rest?"

"That I've wasted my whole life on something that doesn't even exist?" I said, hating the shrillness of my voice. "I'm not ready for Porter to know that. He already thinks I'm weak. Why add stupid?"

David was quiet for a long time. When he finally did speak, his voice was gentle.

"You know," he said, "some wise person once told me not to write the story in advance." He looked up and made a puzzled face. "I can't remember who that was, but it was good advice."

"Har har. But think about it, David. It's humiliating to have people know that you were too dumb to see what was in front of your face."

"You're assuming a lot about other people. Did you hear what I just said about not writing the story in advance?"

David was quoting a story I'd told him, about when I was fresh out of grad school and working for a congressman who'd been a successful businessman prior to running for office. We were doing a phone interview with a financial reporter one day. The congressman was on speaker phone and I was sitting next to him scribbling talking points, and the reporter kept hammering the congressman with questions about the venture capital firm where he'd been Managing Partner, and referring to the company's activities as *leveraged buyouts*, which were very much in the news then and had a negative, predatory connotation. No matter how many times my boss tried to tell him that leveraged buyouts and venture capital investments were not the same thing, the reporter persisted with *LBO* this and *leveraged buyout* that. It was obvious that he had formed his opinion and written the story in advance and refused to be budged from it.

After about five minutes of this line of questioning, my boss lost his cool.

"Listen, buddy," he said. "Do you have any questions that actually pertain to me or my company?"

The reporter said, "Okay, you tell me. What *should* I be asking?

"How about this?" my boss said, not missing a beat. "Is there a God, and am I living my life the right way?" Then he dropped the receiver with a thud.

"I get what you're saying, David," I said, adjusting my body to reach for the box of tile. "And thank you for quoting me back to me. It's always a pleasure to get a dose of my own medicine."

David laughed. "I figured it doesn't happen often enough." He picked up his trowel and then paused. "Here's the thing," he said, the trowel suspended in mid-air. "You've learned the hard way that it's impossible to be in a real relationship with someone who's got a secret. There can't ever be a true emotional intimacy as long as one person isn't fully present and fully authentic."

I nodded. "I definitely know that now."

"And it's been an incredibly painful lesson to learn. But these things happen. People change. They grow and evolve and sometimes they eventually find the strength to tell the truth about who they are and what they want, often as a result of coming face to face with their own mortality. And sometimes those revelations strengthen a relationship, and sometimes they create a crack that widens over time." He set the trowel down and rested his hands on his knees. "I could tell you several stories about people who've decided to quit the rat race and follow their passion, or who've drastically changed their appearance or their habits, and their spouse couldn't handle it. Marriages break down for a million reasons. It happens."

"I know."

"And losing a child...well, sometimes even the strongest marriages don't survive that."

I nodded.

"You can't control these things. All you can do is get out of your own way and create space for joy to find you again."

I adjusted the piece of tile I'd just set down and leaned over to place spacers around it. "So you think I should take the assignment in Assisi?"

"I have no intention of telling you what to do," David said. "But if I were you, I'd give it serious thought."

Diciotto

I flew into Rome three weeks later.

The guide's name is Marco, my editor had written. *He's part of the group working on the Saint Francis project. I've emailed with him a couple of times and his English is pretty good. He knows the city inside and out—his family's been there for centuries. I think you'll like him.*

Marco picked me up at the airport. He was very tall and very talkative and drifted in and out of our lane of traffic as he narrated the entire two-and-a-half-hour drive to Assisi, gesticulating wildly as he pointed out towns and buildings and interesting scenery. Following his conversation was exhausting, like trying to track a fly, and more than once I had to ask him to back up and finish a thought he'd left dangling in mid-air.

"Wait. What were you saying about the Etruscans? Before the part about the Communists?"

Marco looked over at me. "I don't know. I forget already. I am old man."

"How old are you?"

"Fifty-six."

"So, basically almost dead."

Marco laughed. "Yes, is true," he said, nodding. "If I die in car, you can drive this?"

"Yes, I can drive a manual."

"Good," he said. "Now I feel better. But my stomach is talking. There is sushi in Perugia. This is something Americans like, yes?"

"We're pretty far from the ocean for sushi."

"Two hours only. And they have also the ice here in Italy. We are not so primitive, you know."

"Really? Ice? I thought you all built the viaducts and stopped there."

"Was important, viaducts! But also we have the ice."

"Fine," I said. "Let's go eat sushi. Whoever survives has to drive the rest of the way."

I was relieved to see that the sushi chef was Japanese, and the food turned out to be quite good, despite the sketchy location in a strip of shops just off the highway in Perugia. As we ate, I filled Marco in on the article I was writing.

"There are a lot of threads I'll be following. Historical threads, travel threads, all kinds of different subjects I'll weave together. The writing I do for this project will hopefully end up making several pieces for several publications and really give your project some exposure. Did you get the list of places I need to visit?"

He nodded. "I add some places. For threads."

"Like what?"

Marco smiled. "Surprises. I tell you first and if you don't want, we don't go, I promise."

His phone chirped.

"You're a popular guy. Your phone hasn't stopped since I got in the car."

He glanced at the phone before stuffing it back into the pocket of his blue parka.

"Is okay. No problem. Come, we go now."

Marco exited the highway at Santa Maria degli Angeli and zoomed up the winding road to Assisi. He passed under the stone arch that marked the entrance to the historical center of the city, sped up the street, and then made a sharp right around the fountain before speeding down a cobblestone street, careening down a steep hill, and coming to an abrupt stop in front of a stone building.

The apartment I'd rented belonged to an English priest who was an old friend of David's.

"Is there," Marco said, pointing to a door on the left side of the street.

He jumped out of the car, rang the buzzer next to the door, then hoisted my suitcase out of the trunk and set it on the street. When Father Michael opened the door, Marco introduced himself and shook the priest's hand, then turned to me.

"I see you tomorrow at eight," he said, and kissed my cheek.

"*Ciao, Marco. Ci vediamo domani mattina alle otto.*"

His eyes widened. "Why you did not tell me you speak Italian?"

I shook my head. "I don't really. That was it."

"You are a surprise to me." He waved. "Okay, *ciao.*"

The apartment I was renting from Father Michael was perfect. It had a kitchen, a bedroom, a small living room, and a patio. I knew that if I sat down I would fall asleep, so I made myself hang my clothes in the wardrobe and organize my toiletries in the bathroom, then I headed out to find the grocery store Father Michael had marked for me on a map.

The church of Santa Chiara was at the bottom of the street, and I stopped to look in for a few minutes before continuing on. As I passed under the stone arch that Marco had so recently driven through, I caught a snippet of Vivaldi from a passing car, and instantly, Porter pushed into my thoughts.

"*La Follia?* It means madness," he'd said when I asked about the name of his house. "It's also the name of the Vivaldi piece I was listening to when I first saw this place. I guess I took it as some kind of sign."

"I don't think I've ever known anyone who loves classical music as much as you do," I said.

"Yeh, well, it never won me any cool points."

"Did you care?"

"Not at all," he laughed. "The name makes perfect sense, too. You have to be a little bit mad to love a house like this because the projects never stop. There's always something that needs to be done."

"Do you ever regret buying it?"

"Not even once," he said without hesitation, and I immediately wondered if I'd ever been that sure about anything. "But I'm willing to make changes, if there's anything you want to change. I never really gave much thought to the inside, to tell you the truth."

"I can't think of anything I would change," I said, surprising myself. I think I rearranged our house in London at least once a month, probably because I never realized that the problem wasn't the house, but the inhabitants. "And besides, it's not my house, Porter," I said. "If there's something you want my help with, I'm happy to help, of course. I'll never be able to repay your—" I turned around then from the shelf of books I was straightening and saw that he'd left the room.

I found the *Tigre* grocery store and went in to gather some necessities. Coffee, milk, sugar. Slices of grilled eggplant soaked in olive oil, bread, pecorino cheese. On the way to the counter I paused in front of the olive oil display. The first time I'd tasted one of the oils that came from a farm close to Porter's house, the viscous, greenish-yellow, intensely flavored oil had come as a shock. I could taste the sunlight and peppery grass and rich soil the olives grew in. I put it on everything when I was staying at Porter's, and gave Oliver a teaspoon with every meal, too, to keep his joints limber.

I grabbed a metal tin of oil from nearby Bevagna and dumped my groceries on the counter. A song I recognized, "Le tasche piene di sassi," was playing on the store's intercom system. For a couple of months the previous summer, you couldn't turn on *Radio Subasio* without hearing it.

"My God, I haven't heard this song in ages!" Porter would say every time it came on.

"It sounds familiar," I would say, "but there are so many songs about having pockets full of rocks that I can't be sure I've ever heard this particular one before."

As I unpacked my carrier bag of groceries back at the apartment, I realized that the odd feeling I'd had all day wasn't as much about jet lag as it was about the strangeness of being in Italy without Porter.

I could remedy that, of course. I could send him a WhatsApp and tell him where I was, and if I took the train, I could even be at the village station near his house in less than three hours.

But I just couldn't bring myself to do it.

Diciannove

The next morning, Marco picked me up in front of the apartment and we headed towards San Marino in his little Fiat Panda.

"Today we do the *Passo delle Streghe*, yes?"

"Right," I said, checking my notes. "We're doing The Witches Walk between the *Torre Guaita* and the *Torre Cesta* of Mount Titano. The book says the name of the path comes from the wind making it sound like people are talking."

"No, is not true. Is called this because the witch do magic there and then *all'alba*—how you say in English?"

"At dawn."

"At dawn the witch become the cat and run away!"

"You don't really believe in witches, do you?"

"*Sì, perché conosco una,*" he said under his breath, looking away.

Yes, because I know one. I pretended I hadn't heard him.

"Then we can have some lunch and at two o'clock I have an appointment with the head of the tourism agency. I'll need you to help translate."

"Maybe she lie to make San Marino more interesting."

"Do you think she has to lie? Is San Marino that boring?"

He shrugged. "Is not Assisi."

The views from the Witches' Walk were amazing, cloudless and clear, and the fairly gentle rise of the path was a nice change from the steep stairs you had to take to get to it. I loosened my scarf from around my neck and pulled off my gloves and stuffed them in my pockets, but Marco stayed bundled up as if we were going to the North Pole. He'd already given me a lecture on the thousand different ways a breeze could kill you, and as we started walking, I thought of a funny list I'd once seen about the ways women died in Victorian literature, from things like reading a letter containing shocking news to being caught in a sudden downpour or spending too much time in London. Nineteenth century literature had nothing on the modern Italian, though, who saw imminent death in the slightest draft, particularly if it hit the back of your neck.

"There is Croatia," Marco said, pointing across the blue expanse of the Adriatic Sea in the distance. "I never go there, but one time I go to Jamaica."

"That makes sense, seeing as how Croatia is next door and Jamaica is halfway around the world."

"I smoke ganja and dance all night with girls," Marco said. "My wife, she want to kill me. I think she is going to cut it off when I am sleeping."

"Huh."

"I like the spice food in Jamaica. In Italy we eat only Italian food. One day I will go to Turkey and smoke hashish. Have you done this? Is nice, but only if you are calm in your mind."

I was getting used to these verbal non-sequiturs with Marco, who said whatever came into his head as soon as it arrived. He reminded me of Mac that way, and for an instant I felt a pang of sorrow about Mac and Hugh, both of whom would be resigned to my past now that Crawford and I were divorced.

I shook off the thought and started walking again, snapping photos and making notes. After a while, Marco and I went back down to the main street of San Marino and found a *trattoria* to have lunch in. While we ate, Marco told me that in several weeks, he would start picking olives.

"This work, it is hard," he said.

"I've done it," I told him. "I couldn't move for a week afterwards."

"Where have you done this?"

I told Marco about the town where Porter lived and the arrival of a new stainless-steel olive press the previous fall that had replaced the one that had been there for centuries, two huge wheels of thick stone that ground the olives together. The modern machine promised a greater yield, which was the key. Olive oil production is so labor intensive and time consuming that just the promise of squeezing a bit more oil out of each piece of fruit made those rural Italians willing to overlook the fact that, despite their ability to do everything better than everyone else in the world, the new machine came from Germany.

"*Un frantoio tedesco?*" Marco said.

I nodded. "Yes. They trucked it in from Germany."

He made a face. "Is not right. Should be Italian."

I'd never seen, or even really considered, how olives were harvested before I stayed with Porter. The old-fashioned way of picking, climbing ladders and removing the olives by hand and dropping them into canvas bags that you wore strapped across your chest like a bandolier, was how Porter and I cleared his trees, and even with the special poles for removing the olives from the top branches, you couldn't avoid getting poked and scratched.

There were other ways to get the olives off the trees, like hiring the tree shaker. I'm sure there's a technical name for the machine that unfolds from the back of a truck and wraps its arms around the trunk and literally shakes the olives off the branches and into waiting canvas tarps, but I never knew it and just called it the tree shaker. Porter never corrected me. He also, being something of a purist in several surprising ways, said he would never use one on his trees.

"These trees have been here for hundreds of years. They deserve respect, not to be brutalized by some machine in the name of efficiency."

"I agree, but I'm wondering how far you're going to go, though?" I said, teasing him. "You're getting sheep. We're picking olives by hand. My blisters have blisters from turning over the garden. Next you'll be trading in the tractor for a team of mules and going full Wendell Berry."

Porter laughed. I'd given him Berry's *The Mad Farmer Poems*, which I found in a used bookstore in Lucca, for his birthday.

"Not a chance," he said. "I love my tractor. But I agree with Wendell Berry that you have to look more than five minutes into the future, and have some respect for the fact that you're just a temporary caretaker of the land."

"These machines are everywhere in Assisi," Marco said, ignoring my question when I asked him the name of the tree shaker. "Is useful, but I only pick with hands."

It takes something close to a hundred pounds of olives to get a gallon of oil, and the pressing has to be done within three days of getting the olives off the trees, which is why the whole midsection of Italy seems to erupt into activity all at once in the fall. Trucks loaded down with crates of olives snake their way across the valley to the mill, where the crates are weighed. That weight determines how much you have to pay to have your olives pressed. If there has been too much rain, the olives swell with water and the pressing cost is higher and the oil yield is lower. If there has been a drought, the undersized olives weigh less and cost less to press, but also yield little in the way of usable oil.

The men stand around in jeans and muddy boots and stained coats at the mill, their wool hats pulled down low, and smoke and talk, occasionally scratching out complicated equations on scraps of paper to determine the cost of pressing and the eventual cost per liter of the finished product. Talk of the weather and predictions about the future are constant, as is the basic assumption that the mill owner is a lying SOB who is cheating all and sundry.

"Is true," Marco said when I asked if he also thought the mill owners routinely cheated the farmers. "I have to watch them in continuous when I take my olives," he said, shoveling a spoonful of *lampredotto* into his mouth. "These guys, they are all fucking their mothers."

I started laughing and couldn't stop. Tears were running down my face before I was able to pull myself together.

"I think you drink too much wine," Marco said, refilling my glass.

I wiped my face with a balled-up tissue from my pocket. "I'm sorry. It's just that what you meant to say is they are all motherfuckers."

He nodded. "Is what I said, no? Anyway, come on, crazy woman. Finish your lunch. Is time to hear the lies about San Marino."

The head of tourism was a no-nonsense woman in her sixties who was insistent that San Marino should be front and center in any piece I might write about Italy. Marco stood behind her rolling his eyes as she talked and refused to translate most of what she said. On our way out of her office, he elbowed me in the side.

"She want me bad. You see this, too? She tell lies with her mouth, but with her eyes she say, *"Take me to the bed, Marco.'"*

For the second time that day, I couldn't stop laughing.

When Marco dropped me off at the apartment that evening, I made myself an eggplant and pecorino sandwich and logged into my email.

> *Most Highly Favored Niece,*
>
> *Glad you arrived safely and are happy with the apartment. I envy you, spending time with Michael, about whom I have the fondest memories. Please give him my regards and ask if he is still writing poetry?*
>
> *I've been thinking a great deal lately about some of the conversations we had while you were here. What you said, about feeling as though your past had been erased, has stuck with me. I know it's impossible to see now, but there is a path ahead, kiddo. Your job is to find it—but I urge you to give yourself grace as you do so.*
>
> *Do you know of Corrie ten Boom? She was a young woman when WWII began, and her family hid Jews when the Nazis moved into the Netherlands. Eventually someone turned them in, and the ten Booms were put in concentration camps. But despite the horror around her, Corrie ten Boom kept her faith – and kept believing that, despite her inability to understand why things were unfolding the way they were, her life had meaning and purpose, and that she lived every day, even the most horrific ones, within God's sight.*
>
> *Two years after the war, ten Boom was speaking in a church in Munich and a man approached her. He'd*

been a guard at Ravensbruck, where Corrie and her sister were prisoners, and she remembered him. She remembered being made to walk naked in front of him and the other guards, she remembered their cruel callousness as her sister Betsie starved to death.

The guard told Corrie that he had been forgiven by God, and asked whether she could forgive him, too. You know what she said? She said she could not. Not alone, anyway. And right then and there, she turned away from the man and asked God for help. She told God that all she could do was extend her hand to the man, and that God would have to do the rest. And that's exactly what happened. She extended her hand, and then she got out of her own way and let God go to work.

My point is, kiddo, now is the time when you need to ask God for help to forgive the pilot, the drunk driver, the cyclist, Crawford. To forgive yourself for the choices you made in the past that seem misguided to you now. To forgive Porter, if that's also required. You are standing on the brink of your future, and you have to do what Corrie ten Boom did and extend your hand to the people who have hurt you and leave the rest to God. Move on. Focus on you, and on figuring out what you want, and what steps you need to take to get there. And remember that I am here to help you.

You are not alone in this world, and nothing that has occurred in your life is without meaning. However, it is up to _you_ to decide what that meaning will be.

Enjoy Assisi!

Love from your favorite uncle,

David

I read David's email twice then closed my laptop. I started to text Porter, but decided to go for a walk and think about what I wanted to say first.

My footsteps echoed on the stones as I made my way across the *Piazza del Comune* to the Basilica of Saint Francis. Without the hordes of day-tripping tourists, Assisi is a very quiet place, and the Basilica was empty, save for four nuns sitting towards the front.

I slipped into a pew in the middle of the sanctuary and bowed my head, praying a clumsy laundry list of gratitude for David, who had stepped into my life as both a father and a friend, and for Jenny, who, since we'd shared a nap mat in preschool, had only ever wanted the best for me. I thanked God for Porter, and prayed that we might find a way to be friends again, and for Marco, who had made me laugh more in the past two days than I had in the past two years.

And then I said a prayer for peace between me and Crawford.

We'd been at odds before, Crawford and I, and had come back from it. When I moved to Raleigh, I'd been incredibly angry about the way things had ended between us on my last night in D.C. and I had vowed to forget about Crawford. As I settled into my new life, it had become easier and easier not to pick up the phone, not to send an email, not be in contact with him. With time, he wasn't the first person I thought about telling when I saw or heard something interesting.

But early one morning, I woke to the sound of knocking on my door. I pulled on my robe and opened the door to my neighbor, who was holding a small parcel.

"Sorry to bother you so early," he said. "This was in my box yesterday, but it's for you."

I thanked him and took the package, pushed the door closed with my foot, and grabbed a steak knife to slice the tape on the box. Inside was a parcel wrapped in thick brown paper and tied with a white string, and I knew immediately that it was from Crawford because there was a store we used to go to in D.C., a dusty stationary shop tucked on a side street, where I'd lust after the ornate metal paper roller and cast-iron string cage mounted on the wall while Crawford tested all of the black pens before settling on the same one he'd been using since Georgetown. Crawford, more than anyone, knew how much I preferred the simplicity of brown paper to wrapping paper.

Inside the package was a hardcover copy of *East of Eden*.

The last time I'd read it, I was stretched out on the couch at Hugh's parents' cabin with my feet in Crawford's lap. The only noise was the occasional scratching of his pen on a legal pad and the low murmur of conversation and repetitive *thunk* as Mac and Hugh hit golf balls off the front porch.

The four of us had been trying to arrange a weekend at the cabin forever, but somebody always had studying to do or a paper to write or a date that couldn't be missed. Finally, one night over pizza, Hugh announced that if we weren't in front of his apartment the following Friday by five, our friendship would be over, no questions asked. Apparently we all just needed the pressure, because when I arrived at exactly five, having run all the way from class to the Metro station and then to Hugh's building, Crawford was already ensconced in the backseat of Hugh's Audi, which was parked in a loading zone, and Mac was teetering towards the curb carrying three cases of Foster's.

"Right, we're off," he said, dropping the beer into the trunk and slamming it closed.

"Where's your stuff?" Hugh asked.

"Did you not just see me put the beer in the boot, mate?"

"Your clothes, dumbass."

"Don't need any," Mac said. "We're going to the country, so I'll be in the nuddy. You're welcome."

We made him wear Hugh's mother's floral bathrobe all weekend.

Crawford and I were the designated kitchen team at the cabin, since Hugh was hosting and Mac was incapable of even microwaving a hot dog, and when the food was ready, we all piled onto the couch to watch a movie, which would have been nice except that the guys had only brought slasher movies. When I said that I preferred not to watch someone get chainsawed in half while I was eating a steak, Hugh got up and pawed through the cabinet.

"Here's a chick flick," he said, holding up a copy of *Love Story*.

"No," I said. "No, no, no. I hate that movie. Let's go back to the chainsaws."

"I've actually never seen it," Hugh said, opening the cover and sliding the movie into the player.

"I like the looks of this one," Mac said, pointing to Ali McGraw.

"She does yoga videos now," I said. "I'll get you one for Christmas if we don't have to watch this movie." I turned to Crawford. "Please don't let this happen."

He shrugged. "I'm just trying to eat. These green beans are great, by the way."

We didn't get more than fifteen minutes into the movie before Mac groaned and chucked an empty beer can at the TV.

"I told you!" I said. "You guys should listen to me once in a while."

"You just hate it because Robert Duvall's not in it," Crawford said.

"He would never be in something that sucked," I said.

"Why's this movie even famous?" Mac asked.

"Because love means never having to say you're sorry," Hugh said.

I groaned. "Erich Segal should be shot for writing that line."

"That's actually a good plan," Mac said. "I'm never saying sorry again."

"You never say you're sorry now," Hugh said.

"I know," Mac said. "Sorry about that."

We ran that joke into the ground.

Later that weekend, we all went down to the pond. I was lying on a raft reading when Mac cannonballed into the water, sending me and *East of Eden* to the bottom. I'd never had another copy until the package arrived from Crawford.

I could hear the cab's dispatch radio in the background when Crawford answered his cell phone.

"I'm stuck in traffic on the bridge," he said.

"I just this minute got the book. It's really beautiful, and it reminds me of the weekend at the cabin... I miss you guys so much."

"We miss you, too. It's not the same without you. But nothing lasts forever, right?" he said. "Someone was going to move on."

"I just didn't think it would be me. I thought Mac would go back to Australia."

"At the suggestion of the U.S. government," Crawford said.

"Or on tour with AC/DC."

We both laughed. Mac considered AC/DC, which he called *Acca Dacca*, God's gift to music.

"The book's a long overdue apology," Crawford said. "I shouldn't have kicked you when you were down, and I hate that you left angry."

"It's okay," I said. "Water under the bridge."

Crawford was quiet for a minute. "So are you done with this experiment?"

"What experiment?"

"Raleigh. The whole thing."

"I like my job here."

"There are jobs in D.C. Even ones outside of politics. I think you should come back before no one remembers who you are."

"Including you, Crawford?"

There was an uncomfortable silence. "Sure. Including me."

I let his answer hang in the air a bit before responding.

"I'll take that under advisement. I better go now."

Later that day, while I was eating a turkey sandwich at my desk with the phone muted and the door closed, I dug *East of Eden* out of my work bag and flipped it open to re-read Steinbeck's description of Cathy. Steinbeck calls Cathy a monster and says that while Cathy's lack of a conscience is an invisible defect, others are born monstrous in ways that we can see. Echoing the Old Testament thinking that equated physical defects and illness with divine punishment, Steinbeck says that the defects we can see were once thought to be the "visible punishment for concealed sins."

I looked up at the frescoed walls of the Basilica, my thoughts a tangle of *East of Eden* and Crawford and my own past.

I never believed that homosexuality was a sin, by any stretch. After all, I'd never made a choice to be heterosexual. I'd been born that way. And I'd always believed that sexuality was a question of biology, not choice, despite what we were taught at school by Sister Mary Michael, who had lived with the same female "roommate" for decades and was a study in repressed lesbianism if there ever was one. But I also knew that Blythe and Number Three would never really accept that their golden boy didn't fit the social mold, and I wondered if Crawford had grown to see me, the wife he had to support and share a home with, as the visible punishment for what the church and his parents and society told him were his concealed sins. Had I been the cross Crawford believed he had to bear so he could move freely in the world?

I sat in the empty Basilica for a long time, pondering these mysteries, then tightened my scarf around my throat, buttoned up my jacket, and walked home.

Venti

A couple of times a week for nearly two months, Marco
pulled up in front of the apartment and we set off on a
new adventure or went for a walk on Mount Subasio, where
Marco would tell me stories about his life and point out where
asparagus and nettles and truffles grew.

"When I was a young man, I liked to travel," he said one
afternoon as we trekked across a meadow. "Not to write about,
like you, just to enjoy life. But when I go from here, I have
nostalgia." He elbowed me in the side. "You are surprised I
know this word in English, no?"

"Yes."

"Is the same word in Italian," he said, and laughed.

"Did you know that nostalgia was originally thought to be
something only Swiss people got?"

"No. Explain me."

I told Marco about the Swiss soldiers in the Thirty Years' War who'd shared a mysterious set of symptoms—fatigue, fever, indigestion, insomnia, and an intense yearning for home—and the doctor who saw the same symptoms in Swiss mercenaries years later and surmised that there were two particularly Swiss causes of nostalgia: frequent changes in altitude and the constant clanging of cow bells.

"Is not true. Also Italians can have this feeling," Marco said. "In Italy, Italian people complain in continuous about this country. But when they go away? No place is good."

I laughed. "I think that's just human nature. The grass is always greener, right?"

"Si. L'erba del vicino è sempre più verde."

"Hey, did you hear the bells just now?"

"From the basilica?" Marco looked at his watch. "Is not time."

"No, from the cows up there."

He glanced at the side of the mountain where a quartet of cows were regarding us placidly and made a face. "I do not like cows. You cannot get inside the head of them. Who can know what a cow will do?"

The fact that this six-foot-four former soccer player found cows threateningly unpredictable made me laugh out loud until I remembered what he'd told me about his home life over lunch one day. No wonder he valued predictability.

He had married someone, he told me, just like his mother.

"She is one minute calm, one minute furious," he said. "Is no peace with her."

"Did you think she would change? That you could fix her?"

He shrugged. "Who can say? I do not remember. But what can I do? We have a child together."

"Your child is a grown man. You could leave."

"I leave many times," he said. "But you know how it is. First you talk, then you kiss, then you bring your suitcase home."

"I actually don't know, Marco, but I'll take your word for it. You must love her, though, if you keep going back."

"Yes, but she ruin my life. She say, 'Sweep the floor' and then she tell me where is broom, how to use broom, why I use this broom wrong and how I am stupid."

"But you stay because you think you're trapped?"

"I don't think. I just try to survive. Life is hard."

"It's hard for everyone, Marco. You don't have a monopoly on a hard life."

He stopped eating and tilted his head to the side. "What do you mean by this? Monopoly is a game, yes? You want to say that my life is a game?"

"I mean that you're not the only person whose life is difficult."

"I know this," he said, nodding.

"If she makes you so unhappy, leave," I said. "Here, do you want this? I can't finish all this food."

"Is not so easy to leave."

"Of course not. But this is your only life. Why stay with someone who makes you unhappy?"

Even as I said it, I recognized my own hypocrisy. If I'd never found the evidence of Crawford's secret, I would still be with him, wondering what I'd done wrong that day to make him not want to spend time with me.

"I am Buddhist, you know. Maybe is not my only life. In next life I am bird," Marco said. "I fly to your house and sing to you all day and night."

I told him about a Harvard study David and I had read about. The study followed around seven hundred men for several decades to see how their lives played out.

"They wanted to see what contributed to their happiness and quality of life. What made their lives good."

"And? The answer is what?"

"The one thing critical to happiness is a good relationship."

"To be happy in the bed."

"No, Marco. Not everything is about sex."

"Is important, *la vita sessuale*."

"Okay, but you can be happy without being in bed all day."

"Is not necessary all day," he said. "Only you need to visit two or three times."

I rolled my eyes. "You remind me so much of someone I know."

"He is perfect to look at, like me?"

I had to laugh. "Exactly."

"Thank you. Tell me more about this study."

It started in 1938, I told him, and is still going on, with the descendants of the original participants. The whole point was to find out what aspects of their lives had contributed to happiness and personal satisfaction. The men's lives had been wildly different, but the critical factor for all of them was a good relationship.

"The head of the study said that if you live in conflict, like a marriage with a lot of fights or one that isn't affectionate, it's worse for your health than being alone."

Marco nodded. "Is true."

"Okay, so can I ask you something? How do you have sex all the time with someone who tells you that you're stupid? How can you keep sleeping with someone if you don't feel loved and appreciated?"

Marco looked confused. "Are two different things, sex and love," he said. "One is water, one is wine. Is nice if both are on the table, but is not always together."

"I will never understand men," I said, shaking my head.

"What is to understand? I explain you. Is like this. You are fun, you make me laugh, we like history and music and books the same. I like the way you look, the way you smell, the way you dress yourself. When you smile, you have beautiful American teeth. When you laugh, is to me like a music. I am happy with you." He shrugged. "So is a kind of love I have for you. But we do not make sex."

"No, we don't."

"But we can, if you say yes."

I laughed out loud. "I am still holding out for sex and love together, Marco. Sorry."

He shrugged. "Is because you are woman."

"I guess so."

"Let me know when you start to love Marco. Then we go to bed and you love me even more."

When Marco dropped me off late that afternoon, I sat down with the short story I'd been working on since I arrived in Assisi. I'd promised Marco I would let him choose what he wanted to be called in the story, and earlier that afternoon, as we crossed the meadow on Mount Subasio, he'd announced his decision.

"I want to be called Rocco," he said. "Is a good name. Strong."

"Is Rocco a saint?"

Marco shook his head. "Is Italian porn star. Rocco Siffredi."

Like Hannibal Over the Alps

O*n an August evening in 1985, over ninety thousand people packed Nairobi's Uhuru Park for a Mass said by Pope John Paul II. It was the culminating event of a week-long Eucharistic Congress attended by Catholics from around the globe, and as the Pope offered the final benediction and brought the three-hour* *service to a close, the crowd began to disperse under a blanket of darkness. A priest named Michael from northern England was chatting with a bishop as they moved slowly towards the exit when he noticed a white Land Rover off to his left. In the weak halo of the car's interior light, he could see that the passengers were wearing the saris of the Order of Missionaries of Charity. The founder of the Calcutta-based Order, Mother Teresa, was his hero, and the Land Rover, hemmed in on all sides by the crowd, presented an unmissable opportunity for Father Michael to hear from the sisters what it was like to work with the Nobel Prize-winning holy woman.*

Michael excused himself from the bishop, waded through the crowd, and tapped on the passenger window of the car. When the glass lowered, he had a conversation with a nun that changed the course of his life forever.

"What did you talk about?" I ask. It is forty years after the events in Nairobi, but Father Michael is visibly animated as he tells me the story.

"I told her about my work," he says. "I was overseeing a program that cared for the children of unwed mothers and provided meals for the elderly. She listened intently, but then she did something very odd."

"What was that?"

"She took both of my hands in hers and squeezed them and said, 'But what do you want to do?'"

"Isn't that what you had just been telling her?"

"I thought so. And I was quite taken aback by her question," he says. "But I assumed she was asking what I hoped for the future of the program, so I told her of our plans to expand."

"And?"

"And she shook her head, as if my answer displeased her. Then she locked her eyes onto mine, squeezed my hands again, and repeated her question, 'But what do you want to do?'"

Startled by the nun's insistence, Father Michael confessed the secret he had closely guarded for years.

"Truthfully," he told her, "I've always wanted to be a bit of a hermit and write. And I've always loved Italy."

Her response was immediate. "Then you must do what has been put in your heart to do."

"Oh, but I couldn't," he protested. "I'm helping the children!"

"And have you no faith?" the nun demanded. "Those are Jesus's children, and he will look after them. But you must do what has been put in your heart to do."

At that moment, the Land Rover's driver found an opening. The nun let go of Father Michael's hands as the vehicle rolled forward, and he stepped backwards into the crowd.

"That chance encounter in Nairobi changed my life," he tells me. "It took four years to make it happen, but several books and thirty years later, I'm still here."

Here is a small stone house in an unassuming village twenty minutes from Assisi. The road to the village is a narrow, serpentine track that undulates through a patchwork of vivid yellow ginestra flowers, gnarled olive trees, and fields of hay that emit a golden glow in the early evening light. A stone arch marks the entrance to the village, and a few feet beyond it, the road ends abruptly inside a cluster of buildings, all constructed from the same local pink-hued stone. There is a chapel, the flaking interior of which shows signs of recurring water damage, and just beyond the chapel, a small vertical structure that served as a communal toilet until 1997, when an earthquake knocked it off its foundation.

A snowstorm had stranded him for nearly two weeks when he first arrived, Father Michael tells me, pointing to a hilltop in the distance where the shape of a building is barely visible through the trees.

"That is the nearest neighbor," he says. *"It's a spiritual community. One of many in the area."*

For centuries, this corner of Umbria has been a destination for seekers from around the globe. Italy's patron saint, San Francesco, is Assisi's native son, and Assisi and the surrounding countryside hold spiritual significance for millions of Christians. Thousands of people visit the Basilica built to honor St. Francis every year, and as their taxis and tour buses strain uphill towards Assisi's historical center, the fifty-three Romanesque arches of the church come into view, revealing the scale of the Basilica and the friary attached to it. Begun in 1228, two years after Francis's death, the Basilica is actually two churches, one atop another, each containing a treasure trove of exquisite frescoes, ornate monastic stalls, and painted barrel-vaulted ceilings; all of which, coupled with the structure's sheer size, make the Basilica a decidedly odd monument to a man who embraced a life of poverty and railed against the excesses of the Catholic Church.

Chiara di Favarone, better known as Saint Clare, was a contemporary of Francis, and Assisi is her hometown, too. Legend has it that Clare was so inspired by hearing Francis preach that she abandoned her life of wealth and comfort to establish an Order of contemplation and poverty at the convent in San Damiano just outside the walls of Assisi. The convent's residents were first known as the Order of Poor Ladies but are now better known as the Poor Clares. There is a basilica honoring Clare in Assisi, as well, but it is a fraction of the size of the one named for Francis, and far less ornate. Clare's body is displayed on its lower level, along with personal items that belonged to both Clare and Francis, who were reportedly the closest of friends, but the most important item in Clare's church is upstairs, in the Cappella del Crocifisso.

The Chapel of the Crucifix is named for the 12th century San Damiano crucifix that hangs there, the same crucifix

Francesco di Pietro di Bernadone, the future Saint Francis, knelt before to ask for God's guidance. He had just returned to Assisi after being imprisoned for a year in Perugia, and as he prayed, the figure of the crucified Christ reportedly locked his eyes on Francis and said, "Go, rebuild my house; as you see, it is all being destroyed." Francis initially interpreted this as a directive to repair the decaying church buildings in the area, but soon realized that the ecclesial corrections that were needed were spiritual, not structural. The words Francis heard that day formed the foundation of the Franciscan Order, which now spans the globe and has tens of thousands of members.

Midway between the basilicas of Saint Francis and Saint Clare, the Piazza del Comune, Assisi's central square, hums with activity. Children chase pigeons, tourists drink wine and snap photos, clusters of nuns in sensible shoes speak languages from all corners of the world, and monks in cinctured brown robes exchange greetings as they crisscross the piazza and dart down the stone passageways that scale and slope throughout the town. There are Francis-related goods for sale on the streets radiating from the square—wooden Tau symbols, tea-towels, sandals—but no matter how cynical one might want to be about the enormous Basilica or the industry that surrounds the memory of the impoverished saint, there is something undeniably extraordinary about his hometown, as if every stone in Assisi is saturated by spirituality and every breeze is redolent with the numinous. Beneath the watchful eye of the Rocca Maggiore castle that was already standing when Francis entered the world, Assisi continues to welcome seekers with a hospitality that is both genuine and tolerant.

There are multiple signs on the road to Assisi declaring it la città della pace, but the history of this city of peace is actually far from serene. Trampled by invaders and frequently at loggerheads with its powerful neighbors, Assisi's efforts to remain independent from papal and imperial powers required *centuries of bloodshed. The armies of nearby Perugia, for instance, invaded regularly, and even the future Saint Francis served as a cavaliere as a young man.*

Yet the threats to Assisi's peace have not all been political or military. Some have come from the Earth itself.

Italy has two fault lines, making it one of the most earthquake-prone countries in the world. As a result, the majority of Assisi's homes and public buildings have been retrofitted with enormous iron tie-rods designed to hold the stone structures in place. On September 26ᵗʰ of 1997, coincidentally the eight hundred and fifteenth anniversary of Francis's birth, those tie rods were put to the test when an earthquake measuring 5.5 on the Richter scale struck Assisi around two a.m., followed by over one hundred measurable tremors and a second quake registering a whopping 6.1.

The earthquakes damaged over eight thousand structures and displaced thousands of residents, but remarkably, only ten lives were lost. Four of those ten deaths occurred during an aftershock, when a group of priests, conservationists, local officials, and a television crew were inside the Basilica of Saint Francis surveying the damage to the church. As the ground began to shift yet again, a portion of the Basilica's ceiling above the high altar crashed to the floor, crushing four members of the group and killing them instantly.

Restoring the Basilica took several years and millions of dollars, and the effort was not without its detractors. Experts painstakingly pieced miniscule fragments of the church's frescoes, believed to be some of the earliest work of the Florentine painter Giotto, back together again, and some art historians argued that the repairs were heavy-handed and clumsy. Meanwhile, many citizens of the town, frustrated by the lack of emphasis on residential repairs, chose to rebuild their lives elsewhere, leaving the heart of Assisi with only a few hundred permanent inhabitants.

Rocco, a local historian whose roots in Assisi extend for generations, is one of them. He brings his three-wheeled Ape cart to a stop in front of an unassuming building a few minutes from the Basilica and turns to tap my hand.

"Look inside," he says. "Is something good."

I clamber out and press my face against the iron bars that cover the ground-floor window Rocco has indicated. Inside, there are tables dressed in white linen and laid with silver, and for a moment I wonder what it is about the settings of an expensive restaurant that Rocco wants me to see. Then I look down. Lying below the restaurant's floor, which is made entirely of glass, is the interior of a Roman villa.

The 1997 earthquake opened a portal to Assisi's past, when it was known as Assisium. Just a few minutes away from the restaurant with the glass floor, for instance, at the 11th century church of San Rufino where both Francis and Clare were baptized, the earthquake widened a crack in the floor, displacing four skeletons that had been wedged into the walls. Tests revealed that the skeletons belonged to tall, blond, blue-eyed Goths, the Germanic nomads who helped bring about the downfall of the Roman Empire in the 5th century C.E.

The Goths' influence, Rocco tells me, is still evident in the many private gardens in town. Prior to the Goths' arrival, Assisi's wealthy residents purchased food in the nearby village of Foligno, which allowed Foligno to fund an army to attack Assisi.

"The Goths say, 'Do not buy food in Foligno. Have garden instead.' Then Foligno people cannot make the army, and Assisi people have peace," Rocco says. "And also beautiful gardens."

"Very clever," I say.

"They are smart, the Goths," Rocco says, tapping his temple. "Savage like animal and cannot read, but smart."

Rocco guides the Ape down a side street near Piazza Matteotti, on the upper end of Assisi's historical center, and points to the outer wall of an enclosed garden.

"This wall belong to a Roman amphitheater. The earthquake uncover more of this wall, and also many ancient pots and tools. Is normal like this."

I have been distracted by a handsome orange cat sunning himself on the amphitheater wall and have to ask Rocco to repeat himself.

"Sorry, Rocco. What's normal?"

"That from something bad come something good," Rocco says. "Earthquake is bad, but he uncover many good things." He shrugs. "Lose something, find something. Life is like this always."

A few days later, we go trekking on Mount Subasio. The only other people we see are two old men with burlap bags slung across their chests, foraging in the underbrush.

We are having a lively discussion about Hannibal, the Carthaginian general who infamously led an attack on Roman forces with a team of African war elephants two centuries before Christ. One of Hannibal's most decisive victories happened at Lago Trasimeno, close to Assisi, and Rocco has suggested that we visit the lake on our next excursion.

Now he gestures across the expanse of meadow that lies before us, to the narrow path that ascends on the other side.

"This is Sasso Piano," he says. "There is a reward ahead, something metafisica. But we must work to get it."

After an uphill climb that leaves us both out of breath, we reach a plateau strewn with rocks. To the left, the peak of Mount Subasio looms above us, and to the right, the ground disappears into the valley below. An enormous wooden cross stands sentry over the terrain, as if to claim the whole area for Christ.

Rocco points below us and to the right. "There is Assisi. Can you see the tower of Santa Chiara in the clouds? And beyond is the Basilica."

He leaves me to admire the scenery while he goes to the base of the cross, opens a box, and removes a book from a plastic bag. He brings it to me, telling me that he placed the book there years earlier.

I perch on a rock to skim the book's entries. Pilgrims from around the world have paused to write while walking the Via di San Francesco, a nearly three-hundred-and-fifty-mile track from Florence to Rome. Virtually all of their notes refer to peace: peace sought by the travelers, peace found in the footsteps of the saint, peace wished for others and for the world. I close my eyes and lift my face to the sunshine, wondering if that peace is available to everyone, even me.

As we begin our trek back across Sasso Piano, Rocco tells me about a friend of his, an Englishman who has lived in Assisi for years and is now approaching his ninetieth birthday.

"I do not see him for many days, so I worry," Rocco says. "I go to his house and I find him at his desk with a book, the kind with no words, only maps."

"An atlas."

"My friend have this atlas, and on the computer is his friend in England," Rocco says. "This atlas is very old, like my friend, with colors to show a big country who owns little countries."

"Colonies, you mean."

"Si, esattamente. England and her colonies, they are pink. France and her colonies are blue, Holland are orange. But my friend and the old man in England, they cry! I say, 'Why do you cry?' And my friend say, 'We cry because we remember when the whole map was pink!'" Rocco throws his head back and laughs out loud. "This is a crazy, no? These old men cry for England."

"It's a strange thing to be sentimental about," I agree. "Everything changes."

"Chissà il futuro dove ci porterà. We say this every day in Italy."

I nod. "Who knows where the future will take us? The key is to adapt. Like Francis figuring out that the Church needed spiritual repairs, or the Goths telling people to have gardens."

"Yes, but most important is not to be a robber."

"What do you mean, Rocco? Don't steal from someone else?"

"No. Steal from someone else is normal. The Perugians, per esempio, they steal land from Assisi, they try to steal the body of Saint Francis when he die. Is normal," he says. "But some people steal from their own life. They have chance to be happy and say no. They have a chance to love and say no. They have a chance for adventure and say no. They hide from life to stay safe. They are robbers who are...i peggiori?"

"The worst."

"They are worst robbers because they rob from their own life."

I think about this as we enter a wooded area where the temperature drops considerably.

"I definitely don't want to be that kind of person," I say, pulling my fleece over my head. "I'd rather be brave than a robber. I'd rather be like Hannibal, riding his elephant over the Alps."

"Hannibal maybe is brave, maybe is crazy. But I know you want to be Hannibal because you love elephants, not because you wish to destroy Rome," Rocco says, and laughs.

That evening, I meet Father Michael in the Piazza del Comune for a glass of the local Sagrantino wine.

"Can I ask you something about Nairobi? Did you know immediately that the conversation with the nun had changed your life?"

Father Michael thinks for a moment before answering.

"I suspected it immediately, yes," he says, nodding. "And as I began to follow her advice and pursue what was in my heart, things began to fall into place."

I tell him about Rocco's idea that destruction and discovery go hand in hand. "We were talking about the earthquake in 1997," I say, "and Rocco said that loss and gain are inextricably coupled. He said that when you are in a period of destruction, there are always positive discoveries to be made, and the job is to find them. And I'm guessing that in a lot of ways, it felt like destruction for you to leave the life you'd built in England."

Father Michael nods again. "Oh yes, it did. There were several very difficult conversations that were necessary."

"But when you finally made it here to Italy, did you ever doubt what you'd done?"

"Not what I'd done," he says, "but perhaps what I'd left undone."

I think back to my conversation with Rocco on the mountain and ask Father Michael if he feels nostalgic for England.

"Not for England, no," he says. "But occasionally for India, where I lived as a young boy. The smell of the frangipani and jasmine outside my bedroom window, the geckos on the wall and monkeys in the garden, our journeys on the rack-railway up to the Nilgiris to escape the heat... My childhood was spent in complete freedom in a rather Edenic setting." He pauses for a sip of wine. "I was insulated from the atrocities of colonialism, being a young boy, so the nostalgia I feel is for that freedom, and that place, and the innocence of childhood."

Father Michael's family left India one day after the country attained independence from the United Kingdom. Most British expatriates returned to England, but his family immigrated to Australia.

"When I finally returned to India some years ago," he says, "I discovered that my childhood home had been converted to a school. I was able to find the church where I was baptized, but everything else was unrecognizable."

"That must have been disconcerting," I say.

He nods. *"It was. But I'd left so long ago, it was to be expected."*

"I've been thinking," I tell him, *"that maybe for some of us, leaving is the first step to creating the life we are actually meant to have."*

"It's certainly possible."

"Maybe Rocco is right," I continue. *"Maybe destruction and discovery do go hand in hand, and if you want to make the discovery, you have to initiate the destruction. You have to jump without a safety net."*

"Isn't that the same thing as having faith?" Father Michael asks. *"We're called to align ourselves with God's will and trust that God will take care of the details, which is an awful lot like jumping... Of course, God is our safety net, but that net is so rarely visible in the way that we crave."*

"But what was it about Italy that made you willing to jump?" I ask. *"I mean, there are a thousand reasons to love Italy, but visiting here and living here are two very different things."*

"This is where the life I was meant to lead could unfold," Father Michael says. *"Why that is, I am not entirely sure. But the pull towards this life was from God, not from Italy, make no mistake about that."*

"There must have been people trying to dissuade you, though? Telling you that leaving England, leaving the programs and the life you'd built, was crazy."

"Of course," Father Michael says. *"But when you are following God's will for your life and doing what God has put in your heart to do, those other voices and concerns become background noise."* He is quiet for a moment, then sighs. *"I will admit, however, that it was heartbreaking to learn that the home I'd founded in England closed not long after I left."*

"The home for the children?"

He nods. *"And the program to feed the elderly. We'd worked so hard, yet both programs closed within a year."*

"That had to be a terrible feeling," I say. "But maybe it would have happened anyway."

"Maybe so," he says. "And of course it's our ego that makes us think we are central to any endeavor, isn't it? Some situations aren't meant to be saved."

"Do you know Rabbi Nachman's story of The Lost Princess?" I ask Father Michael.

"I'm not sure I do."

"It's an allegory. Basically, a princess goes missing, and the king dispatches a servant to find her, but the servant gets distracted and makes several wrong turns. The lost princess represents the shekinah, that little bit of God we all retain at birth, and the servant represents each of us, seeking the divine spark, but taking all kinds of wrong turns along the way to finding it."

"The divine spark being what has been put in our hearts to do," Father Michael says.

"Exactly. And if the whole point of living is to find that nexus where God's will and our talents come together, because that's where the divine spark lives, then writing in Italy is what you had to do."

"That was certainly my takeaway from Nairobi," Father Michael says. "And considering the source, I took that counsel very seriously."

Father Michael took the advice he received seriously because when he excused himself from the bishop on that dark evening in 1985, hoping to ask one of the nuns in the Land Rover what it was like to work with his hero, it wasn't a sister of the Order who rolled down the window and reached out to take Father Michael's hands.

It was Mother Teresa herself.

"I was ecstatic," Father Michael said when he first told me this story. "She took my hands in hers and kissed them and *held them fast. I couldn't believe I was having a conversation with Mother Teresa! I was thrilled beyond words. And after the initial shock wore off, I couldn't wait to tell my Bishop that these very hands had been kissed by the holy Mother." He held his up hands to show me, the knuckles knotted and the veins a blue web under paper-thin skin. "I phoned as soon as I returned to England."*

"Was the Bishop jealous that you got to meet Mother Teresa?" I asked.

"He hung up on me."

"You're not serious?"

"It's true," Father Michael said. "He hung up on me. And when I phoned again a few days later, he said, 'You know, it's all good and well for holy women to say things like that.... but, my lad, there is work to be done here!'"

I laughed out loud at that. "Holy women are the worst. Full of bad advice. Everyone knows that."

Father Michael smiled. "You know, Mother Teresa had changed course more than once," he reminded me. "If anyone could advocate following your heart, it was she."

Mother Teresa was born Agnes Gonxha Bojaxhiu in Skopje, Macedonia, to devout Catholic parents. At age eighteen, she joined the Sisters of Loreto in Dublin, Ireland, before being sent to India for her novitiate period, where she taught the daughters of wealthy families in a Calcutta convent school. But after fifteen years of this work, Sister Mary Teresa, as she was then known, recognized what had been put in her heart to do, as she would characterize it so many years later in Nairobi. It took nearly two years to organize, but in August of 1948, Mother Teresa walked away from her position as the convent school's principal to work with the city's neediest citizens in the slums of Calcutta.

"*I'm sure her fellow nuns thought she was crazy,*" *Father Michael says.* "*But she followed her heart and look how that turned out.*"

We are standing together in the Piazza del Comune, washed in the soft pink light of the setting sun, and I want to say something meaningful to Father Michael, to convey how much our time together has meant to me, but all that comes out is, "*Thank you. Thank you for sharing your story with me.*"

He takes my hands in his and says softly, "*You know, I'm still here.*"

I understand what he is saying.

Father Michael is still in Italy because no matter when it arrives, no matter where you receive it, when the calling of your life is revealed to you, when you find that nexus where God's will and your talents meet, you must respond.

In his own gentle way, he is asking me to consider the same question Mother Teresa asked him in Nairobi: What do you want to do?

When I got to that part of the story, I sat back in my chair and crossed my arms over my chest. I had no idea how to answer that question and bring the story to an end.

Ventuno

I emailed the story about Assisi to Porter.

I haven't finished it, I wrote, but I'm hoping to soon. And I wanted to let you know where I am and what I'm doing. I hope you're well. Give Oliver a treat for me, please. x Beth

I sent the email and closed my laptop, laced up my tennis shoes, pulled on a jacket and scarf and gloves, shoved a granola bar and a bottle of water into the pocket of my jacket, and headed out the door. I walked up the steep stone streets, past the church of *San Rufino* to *Piazza Matteotti*, past the luxurious *Nun Spa* where you could get a massage and swim in a former Roman bath, and up and under the stone archway that marked the upper edge of Assisi's historical center. There was no one else on the street, save for the occasional *Vespa* buzzing past, and I pushed

227

myself to keep going, even as the road became ridiculously steep and my leg muscles burned with every step. By the time I arrived at the *Eremo delle Carceri*, the hermitage of Saint Francis two and a half miles above Assisi, I was huffing like a freight train and my legs were on fire.

I sat on the stone wall in front of the hermitage to drink my water and let my leg muscles rest. The sanctuary was closed for the season, but the view over the valley, normally obscured by leafy trees, was beautiful.

Mother Teresa's question to Father Michael had echoed in my head with every step up the mountain. *What do you want to do?*

When Crawford and I married, I knew the answer to that question. All that had been important to me was being a good wife and mother, making our home as comfortable as possible, marking every holiday and milestone with a celebration, and entertaining our friends. Those were my priorities, all the things I'd wanted as a child. But that life was gone now.

You're free to create a new life, and find your own way forward, David had emailed a few weeks earlier. *It won't be easy, but it will be worthwhile.*

I'm only free because I've lost everything that mattered, David. It's like Janis Joplin said—freedom's just nothing left to lose.

Sometimes it's about changing the tuning, kiddo. Singing the same song in a different key. Try thinking of this as the beginning of a new life, not the end of an old one.

David had a point, of course. I was completely, utterly free, with no one to answer to but myself and, occasionally, my lawyer's billing office and my assignment editor. But the cost of that freedom was way too high, and when I thought about the future, the uncertainty of it all still filled me with terror.

I stretched out my legs, trying to ease the pain in my thighs, and thought about what the therapist in Washington had told me on my one and only visit all those years ago.

"Worrying about the future can be paralyzing," she said. "We're so afraid of what might be right that we settle for what we know is wrong, just because it's familiar."

"So how are you supposed to move past that?" I'd asked.

"You have to learn how to evaluate your choices differently. Think about this: If you're considering your options, wouldn't it be more helpful to concentrate on the possible upsides rather than the potential difficulties? Yet we give all of our attention to the possibility of failure instead of the likelihood of success. We should be thinking, *What if this does work out? How wonderful would that be?* Fear really is our biggest enemy."

"That all sounds good, but how do you actually *do* it?"

"Start with a small decision and focus on *what could go right* instead of *what could go wrong*. If there's a reasonable chance that things could go right, isn't it worth the risk?"

It was getting dark and the chill from the stone wall beneath me was making my whole body cold. I stood up, brushed the granola crumbs off my jacket, and pushed my water bottle and wrapper into the trash can before starting downhill. I was only about five minutes into the walk back when I heard rustling in the bushes and stopped dead in my tracks, my heart pounding in my chest.

There was more rustling, and then a goat emerged from the bushes with a leafy branch in its mouth. It stopped and stared at me, its mouth still grinding leaves in sideways circles, before bleating and trotting to the other side of the road, where it disappeared into the underbrush. I was so relieved that I laughed out loud.

When I got back to the apartment, I sat down to write David.

I've been thinking about my role in everything that's happened. All the things I ignored about my life with

Crawford because I wanted so badly to have a peaceful home life. I think I convinced myself along the way that I could only have one—either a comfortable home or a good relationship, but not both. I didn't realize how connected they were. And I thought if I stayed busy, the glaring disconnect between me and Crawford would go away, or at least not hurt so bad, but that was a lie, too.

Maybe the goat I saw tonight was a scapegoat, and I should have loaded all those thoughts on its back and run it off the side of the mountain. But I missed my chance and now I'm left here in Saint Francis's hometown feeling like a modern-day Job. What else can go wrong? Will it help if I repent? What do you think, David—should I go sit in the square and scrape myself with potsherds? Or go get something to eat? I can't decide. xo Beth

I hit Send and checked my watch.

It was after eight, which meant the grocery store was closed. I had a little bit of bread and cheese left and could make a sandwich, but I decided to treat myself to dinner at my favorite restaurant, the *Taverna dei Consoli* right above the main piazza. I traded my fleece for a new blue cashmere sweater and swiped on mascara and blush, then pulled on my jacket, grabbed my purse, and headed out. The walk from the apartment to the restaurant was no more than five minutes, and as soon as I saw that the lights of the restaurant were on, my stomach started growling.

The waiter greeted me the way he always did—*Eccola scrittrice americana!*—and pointed to the small table in the corner I liked. He brought me a glass of *Sagrantino*, and after I'd ordered, I pulled out my phone out to read the news and saw that I already had a reply from David.

Dear Job,

While I'm glad you didn't run the goat off the cliff, I understand the urge. It's certainly convenient to have a scapegoat. But making someone your scapegoat requires a lot of factual cherry-picking and selective exegesis. To blame the Jews for killing Jesus, for instance, you've got to ignore the fact that Jesus himself was a Jew, crucifixion wasn't terribly unusual, and Pontius Pilate was a Roman—basically you've got to pull the entire saga out of context. And maybe there's been a lot of that proof-texting and exegeting going on between you and Crawford, but that's over now.

So while I understand feeling like Job, I can't resist reminding you of a couple of things about that story's context that I think will convince you to leave the potsherds in the cupboard.

First of all, the whole framework of the Job story—that Yahweh makes a bet with the 'satan,' the adversary, the false counselor, to test Job—is so ludicrous, so beyond the way that Yahweh was known to act, that the earliest audience of this story would have recognized it immediately as a satire. A farce. And your life has not been a farce, my dear.

Secondly, in 42:6 when Job supposedly says, "I despise myself and repent in dust and ashes," the Hebrew doesn't support that translation. There's a perfectly good word for 'repent' that's used multiple times in the Old Testament, but it's not used here. The word that's used here means 'to take comfort,' and the reference to dust and ashes recalls Abraham arguing with the Lord to save Sodom and Gomorrah because of the righteous people there. Since the entire Bible is a spider web of self-referential signals to the audience to remember a passage or tale they'd heard previously, it only makes sense that "dust and ashes" is a deliberate reminder of Abraham speaking to God as if they are equals and saying, "I have been so bold to speak to the Lord though I am merely dust and ashes." I don't think Job repents at all. I think he is comforted.

But why does it matter if Job is comforted after speaking to God as an equal, despite being made of dust and ashes? It matters because it means that Job understands something critical: God is God, and Job is only human, and there's a vast, unbreachable gulf between what the omniscient, omnipotent God can know and do and what Job—a mere man—can know and do. How is this comforting? It's comforting because while Job recognizes the difference between himself and God and acknowledges that he doesn't understand why bad things happen, he knows that God is with him, listening and responding in his darkest moments. Job takes comfort in God's steadfast presence. He understands that he doesn't need to ask why anymore, because he knows the answer is not available to him in his life on earth.

That same comfort is available to you, Beth.

Stop looking for a scapegoat, and stop driving yourself crazy asking why. You're in a marvelous place to experience the comforting presence of God, who is with you always. So put the potsherds away, kiddo. I hope you got something to eat?

xo

David

The waiter arrived with the breadbasket while I was thinking about David's email and the long letter Jude sent me after we split up. This was a couple of years before Jude took the job at the *Post* and started investigating my boss, and in his letter, he blamed me for virtually everything that had gone wrong between us. I'd replied with one line: "I didn't realize you'd started writing fiction." I still think that was a really good comeback, maybe my best ever.

I chewed on a piece of bread and let my mind scroll back to a conversation David and I had one afternoon when I was in college. I was stretched out on his office couch, writing a paper on the early Christian understanding of theodicy and availing myself of his library and a tray of cookies from the church kitchen.

"It's not like this idea about divine justice has changed much," I'd said, causing David to look up from the stack of papers he was reading. His glasses were perched on the edge of his nose and his feet were propped on his desk, revealing multicolored palm trees on his black socks. "We're not so overt about it now, but people still think that illnesses and accidents are punishments from God. They may pretend they don't, but when something good happens, they say *Oh, God must have big plans for you!* right?"

"Go on," David said.

"But if good things happening means God is watching out for you, then bad things happening has to mean that God decided you weren't worth the effort."

"You're arguing against the Deuteronomists," David said, removing his glasses and rubbing his eyes. "Pop quiz for a cookie: Which texts are Deuteronomic?"

"That's too easy. The books of law. Deuteronomy, Joshua, Judges, Samuel, and Kings."

"Good job! I get a cookie." He put his glasses back on and held up his hands for me to throw him a cookie.

"Your reward system is weird," I said, tossing him one from the tray. "The chocolate chip ones are insanely good. They have pecans."

"And the Deuteronomic equation?" David said, biting into the cookie and sending a smattering of crumbs down the front of his black clerical shirt.

"Follow God's law and good things will happen, disobey God and bad things will happen."

"Excellent. Another cookie for me. And yes, that understanding is part of our collective western consciousness, whether we realize it or not."

"Hence the nonsense about guardian angels protecting people."

"I'm not saying there are no angels," David said, catching the second cookie I threw. "Nor am I saying that the Deuteronomist equation is untrue, because I do believe that living in accordance with God's will is its own reward. But I would argue that there is another force at play, too."

"The chaos."

David nodded. "Bingo. The chaos. No more cookies, though."

I turned David's copy of *The Problem of Pain* over to look at the photo of C.S. Lewis on the back.

"Are you saying we should just roll over and not hold anyone responsible for anything?" I said. "I shouldn't blame that drunk girl for crossing the center line and killing my mom?"

"I didn't say that," David said, shaking his head. "People are responsible for the choices they make. But what I am saying is that there was no divine plan to place your mom and Celia on the road at that time. The driver made her choice, and it was horrible and illegal and fatal, but as far as your mom being there? That was the chaos. God had no part in that."

The waiter returned then with a bowl of pasta with truffles. He set it front of me and refilled my wine glass, then went to greet the crowd of Italians who had just come in, engaged in the national pastime of talking over one another. One of them was as tall as Marco, and I thought about a book David had recommended to me when I told him about Marco's home life.

"It's called *No Visible Bruises,* and it really opened my eyes to what happens in domestic abuse situations."

"Does it explain why women stay?" I'd asked. "That's what I never understand. Or at least file a police report when the cops show up."

"The book made me understand that these women are playing a long game, particularly when kids are involved. If you file a police report, what's going to happen when he comes home after one night in jail?"

"He's going to beat the hell out of you."

"Exactly. It's a constant chess game for the victims, trying to stay two steps ahead of the abuser while they figure out an exit strategy. And those exit strategies are incredibly hard to come by. Are you going to rip your kids out of school and leave your job and go into hiding? Because that's what it takes for these women to get away. They have to walk away from friends and family if they don't want to be found, but friends and family are the only people who might be able to help if the abuse escalates. So it's a choice between trying to navigate the situation and maintain a safety net, or making a run for it and letting the net fall away."

"I hadn't really thought about it that way, but you're right. Where are they going to go that he won't follow?"

"Another thing this book makes clear is the role shame plays in keeping these women in abusive relationships. Society tells us that women are solely responsible for the emotional well-being of marriages and families, so when those fall apart, it's her fault."

"I feel that way about my own situation," I said.

"I never fully comprehended the price women pay until I read this," David said. "Men move on without a social stigma, but we have this idea that a woman must be too flawed to hold the relationship together if she is divorced. That she failed her husband and children."

"That's absolutely true. He gets to be an eligible bachelor and she gets to be damaged goods," I said. "And other women always think they would have kept him happy."

"Plus, these women have been convinced by the abusers that violence is proof of love. He loves her so much that it makes him lose his temper, right? So when he lashes out at her, it's somehow both her fault *and* evidence of his devotion."

I thought about the idea that women bear the responsibility for maintaining the emotional well-being of the family while I ate. Crawford had felt free to stay at the office until all hours and put himself and his needs first, and he'd had no problem being deaf to my pleas for his time and attention because there was a roof over our heads and food on the table. For Crawford, his responsibility to our family began and ended with financial security. And while I didn't envy him the tremendous pressure our lifestyle put on him and I would never downplay how important financial security is, that approach left a lot to be desired. Companionship. Emotional security. Intimacy. I'd always felt that I had no right to complain because we were well-off, and I'd certainly believed that the emotional welfare of my family was my responsibility.

When the waiter returned to take my empty pasta bowl and deliver the thin slices of steak with rosemary I always ordered, he asked if I wanted another glass of wine.

I spent a moment doing calculations, wondering what I'd earned by walking up to the hermitage, before realizing I didn't have to think like that.

"Absolutely," I said.

Ventidue

In the four years I'd lived in Raleigh, I'd never been brave enough to call Porter, or email him, or go to his restaurant and find him, even though I'd been less than an hour down the road. But I'd thought about him more than I cared to admit. As soon as I'd hit the North Carolina state line in that rattling old U-Haul with its loose brakes and acrid-smelling heat, a floodgate had lifted, unleashing a river of Porter memories. That weird phenomenon called Baader-Meinhof syndrome, when the universe seems to keep sending you reminders of someone? Even the cleaning aisle in the grocery store brought me up short when I bent down to get a tube of Comet off the shelf and saw the Ajax next to it.

Of course, scientists say Baader-Meinhof isn't the universe sending us reminders at all. It's just our brains seeking out patterns, because patterns are how we make sense of our experiences. The minute we encounter something new, an unfamiliar object or event or person, our brains begin to scroll through our catalogue of past experiences, looking for something that matches. We layer this new information on top of what is already embedded, and in the process of doing that, our brains de-emphasize the things that don't fit with the patterns that are already established, and overemphasize the things that do.

Scientists prefer to call this 'frequency illusion', but Baader-Meinhof sounds much cooler and has a great origin story. Back when Germany was split into East and West, Baader and Meinhof were founders of a West German domestic terrorism group. One of the scientists researching frequency illusion heard someone mention the Baader-Meinhof terrorism cell twice in a short period of time, and the repetition jumped out at him as an example of exactly the phenomenon he was researching, so he gave the name to the syndrome.

Whatever you want to call it, I had it bad in Raleigh. Reminders of Porter were everywhere. And every week I would pep-talk myself into calling him, and every week I would chicken out, unable to conjure up the nonchalance that would be required to have a conversation with him. I knew that as soon as I heard his voice, I would pathetically bleat, "Why did you break up with me?" before tearfully confessing that I still thought about him far more than I should.

But as the weeks wore on, the Porter-related memories became a trickle rather than a deluge.

I thought I saw him a few times. Once in traffic on the interstate, once at a Greek restaurant in Chapel Hill, once at the Raleigh-Durham airport, and once at a foreign trade dinner where I was seated between a humorless man from Dortmund and a tiny man from Taipei who had one drink and turned beet red.

"You boss very fat," he said to me when the governor was walking up to the podium.

"Governor Brewer? He's not fat at all. He's very fit," I said. "Very athletic."

"Very fat. Rich man," he said, and then collapsed into giggles.

I stuck it out until the Governor's remarks were finished, then said goodbye to the Taiwanese man, who looked like he was about to drop face-first onto the table, *Auf Wiedersehen* to the stone-faced German, and intercepted the Governor as he glad-handed his way back to his seat.

"Good job, Boss," I said when I finally got next to him.

He looped his arm around my shoulder. "Thanks. You enjoying yourself?"

"It's the most fun I've ever had in my life, sir," I said.

Governor Brewer threw his head back and laughed. "You were made for politics. Scoot out the back door. You've done your time."

On my way to the service door, I darted past the kitchen. That's where I caught sight of Porter, bent over a huge stainless-steel pot. I stopped in my tracks, skidding slightly in my heels on the polished floor, to watch him grab a spoon and taste the contents of the pot. When he lifted his head to toss the spoon into the sink, I saw that it wasn't Porter at all.

It was never Porter.

Now here I was in Assisi, mere hours down the road from him, and once again, I couldn't bring myself to call.

As I left the restaurant and walked down the stairs to the *Piazza del Comune*, I decided to take a walk to the Basilica. I crossed the *piazza* and stopped to look in the windows of the linen store I loved, then the store that sold religious vestments and icons and traveling eucharist kits, and the store with windows full of hand-painted Christmas ornaments from Deruta. Then I continued up the hill, past the Swedish Sisters convent and around the corner to the left, where the bronze statue of Saint Francis the Cavalier in front of the Basilica came into view.

I stood in the cold air looking at the statue for a long time before continuing around the corner. The shops selling souvenirs and snacks were all closed, and I passed quickly and started uphill back towards the *piazza* where I'd begun. But as I passed the *Galleria d'Arte San Francesco*, I couldn't resist peeking in the windows.

The artist who sculpted the statue of Francis on his horse, Norberto Proietti, also painted scenes of monks, and there were several of his works in the windows of the gallery. The monks in his paintings are all doing normal tasks, like picking olives or singing or bundling wheat, but several of them are always floating high in the sky above the scene, their robes trailing behind them, and despite my distaste for anything that could be described as even remotely whimsical, I loved these prints in a way I couldn't explain. Someday, I vowed, I'd own a bunch of them.

I shoved my hands in my pockets and tore myself away, continuing up the hill and across the *Piazza del Comunue* to the *Vialle Galeazzo Alessi*, where I hurried passed the shuttered fruit stand and the tailor's shop and the jewelry store before veering downhill onto *Via Sermei*.

As I came around the corner at the top of the street, I saw a man leaning against the front door of my building, arms crossed against his chest. I clutched the keys in my hand and came to a stop.

He looked up. "Beth? Thank God. I'm freezing."

I hurried to give Porter a hug. "How did you know where I was staying?" I asked, unlocking the door to the building. "Come inside and get warm."

"I implanted a GPS on you last year."

"You called David?"

Porter laughed. "I emailed him, yeh."

"Where's Oliver?"

"With Patrizio and Alberto. They were cooking steaks when I left, so I am guessing he's having a good time."

"Are you staying over?" I asked, unlocking the door to the apartment and gesturing for Porter to go in before me. "Do you have a bag?"

Porter shook his head as he stepped inside. "Nah. I'll drive home. I just wanted to say hello. I was really surprised to find out you were here."

"I know. I'm sorry. I just needed time to sort some stuff out. I was staying with David when this project kind of fell in my lap and I wanted to call you earlier, but... well, honestly, I just felt like I needed to do this by myself."

"Sure," he said, dropping his coat over the back of a chair. "I get it."

"Can I get you anything? I've got a bottle of wine I can open."

Porter shook his head. "No thanks. Gotta drive home."

"Have you eaten?"

"A delicious gas station *panino*. Actually, a glass of water would be great."

"Sit down. I'll get it." I found a clean glass in the cabinet and filled it from the tap. "How are you?" I asked, handing it to him. "I saw an article about hiking in the Dolomites the other day and thought of you. How was it last Christmas?"

"I ended up going to the States, instead."

"You did?"

He nodded. "For a final hurrah at Claire's family home with Ford and Courtney."

"The big house in the painting?"

"Yep. I don't know if I ever told you, but there were all kind of entailments on it. All this stuff Claire's parents set up so that no one who married into the family could get their hands on the place. Claire's sister lived there for years, but she died before Claire did, so Ford and I inherited the house and all the land. It took forever to get all the legal stuff sorted so we could sell it, but we got a buyer right away, a guy from out west who's going to turn it into a hunt club. He bought most of the furniture, too."

"That must have felt good, to get that done."

He nodded. "We sent some paintings to a museum in Richmond, packed some things for storage, and had Goodwill haul a couple loads away. Then we had Christmas dinner with Delia and her family."

"Wow! How is Delia?"

"Dead, now."

"What? When did that happen?"

"Middle of January. I'd just gotten back here. We had a good Christmas, though. I think there were about thirty people there."

"She must have been so happy to see you guys."

Porter nodded. "She was. She was almost blind and pretty hard of hearing, but she was like a queen, sitting in her chair with everyone bringing her food."

"I'm really glad you got to see her."

"Me, too."

"Was it weird, being back in Virginia?"

"The whole trip was weird. But it was great to see Ford and Courtney, and great to see Delia. Then I took care of a few things and came home."

Porter kicked off his shoes and put his feet against the edge of the coffee table. His sock was so worn that I could see his heel through the fabric.

"How is Ford?"

"He's good. They're good."

Porter's expression didn't match his words at all.

"What's going on?"

"He's been talking to our mother."

"Really? Wow. How did that come about?"

Porter let his feet drop to the floor and clapped his hands on the top of his knees. "Maybe a glass of wine would be good. Do you mind?"

I shook my head. "Help yourself. I've only got one bottle, but it's decent."

Porter moved around the small kitchen area, taking two wine glasses from the cabinet and bringing them, and the bottle and an opener, to the coffee table. He set all of it down before dropping onto the couch and leaning forward to uncork the bottle. He filled one glass and handed it to me then poured a glass for himself, leaned back, put his feet up, and threw his free arm over the back of the couch.

"The last time I heard from my mom I was twenty-four," he said. "She came to Chapel Hill looking for money."

"Seriously?"

"Yep. Showed up at the restaurant wearing a tight dress with her hair all poofed out and these ridiculous spiky heels on. I got a call in the kitchen that someone was asking for me and when I saw her, I honest to God thought she was a hooker."

"Wow."

"She missed my whole childhood and then had the nerve to just reappear."

"What happened?"

"I agreed to have dinner with her. At first she played it like she wanted to have a relationship with me, but that didn't last long. I don't even think the entrees had come before she asked for money. Apparently, she'd moved on to husband number three and it wasn't going well."

"Did you give her money?"

He shook his head.

"So she went away?"

"She stayed in town two or three more days. Kept showing up at the restaurant until they threatened to call the cops. I stayed at Pablo's house the whole time so she couldn't find me." Porter glanced at me. "It fucked me up, seeing her."

"I can imagine."

"She told me I was a terrible son for refusing to help her."

"Wow. That's.... I don't even know where to begin with that."

"Right? The night after she left, Pablo threw a party to celebrate and I got hammered."

"Understandable," I said.

"And then I attempted to drive to the store for more beer, hit a parked car, and got a DUI."

"What?"

He exhaled loudly. "Yeh. I was incredibly lucky. Just hit a car, nothing else. But I got arrested." He glanced at me. "Ford left me in jail overnight. He flew in the next day to bail me out and ripped me a new one."

"Wow."

Porter looked at me. "It could have been so much worse, like what happened..." His voice trailed off.

"To my mom."

"To your mom," he said, nodding. "I paid a shit ton of money to lawyers to get it taken care of when I bought the Lake House, because you can't get a liquor license with a DUI on your record. I thought it was all behind me, but now immigration is threatening to revoke my elective residency."

"How do they even know about it?"

"You have to declare that kind of stuff. For some reason, now it's a problem." He took a sip of wine. "I have a lawyer in Milan, and it will be fine. I'll just pay a little something and it will go away."

"Hang on, though. Back up a second. You haven't heard from your mother since then?"

"No."

"But now Ford is talking to her."

Porter nodded.

"Why?"

He shrugged. "Closure? I don't know." He pushed himself off the couch. "I've got to use the bathroom and then I'll fill you in."

While Porter was in the bathroom, I went into the bedroom and changed into pajamas. He was already back on the couch when I came out.

"Sexy," he said, smiling at my flannel pajamas and wool socks.

"Absolutely."

"Want more wine?"

I shook my head and sat down on the couch. "When was all this, Porter? Her coming to visit and the DUI? You said you were twenty-four, but I knew you when you were twenty-four."

"Remember when you came down from D.C. and we had that big fight?"

"That ended everything? Don't remind me."

"I'd just gotten out of jail. Hadn't slept in two days. The Jeep was impounded and my boss was furious because I'd missed a night when we were booked solid. Ford spent the whole ride to the restaurant screaming at me about what a fuck-up I was. I'd thrown up all over myself in jail and he wouldn't stop to let me shower so I had to borrow Pablo's dirty clothes from his work locker. And then you showed up."

"And you chose not to tell me any of this and just let me think you'd met someone else. Why?"

"It was better than the truth. And I thought I could explain later, when things calmed down, and patch things up. But there was so much shit to deal with that I kept putting it off... and then it was too late."

I thought about this for a few minutes.

"There's something missing from this story, Porter. Something was wrong before I came down from D.C. The whole reason I drove down there was because you'd stopped returning my calls."

"I was in the middle of all the stuff with my dad."

"What stuff with your dad?"

"You really don't know?" Porter said, running his hand through his hair. "It was all over the news. I think the whole world saw."

"I have no idea what you're talking about."

"He and some con-man he met in a bar started selling European bonds that were total bullshit. The company was a Ponzi scheme, a Madoff type thing. And when someone started asking questions, he panicked. Took money out of my savings account and Ford's to try to stay out of trouble. Thank God he couldn't touch our trusts, or else we'd be penniless." Porter made a face. "The bastard even hit up Delia!"

"He was selling bonds?"

Porter nodded. "Bonds that didn't exist. It was all a lie. They were cheating investors and using the money to live the high life. Tens of millions of dollars."

"Wow. Did people get their money back?"

"Some."

"What about Delia? You said he hit her up, too?"

"She gave him ten thousand dollars. Her whole life's savings."

"But why would Delia give him money? She knew he was irresponsible."

"She knew better than anyone. But she also basically raised him and he was always a little boy in her eyes. Plus, she tried to see the good in everybody."

"That just makes it so much worse that he stole from her."

"We asked The Colonel for the money to pay her back, but he wouldn't give it to us." Porter lowered his voice. "'I am not bailing out that worthless, no good, indulged little bastard again. Over my dead body.' Ford and I paid her back, don't worry. We sold some stocks." He let out a short laugh. "The fun really started when the FBI came knocking."

"When was that?"

"About two weeks before my mom showed up. It was so weird. First, my dad hit me up for money at Christmas. He'd been drinking his money away for years, but still, there should have been plenty, right? So I knew something was whack."

"And then the FBI shows up."

"Yeh. Ford and I were summoned to the house in Richmond. I had to take off work, Ford had to fly in from Seattle, and there was this big pow wow with lawyers and FBI guys and a couple of investigators from the SEC. Ford and I didn't know anything, so we signed some statements and then went to the Club and got shitfaced."

"I am so sorry, Porter. It must have been incredibly stressful. But I still don't understand."

He looked at me. "Which part?'

"I'm not trying to make this about me, but you're telling me this was all happening when we were engaged," I said. "But you didn't even tell me that he'd hit you up for money, and we spent Christmas together. And did you really think I would see something about your father on the news and not call you?"

"I know. I wasn't thinking straight. I was just—I don't know. Overwhelmed, I guess. I didn't know how to talk about any of it. And then the FBI said not to discuss it." He made a face. "I just felt like a total asshole."

"Why? You didn't do anything."

"I don't know. It wasn't about you, trust me." He met my eyes quickly and then looked away. "I did really stupid shit after you left for Washington. Drank too much, smoked too much weed. Stayed up 'til all hours."

"Other women?"

He shook his head. "No. Not that."

"I would have understood. I know how restaurant kitchens are."

"No, you wouldn't have. I think you would have tried, but ..." He cleared his throat. "You had a new life, and smart friends, and things were going well for you. When I got the DUI, I felt like I'd sunk so far down I would never climb back up again. And you deserved something better. Someone better."

"Oh, Porter."

"Honestly, it was just easier not to tell you. That's cowardly, I know. But I hated myself for being like my old man."

"So where is he now?"

Porter shrugged. "Vanished. Not even Interpol can find him. I'm guessing he's dead."

"And your mom?"

"Micheline is back in Montreal," he said, rolling his eyes. "Did I ever tell you how she left? We got up for school one morning and her wedding rings were on the table next to a box of Fruit Loops." He reached for the wine bottle and started to refill my glass, but I held my hand over it. "No note, nothing. Just a box of cereal."

"I can't imagine, Porter. Nothing would have made me leave my daughter. Absolutely nothing, unless it was to save her life."

"Exactly."

I sighed. "I wish we'd talked about all this stuff when it was happening. I had no idea what was going on with you."

Porter was quiet for a minute. "My life was a pile of shit and I didn't want to drag you down into it."

"Yeh, but instead you broke my heart."

He grimaced. "I know," he said, and leaned his head back against the couch and closed his eyes. "I'm really sorry."

I picked up my wine glass and studied Porter. I could see him so clearly as a little boy, with the cowlick in the front of his hair and a spray of freckles across his permanently sun-pinked nose. A kid who'd had no way to process being abandoned, and had been trapped in a family where keeping up appearances was more important than dealing with reality. A little boy who'd grown into a man thinking that he had no right to emotional support, perpetually terrified that he was turning into his dad.

I was so grateful to have had a father I respected, even if our time together was short. I had always known he loved me. When the officers from his precinct delivered his personal things after the funeral, almost everything in the box was from me. A pencil drawing I'd done of him fishing at Owasco Inlet. My spelling bee ribbons. The lumpy coffee cup I'd made him for Father's Day. My essay on America's centennial that won my school's prize and was printed in the paper. A bunch of candy canes, the only candy he and I really liked.

And a photo, excised from a newspaper and laminated, that had been pinned to the bulletin board over his desk.

"That's Jeremiah Denton," my mom said, taking the photo from me. "When he got home from Vietnam." She put the photo back in the box. "I don't think I have the energy to do this now. I'll put this in the hall closet and go through it later."

"I'll do it," I said. But when I got to the closet, I plucked the photo out of the box and took it to my room.

At school the following week, I went to the library and looked up Jeremiah Denton in the microfiche. He was a Navy Commander who flew eleven missions before being shot down and captured by the North Vietnamese in 1965. He spent almost eight years as a prisoner of war, and because he was the highest-ranking officer in the prison, the North Vietnamese were determined to break him. They kept Denton in solitary confinement, locked him in shackles, put him in boxes no bigger than coffins, and beat him on a regular basis.

But Denton never caved. And he did everything he could to help the other men in the prison stay alive by developing ways for them to communicate, knocking messages on the walls of their cages, rhythmically sweeping brooms, coughing in code, and hiding notes in the toilet drains. He understood that as long as the prisoners had each other, they could find the strength to stay alive.

Just before the end of his first year in captivity, the North Vietnamese sat Denton down in front of a Japanese television crew and ordered him to denounce American involvement in Vietnam. Denton knew that U.S. intelligence officers would be watching. He knew that the United States didn't have any idea whether the protocols of the Geneva Convention, which spelled out the standards for the humane treatment of prisoners of war, were being upheld. So Jeremiah Denton refused to say the words that had been scripted for him, and instead reiterated his support for the American military effort and blinked repeatedly, as if the camera lights hurt his eyes. He spelled out one word over and over in Morse Code as he blinked. TORTURE.

As I turned the handle to advance the microfiche, I remembered going to the precinct with my mom one evening to drop off my dad's dinner when I was very small. I'd asked him who the man in the photograph was.

"That's the bravest man in the world, Bits," my dad said, unpinning the photo from his bulletin board and handing it to me. "That is a man who told the truth even when it would have been much easier not to. Most of the time, that's what being a hero is all about."

I looked back at Porter, whose eyes were still closed, and briefly wondered what life might have been like for us if he had told me the truth instead of letting his family secrets tear us apart.

"Porter?" I said, putting my hand on his shoulder.

His eyes shot open. "Yeh, hey. Sorry."

"I'm going to make up the couch for you and then I need to go to bed, okay?"

"Are you sure? I can head home."

I shook my head. "There's a travel toothbrush in the little blue bag on the shelf that I haven't even touched. I'll grab some blankets."

I dug the extra blanket, pillow, and duvet out of the cupboard and made up the couch, then waited for Porter to finish in the bathroom so I could brush my teeth.

I heard him fill a glass of water from the sink as I was getting into bed, and then he rapped on the doorframe and stuck his head into my room. "Thanks for letting me stay."

"Of course, Porter. It's the least I could do."

"Well, I appreciate it. Sleep well."

"You, too."

I flipped over and faced the wall. Porter was snoring before I'd even begun unpacking everything he'd told me.

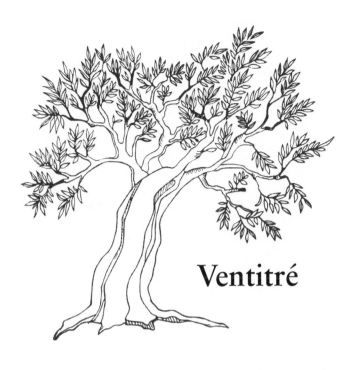

Ventitré

"**I** just can't believe any of this," I said to David the next afternoon when I called him and recounted Porter's visit. "I was lying there listening to Porter snoring in the living room, and all I could think is, what is wrong with me that I managed to find two men who could never tell me the truth? My life was turned upside down by each of them deciding not to come clean with me. If Porter had told me what was going on, I would have helped him. Same with Crawford."

"You've got to give yourself some grace, Beth," David said.

"Seriously, though, I need you to tell me what's wrong with me. Why is my judgment so bad? Or is it something about me? Do I come off as untrustworthy?"

I heard David's chair creak. "I want you to do a little exercise with me," he said. "Imagine you're all actors in a play."

"What do you mean?"

"You're in a play, and with all this going on, the Porter character decides he can't tell you the truth. Why?"

"Because he's ashamed."

"Okay. So where are you in the scene when he's making that decision?"

"Not on stage. In the wings."

"Exactly. And what about Crawford? Why didn't he tell you the truth?"

"Because he didn't want to deal with people's judgment and was afraid of being rejected."

"So where are you in that scene, when he's coming to that conclusion?"

"Lying in a ditch, wishing I was dead."

David was quiet for a minute. "I hate hearing that," he said.

"Sorry. I thought we were truth-telling."

"Is that the truth?"

"Yes."

"Well then we need to come back to that. But what I want you to realize is that in both of these cases, the decisions to keep silent were made without you. In spite of you, as it were. And maybe even to protect you."

"It didn't work."

"It rarely does. But do you understand what I'm saying? Both Porter and Crawford made decisions based on what *they* needed or wanted, what *they* were feeling. Their actions weren't about you, they were about them."

"I get it."

"And Porter did tell you the truth, eventually. It just took some time."

"Thirty years."

"Well, better late than never. And maybe the same will happen with Crawford, eventually. But you can't force him. And you're not responsible for him. He may still have some things he's wrestling with, things that are keeping him from admitting what everyone already knows is true."

"Maybe."

"And I suspect he knows exactly how badly he's hurt you."

"I think he's tried very hard not to know it," I said, switching the phone to my other ear.

"Alright. So what are you doing today? Is Porter still there?"

"He went home earlier. I went for a walk, and Marco's coming in about ten minutes to take me to a seafood restaurant at Lago Trasimeno, and then we're going to look at some Etruscan caves."

"Well that's quite a day. I can't wait to hear all about it."

On the way to Lago Trasimeno, Marco announced that our next trip would be to Montefalco.

"There is a museum with frescoes of Benozzo Gozzoli I like very much, about the life of Saint Francis. Then we go to Bevagna and I show you where Francis teach to the birds, and then we go to a place where they make wine and olive oil."

"Super."

"We will drink *Sagrantino* that you like. The owner is a friend of mine. A little man with a *coda di cavallo*—how do you call this?"

"Ponytail."

"He is short with all muscle, like a primitive man, and the tail of a pony. Downstairs we sit in a wine barrel. Is very romantic."

"We're going to sit in a barrel?"

"Is empty barrel, with a table inside. *Molto romantico*," Marco said, grinning at me. "After this, you will beg me, 'Marco, *per favore, facciamo l'amore.*'"

"Right. Well, don't let me forget to do that. So tell me what the tourism group talked about at the meeting."

"In the castle *Rocca Maggiore* we will do a show about the life of Francis, with food," Marco said. "People learn something about Francis while they eat. Is like theater, but very exciting, with lights and music and horses." He put his hand on my arm. "You will write the play about Francis in English, yes?"

"Sure."

Marco nodded. "Good. We work together for a long time, me and you. We are like Francis and Claire."

"Okay, but I'm not cutting off my hair or taking a vow of poverty for you," I said.

"No, is not necessary. I like this hair." He reached out and patted my bun. "Is nice. Not too much gray and I like how you make the little ball at the back."

As we neared the lake, it started to rain. The parking lot of the restaurant was packed, so we continued down the road to find a place to park. Marco wedged the car into a tiny spot in front of a house and as we got out, an old woman stepped out onto the balcony above us. I thought she was going to tell us that we couldn't park there, but instead, she looked up at the sky and shook her tiny fist.

"*Piove di nuovo?*" she yelled. "*Vaffanculo.*"

Marco and I both started laughing. He grabbed me around the waist and pulled me towards him then flipped his parka up over our heads to shield us from the rain.

"Did she really just tell God to go fuck himself because it's raining again?" I asked as we stepped into the restaurant.

Marco slid off his parka, shook the rain off it, and nodded. "We Italians are like this. Very nice to all people. Everyone is invited to go fuck himself, even God."

I hovered near a four-top that was drinking espressos while Marco stood in line to order. When they finally stood up to leave, I swooped forward and slid onto the bench, still warm from their bodies.

"*Brava*," Marco said when he joined me. "Was very good how you watch this place, like you are big bird."

I laughed. "I have skills."

"Don't be mad but I order everything."

He wasn't kidding. When the waiter arrived, he unloaded plate after plate off his tray until the entire tabletop was covered with food.

"Is there anything left in the lake?"

"Yes, all the Romans that Hannibal made dead. They give a special taste to the fish," Marco said. He thrust a bowl of seafood salad at me. "Is with lemon, you will like."

We ate without talking for a long time.

"So tell me about the caves we're going to see," I said finally, trying to dislodge a fish bone from my molars. "What is special about them?"

Marco shrugged. "Are caves. Look like cave, smell like cave."

"Then why are we going to see them?"

"Because I am a little bit in love with you," he said, grinning at me. "So I pretend things you need to see."

"*Bugiardo.*"

Marco laughed out loud. "Is funny when you call me liar because your accent sound like you are from Rome. I hear this and I wonder who is talking to me."

"Let's skip the caves. Want to go for a walk by the lake?"

"*Fa troppo freddo,*" he said, shuddering.

"You have a big coat, Marco. You're not going to freeze."

"We go to Orvieto. I show you where I was in the Army and we look at the church."

"Okay."

"But first you tell me about this man who come to see you."

"What man?"

"I see you this morning," he said. "You drink your coffee, you talk. This is the man with the house where you pick olives?"

"Wow. I see what you mean about Assisi being small. Yeh," I said, nodding. "He's an old friend."

Marco chewed a lemon cookie silently, a pensive look on his face.

"But he love you," he said finally. "I see this."

I shook my head. "No. We're just old friends. He helped me after—after the accident."

"After your daughter is died."

I nodded. I'd told Marco only the most cursory details of the accident.

"I understand," he said. "Is important, to have a friend like this. But I think you are the *bugiarda*. You lie to me."

"How so?"

"You know that he love you. In the same way you know that I love you."

"You're crazy, Marco. *Sei pazzo.* Are you going to eat all of those cookies, or can I have one?"

A friend of Marco's, someone he knew from Assisi, approached our table. Marco told him that I was a writer for the tourism project, and then they began speaking so fast that I had no chance of keeping up and let my thoughts drift back to my conversation with Porter that morning.

We were standing at the bar, drinking *macchiatos* and pulling apart pastries, when he suddenly said, "Did I ever tell you about going to a psychic?"

I shook my head. "I can't imagine you ever going to a psychic."

"I was a senior at Forten Hall. We were coming back from a team retreat one weekend, looking for Miss Peaches, and got lost."

I licked pastry cream from my fingers. "Miss Peaches?"

Porter nodded. "Pot dealer to pretty much everyone at Forten. She wore house slippers and a bathrobe all day and her trailer smelled like bacon. She had the meanest, ugliest dog I've ever seen tied up in the yard, too. Anyway, we were driving around looking for her place when we saw a sign for a psychic. Madame Helena, I think."

"I'm sure Madame Helena was thrilled to get a carload of gullible rich boys."

"No doubt. Most of the guys asked her stupid stuff about getting laid, but I didn't ask her anything. I just wanted to see what she would say."

"So what did she say?"

"She read my palm," Porter said, laying his hand palm-up on the counter between us, "and said I would have a lot of success, and then a major shift, in my professional life."

"Hmm. Well, that was general enough to be correct."

"And that in my private life, there would only be one."

"One what?"

"One woman."

"Oh." I laughed. "Well, there's your proof that she was a fraud. Obviously she didn't know what a stud you were. Or maybe she meant one hundred?"

Porter laughed and swiped his napkin across his mouth. "Hey," he said, crumpling the napkin into a ball and setting it on the counter. "Thanks for last night. For letting me explain."

"Of course. I'm glad to know, actually. I mean, I know it doesn't matter anymore, but I never could make sense of how things ended between us."

"Stupidest thing I've ever done."

I wasn't sure if he meant the DUI or breaking up with me and didn't want to ask.

After breakfast, we walked up to *Piazza Matteotti* where Porter's car was parked.

"Am I going to see you again?" he asked, digging his car keys out of his pocket.

"Of course," I said. "I just need to finish this project and then figure out my next move. Maybe we could take a day trip? Marco took me to Lucca and I absolutely loved it," I said. "They've turned the top of the Roman walls into a bike path and you can ride all around the city center. We could rent bikes."

"Sounds fun."

"We also went to Todi, which I really liked, and Urbino. Tomorrow we're going to Ferentillo, to a church with mummies in the basement."

"Mummies?"

"Yeh. Something about the soil and the temperature and some kind of bacteria that preserved the people who were buried in the bottom of the church. They're organically mummified."

There was a moment's pause and then we both said, "Band name!"

Porter opened the driver's side door. "Okay. Well, have fun. Be safe. It makes me a little nervous, you driving all over Italy with this random guy."

"Oh, he's a good friend at this point," I said. "You'd like him. He's very funny."

"Just be careful," Porter said, folding himself into the driver's seat. "Do you want a ride back to your apartment?"

I shook my head. "Thanks, but I'm going to take a little walk."

He turned the ignition. "You know," Porter said, holding the car door ajar, "that psychic was right."

"I think they just say whatever and see how you react. It's more about reading your face than your palm, right? And you were a private school kid, so of course she said you'd be successful."

"No," he said. "I mean she was right about the other thing. About my personal life. For me, there has only ever been one woman."

And then he smiled, pulled the door closed, and left.

I was nibbling absent-mindedly on the last cookie, thinking about all of this, when Marco suddenly clapped his hands and said, "*Andiamo*." I hadn't even noticed that his friend was gone. Marco made a stack of our lunch plates and we slid out of the booth.

"I ate way too much," I said as we walked to the car. "I need a nap."

"What this means, nap?"

"*Un pisolino.*"

"Ahh. *Anch'io.*"

I slid into the passenger seat as Marco started the car and put the heater on full blast. I was pulling on my seatbelt when he put his hand on my arm to stop me.

"Give me your hands. I make warm."

I held out my hands and Marco covered them with his giant brown paws.

"I want to say something to you but is necessary I speak Italian, okay?"

"Okay," I said, nodding.

"*Non sono bugiardo. Quello che ti ho detto non era una bugia.*"

"What wasn't a lie?" I asked, but Marco kept talking as though I hadn't spoken.

"*Sei diventata molto importante per me ed è vero che sono inammorato di te. Ma la mia vita è un pasticcio. Troppe responsabilità, troppi problemi. Se le cose fossero state diverse avremmo potuto stare insieme ed essere felici.*"

I stared at him for a minute, wondering if I'd understood correctly.

"Marco," I said finally. "You're very important to me, too. But you don't mean that. You're not in love with me."

He let go of my hands. "Is true, I am a little bit in love with you," he said, throwing the Fiat into reverse. "I have nothing but problems in my life, but to be with you is like festival day all the time. You make me happy. And I know if my life was different, we could stay together. So I love you," he said, and shrugged. "What do you want from me?"

I looked out the window. This day could not possibly get any stranger.

We skipped the caves and went to Orvieto, parking at the bottom of the mountain and taking the funicular up to the historic center. I bought tickets for the cathedral, which was unusually empty, and we spent a long time in the Signorelli chapel, where I had to hold on to Marco's arm so I wouldn't tip over while I admired the paintings on the ceiling.

Afterwards we strolled through the town and went for a coffee, and then it was time for us to head home. We were both exhausted, and Marco seemed agitated as we zoomed down the highway and took the exit to Assisi at top speed.

We didn't speak until we were rounding the corner by Clare's convent at San Damiano.

"Tomorrow we don't have any plans, Marco, so I think I'm going to walk on the path to Spello. But the day after, are you available to go to Gubbio?"

Marco nodded. "*Penso di si.*"

"Should I call you?

"No. Is better that I call you."

I nodded. "Okay. I don't want to make trouble for you."

He glanced at me. "Is my problem, not yours."

When we pulled onto *Via Sermei*, I gathered my jacket and purse and jumped out as soon as Marco stopped in front of the apartment. I went right up the stairs and to the bathroom to wash my face and change into my pajamas, then crawled into bed and propped myself up on the pillows. After searching for ten minutes for something to watch, I finally settled on *Night of the Iguana*. It's a pretty awful film. Richard Burton plays an Episcopal priest who has an affair with a teenager and gets sent to a psychiatric hospital. When he's released, he takes a job leading a tour group in Mexico, but he's a terrible tour guide and the tourists hate him.

By the time the tour bus arrives in the seaside town where Burton's old friend Ava Gardner runs a hotel, Burton is teetering on the edge of a breakdown. He's totally self-destructive, and at one point, Ava Gardner has him trussed to a hammock to keep him safe. Deborah Kerr, who plays a young guest at the hotel, has a crush on him and comes over to talk while he's in the hammock. It's obvious she likes him, and Richard Burton says something like, "I'm broke, spooked, and unemployed; what could you possibly see that's good in me?" Deborah Kerr answers, "But those are just your circumstances — not who you are." When I heard that, I stopped the movie and grabbed my phone.

I had Marco's email address stored in my contacts list. I started typing, trying to explain, in simplified English and my limited Italian, the premise of the movie, and what Deborah Kerr had said.

Marco, I finished, *this is true for you, too. Things are very difficult for you and this is not the best time of your life, but you are a good person—smart, kind, funny, capable—and the bad things happening in your life right now are just your circumstances, not who you are. You deserve to find happiness.*

I hit Send, put my phone back on the nightstand, and restarted the movie.

I was dozing off when my phone buzzed. I rubbed my eyes awake and opened my email. Marco had replied, just one line.

Ma se è vero per me, è vero anche per te, no?

But if this is true for me, is also true for you, no?

Porter emailed a few days later, a chatty note.

B,

How were the mummies?

It's so quiet here. I was in my chair reading last night when Oliver walked into the living room with a rabbit in his mouth. He set it down on his bed and looked at up me like "Now what?" The rabbit sat there for a few minutes, then looked around and hopped away. Oliver just watched it go and went to sleep. I haven't seen it since, so I may have a pet rabbit now.

There is one piece of excitement, though. After seventy-four years, Patrizio and Alberto are moving. Turns out they've got a sister near Castiglione di Lago who's recently widowed, and the three of them have decided to live together in her big house. I went over yesterday to help them make some minor repairs and was pleasantly surprised. The house is in really good shape, save for the doorbell that still doesn't work. They're going to leave some furniture, and what I saw was quality stuff. And there's a huge old stove in the kitchen that I'd kill for.

How are things going with you? I'm attaching a pic of Oliver, who would appreciate some feedback on his new collar.

P

When I finished reading Porter's email, I didn't answer immediately. Instead, I went back to a blog post I'd come across earlier in the day and bookmarked to read again.

It was written by an Australian palliative care nurse named Bronnie Ware. As her patients neared the end of their lives, Ware would ask them what they wished they'd done differently, and she noticed that she heard the same five responses over and over, all of which centered around the fact that people regretted having denied themselves happiness over the course of their lives. They'd made their lives smaller and less joyful because they feared what was unfamiliar, and they'd let themselves be constrained by other people's expectations.

I thought about Marco as I read.

Gubbio had been our last trip together. My research was done, and while there were plenty of other places I wanted to see, Marco, from what I could gather, had been getting it with both barrels at home.

"My wife think I spend too much time with you," he'd said as we rode up the mountain to the monastery perched above Gubbio. We were in a cable car that looked like a metal bird cage. "She ask why you need to see so much to write." He shook his head. "She is stupid. But she is also not stupid, because she see that I am in love with you," he said and shrugged. "What can I do?"

I thought about the advice I'd gotten from the therapist all those years earlier: *Instead of focusing on the downsides, look at the potential upsides and ask yourself, "If this works, how wonderful might it be?"*

Then I clicked back into my Inbox and reread Porter's email. My heart was beating out of my chest as I typed.

Could you do me a favor, Porter? Could you ask P & A if they'd be willing to rent me their house?

Sure. But you know you can stay here with me as long as you want?

I do, and I appreciate it, I wrote. *But I need to be on my own. I can't afford to buy anything until the house in France sells, but I can pay them a fair rent and take over the utilities and keep it nice until they find a buyer. And we could be neighbors! Maybe they'll go for it?*

Am I authorized to tell them you'll throw in some banana bread? Porter replied.

Absolutely. And some for you, too, for brokering the deal.

I'll go over there now and get back to you asap, he wrote.

I didn't see much of Marco in my last three weeks in Assisi. I was busy writing and organizing my move, and he went to Rimini for a tourism conference and then visited an uncle in Bologna. But earlier in the day, I'd passed him on the street.

"I cannot talk to you long," he said, bringing the *Ape* to a stop next to me. "Everyone in Assisi know me. Does not look right."

"Okay. I just wanted to let you know I'm leaving," I said, and filled him in on my plans.

"I think a lot about this Mother Teresa story you tell me," he said when I finished. "She is like Saint Francis and Saint Clare. They have to leave one life to find another. Is good example for you, for your plan."

"I'm no saint, Marco," I said, crossing my arms over my chest against the chill. "And I'm really scared."

"Is life," he said. "Scary is how you know it matters. But you will find your way. And I am always your friend."

I leaned into the *Ape* to give him a quick hug. "I do love you, Marco. I want only the best for you."

He nodded. "We still have a show of Saint Francis to write together. *Allora, non è un saluto. È un arrivaderci,*" he said. "We see each other again."

Later, as I cleaned the apartment, I thought about Mother Teresa and what it must have been like for her to walk away from the security of the convent school and go live in the slums of Calcutta. I thought about Saint Francis, when he was fresh out of prison and praying at the foot of the San Damiano crucifix, desperate for guidance, and Saint Clare, who abandoned her life of privilege to follow Francis into the unknown. I thought about Father Michael wading through a mass of people to knock on the window of the Land Rover, hoping for a second-hand testimonial and coming face to face with his hero, whose question changed his life.

Before Marco had gunned the *Ape* down the narrow street that afternoon, he'd said, "I need that you promise me something, crazy American. Only just one thing."

"Of course. What is it?"

"Do not be a robber," he said. "No matter how scary things will be, promise me this."

"Okay," I'd said, blinking back unexpected tears.

He'd reached into the pocket of his jacket and extracted a tightly folded square of paper and pressed it into my hand. "Is living in my pocket for weeks, this paper. Is for you. A souvenir, to remember Marco."

My cell phone had begun ringing then, so I'd shoved the paper into my own pocket and forgotten about it as I went about my day.

Now I took off the plastic cleaning gloves I was wearing, reached into my jeans, extracted the piece of paper, and unfolded it on the tabletop.

What Marco had given me was the sort of map you might find at a tourist office or in the lobby of a museum, a replica of an antique. The map showed the area around Lago Trasimeno and the route Hannibal and his army had taken to their unlikely victory, the same place where we'd eaten in the seafood restaurant and Marco had told me he was in love with me.

Across the yellow fields of the map, he'd scrawled: *Piove di nuove? Non permetterle di fermarti. Prendi il tuo elefante Annibale. È arrivato il momento di attraversare le Alpi.*

Raining again? Don't let that stop you. Get your elephant, Hannibal. It's time for you to cross the Alps.

Ventiquattro

Porter put in endless hours helping me scrub the floors and walls and paint every square inch of Patrizio and Alberto's house before my furniture arrived from France. We listened to classic rock and chatted while we worked, and it felt like the most normal thing in the world.

We were sitting in the kitchen taking a break one afternoon when Porter suggested that we take a day off to go explore someplace new.

"Stop rolling over, Oliver," I said, picking white trim paint out of his fur. "I'm trying to help you, not pet you."

"How about Pitigliano?" Porter said. "It's not far and we've never been."

"That sounds good. I'm definitely ready to get away from working on the house for a day. Every part of me hurts."

"It's really coming along, though, don't you think?"

"Have I mentioned how excited I am to have a fireplace in the dining room *and* in my bedroom?"

"Only a couple dozen times."

"I mean, it's not bad for my first house. The view's incredible," I said, gesturing to the window. "The neighbor's an ass, but you can't have everything."

Porter laughed. "I'm excited to see what you're going to do with this place. And I cannot wait to start cooking on that stove." He looked down at Oliver. "I think he painted himself just to get this spa treatment. Look how happy he is."

On the way to Pitigliano, I read a Zen koan for us to discuss, which was a weird thing we'd started doing after taking what was supposed to be a quick trip to Montepulciano. We'd done sort of a backwards tour of the town to avoid the crowds, starting at the *Tempio di San Biagio* church and then walking up a steep back street to join the pedestrian traffic on the *Via di Gracciano nel Corso*, and had bought a dozen bottles of wine in a shop before deciding we didn't need to hurry home. We were sitting in the front window of the wine store, eating olives and tucking into a bottle of *Avignonesi Vino Nobile*, when I found a pamphlet about Buddhism someone had left on the windowsill. There was a koan at the end and we'd had a lively discussion about what it was supposed to mean.

"Okay," I said. "Are you ready for today's existential riddle?"

Porter nodded. "Bring it."

Buddha told this parable: A traveler was fleeing a tiger and ran until he came to the edge of a cliff. He caught hold of a thick vine and swung himself over the edge. Above him on the cliff, the tiger snarled. From below there was a snarl, another tiger. The traveler hung from the vine between the two tigers. Two mice, one white and one black, began to chew the vine. The traveler could see that the vine would soon give way. In front of him, he saw a beautiful bunch of grapes. Holding onto the vine with one hand, he reached out and picked a grape. Delicious!

"You start," Porter said, steering the car onto the shoulder so a BMW could pass.

"Hmm." I folded my arms over my chest. "It's noteworthy, maybe, that the main character is called a traveler, someone who is just passing through the scene."

"Why would that matter?"

"I don't know," I said, laughing. "I'm just trying to get this ball rolling. Maybe it's important that the mice are black and white. They could represent good and bad."

"So the traveler is caught between two extremes?"

"Yeh, and with a tiger above and a tiger below, he's trapped between the two aspects of his nature."

"You may be right," Porter said. "But why put the poor guy in danger in the first place?"

"Because he's not supposed to be attached to his mortal life. Isn't that part of Zen Buddhism?"

Porter scratched his beard, his latest project. I never thought I would like a beard on him, but it looks quite handsome. "I think so."

"What about the grapes?" I said.

"Maybe this is too simplistic, but I was thinking that it's a reminder that when you have the chance to reach for something good, you should do it."

"Even when you're dangling on a vine, about to be eaten by tigers?"

"Especially then," Porter said.

I looked out the window at the landscape and thought about that for a few minutes. My mind went back to that bleak time after the accident, when there was nothing in the world that wasn't shrouded in gray.

"That's exactly what I did when I answered the phone," I said finally. "When I heard your voice after thirty years, I reached for the only thing that had the potential to be good. Thank God you called me."

Porter reached over and squeezed my hand. "Thank God you picked up."

I squeezed back. "Porter?"

"Yeh?"

"You just missed the turn to Pitigliano."

He laughed. "Stop distracting me, woman."

Pitigliano is a small town carved out of a tufa cliff in the part of Tuscany called Maremma, the same area where Patrizio and Alberto used to hunt mushrooms.

In 1556, Count Orsini, who ruled the area, gave his personal doctor, who was Jewish, a piece of land for a Jewish cemetery. A couple decades later, the town built a synagogue, and so many Jews left the ghettoes of Florence and Rome to enjoy the relative freedom of life in Pitigliano that people began calling it *La Piccola Gerusalemme*, little Jerusalem.

Porter and I visited the synagogue and kosher bakery and the bathhouse, and then we went down under the town, where there are Etruscan caves and passageways called *Vie Cave* that connect Pitigliano to nearby Sovana.

We were walking in the *Vie Cave* when Porter started talking about the anger that had eaten at him for years. Anger at his mother for deserting the family and his father for being so irresponsible, and at his grandparents for leaving Porter and Ford to live in the mess they'd been born into. With the exception of Ford, Porter said, he'd been abandoned by everyone he'd ever counted on.

"Including me," I said.

"But I caused that."

"Think about how different our lives might have been if we'd just talked thirty years ago," I said.

"I don't let myself think about that," Porter said. "I never have."

By the time he owned his restaurant, Porter was staying at work too long, drinking too much, and indulging his base desires with a succession of vapid young women who liked him for his generosity with his American Express card. Eventually, he was hospitalized with gastric ulcers, and, trapped in a hospital bed, took a long, hard look at his life.

"I had turned into everything I'd tried so hard not to be," he said. "A loser with a beer gut, a Porsche, and an STD. No meaningful relationships, and a line cook selling me more and more weed every week so I could sleep at night." He shook his head and made a face. "When I got out of the hospital, I called up Ford and flew out to Seattle."

Long talks with his brother on the back deck overlooking Puget Sound gave him clarity, Porter said, and as soon as he returned to Chapel Hill, he hired a firm to put together a prospectus for the restaurant.

"It took about eight months to find the right buyer, and another four or five months for due diligence, but at the end it all came together. I paid Ford back his investment in the restaurant, sold my house and furniture, sold the car, and applied to retire here with enough money in the bank to satisfy the Italian government. I looked around for about two months with an agent out of Rome, and the minute I walked in to *La Follia,* I knew it was mine."

He paused for a minute, looking up at the moss-covered walls. "I figured I'd grow old alone here, and I was okay with that. I felt okay about everything, really. All that anger I'd bottled up, all those regrets, I don't know.... It's like I left them back in the States. I left the old me behind."

I nodded.

"I never stopped wondering how you were, though."

I hopped down off the rock I was standing on and grabbed his arm. "You saved my life, Porter. I can't tell you how many times I walked over Westminster Bridge and thought about jumping. You gave me something to wake up for."

"I think calling you was the best decision I ever made," Porter said, and slung his arm around me.

We started walking again.

"Did I ever tell you what happened at Heathrow on my way here that first time?"

Porter shook his head. "You didn't say much of anything back then."

"I went into the bookstore before my flight. Two American women were having a conversation about some friend of theirs who'd gotten in a car wreck, and I guess the person hadn't been hurt, or not too badly, anyway, and one of them said, 'Oh, she must have had a guardian angel with her!'"

Porter rolled his eyes. "Oh God."

"Porter, I ripped into that poor woman. A total stranger! But I thought about my beautiful daughter and I just saw red."

"Maybe you did those women a favor. Took some of the bullshit out of their lives."

"I doubt they saw it that way."

"This is my problem with religion," he said. "I know you love David, and he always seemed like a really good guy, but I can't stand this kind of holier than thou religious bullshit. I mean, what is God doing up there? Sitting on a cloud watching a car wreck and saying, 'Oh, damn. I have plans for Linda to save a kitten next Thursday, so I'll send an angel to protect *her,* and just let the other driver die?'"

I told Porter about an incident a few months after my dad died. My mom and I were standing in the cereal aisle when a woman we knew from church came up and told us that we should feel honored that my dad and Kirk had been taken, because obviously God needed them in heaven.

"My mom's face got deep red, and she started shaking. She said, 'I don't know what kind of God you believe in, but the day I think that the Lord took my husband and brother for his own personal convenience will be a cold day in hell!' And then she grabbed my hand and practically dragged me out of the store. Left our shopping cart right there in the middle of the aisle."

"I would have, too," Porter said. "It's so stupid. I mean, how many times have you seen some poor town in Kansas get blown apart by a tornado and all the people whose homes were spared are like, *God was really looking out for me!* and meanwhile Bob down the street is pinned under a Buick?"

"Well, you know, God always had a problem with Bob."

"Fuck Bob."

I laughed. "Poor Bob. But imagine someone saying that to you, that your husband and brother are gone forever because, ya know, there was a cold case and a brushfire that needed attention in heaven?"

"It's ridiculous. Shit happens, and not everything has some higher purpose. If your house is still standing, that's because the tornado changed course, not because you're so special."

I nodded. "David says that if our faith is based on the expectation of God's favor and protection, then we are on thin ice, because as soon as something bad happens—which it will— our faith will fall apart."

Porter started to respond, but before he could, his cell phone rang.

"I can't believe I have reception in here," he said, tugging the phone out of his jacket pocket. He looked at the screen, smiled, and held the phone to his ear. "What up, loser? Say hello to Beth," he said, and thrust the phone at me.

"Hello?"

"Beth? It's Ford Haven."

I stuck my tongue out at Porter, who was standing with his arms folded over his chest, smiling.

"Wow. Hi, Ford." His voice sounded just like Porter's.

"I want to start by saying that whatever my dumbass little brother did to run you off back in the day, I'm really sorry. He's a moron," Ford said. "I tried to raise him right, but he didn't make it easy."

I looked at Porter and laughed. "No worries. He's more than made up for it."

Porter rolled his eyes.

"Courtney and I are thinking of coming over in the spring," Ford said, then paused for a second. "Porter said you're renting the house next door, so I hope I'm not wrong in thinking you'll still be there?"

"I'll still be here."

"Good. We'll be looking forward to it. Tell my little brother I expect to be wined and dined."

I laughed. "Oh, I'm sure he knows that."

We said goodbye and Porter tucked the phone back inside his jacket. Then he reached for me, pulling me into a hug.

I wrapped my arms around Porter's back. I could feel his heart beating against my cheek as I breathed in the scent of the woods and tobacco and spice.

The smell of home.

Venticinque

Our last outing before the lockdown was to Florence, to buy Porter a new pair of leather work gloves from a shop near the *Ponte Vecchio*. We parked in a lot outside town and took the tram to *Santa Maria Novella*, then wound our way around the clusters of backpackers and tourists into the city center.

"Want to climb the *Duomo* again?" Porter asked, gesturing to the line of people waiting to get into the Cathedral.

We'd climbed the four hundred and sixty-three stairs to the top a month earlier, ducking and weaving through the narrow passageways and pressing ourselves against the stone walls to let people squeeze past. Going down had been even more crowded, and to add insult to injury, I'd forgotten about the new sunglasses perched on top of my head and ducked under a stone archway, scraping both lenses beyond repair. I ended up tossing them in the trash outside the church.

"No thanks," I said. "I'm still recovering from last time."

We paused to admire the statues outside *L'Accademia*, then doubled back on a side street to the leather shop where Porter bought his new gloves. Afterwards we stopped for a coffee, then continued across town to the church of *Santa Croce*, making a quick circuit of the interior before heading out to the refectory and the 13th century crucifix by the Florentine painter Cimabue that I love. It's an incredibly poignant rendering of Jesus, whose body is slumped after agonizing hours of suffering. Porter doesn't like it and calls it "defeated Jesus", but to me it's a reminder that even Jesus must have doubted that things would get better.

"That crucifix has survived three floods," I said when Porter repeated how depressed it made him. "Does that make you appreciate it a little bit more?"

Porter was reading the plaque on the wall. "It says when the Arno River burst its banks, this church was filled with twenty-two feet of water in the 1966 flood."

"Can you imagine that much mud?"

We stopped in the *Capella dei Pazzi* to see the della Robbia ceramics, then left *Santa Croce* and spent the rest of the day eating gelato and strolling around town.

When the stay-at-home orders came from the Italian government a few days later, I was so grateful that we'd had that last day out before everything became complicated. We say every day now how lucky we are to have room to roam. Porter works in the fields and in the barn and tends his sheep, which is pretty much exactly what he did before the lockdown, and other than having to move my Italian lesson online and carefully coordinate trips to the grocery store and pharmacy, my life isn't too much different than before. And there are always projects to do. Last week, we scraped and repainted all the shutters, first on Porter's house and then on mine, and next week we are tackling the exterior doors.

This situation, living next door to Porter, might be temporary. Maybe someday I'll decide to sell Patrizio and Alberto's house and move in with him, which I know is what he wants. But for now, this feels right. We spend at least part of each day together, and then, when I need to be alone with my grief and my memories, I have the space to do that.

Oliver has the run of both places, and Porter and I realized pretty quickly that he was taking full advantage of the situation, eating breakfast at one house then going to stand over his bowl and wag his tail as if he hadn't already been fed at the other. Now we text for confirmation before we feed him.

Movies have become a much bigger part of our lives during lockdown, and the DVD player and copy of *Lonesome Dove* Porter gave me as a housewarming gift turned out to be prescient.

"We can only watch up to the point that Robert Duvall gets his leg amputated, okay?" I said, as Porter slid the DVD into its slot the first time we sat down to watch it. "That's the deal."

"I remember, I remember. You can't stand to see the object of your obsession get hurt, even though you know it's just a movie."

"Okay, well, first of all, *Lonesome Dove* is a masterpiece, not just a movie."

Porter laughed. "Sit down, stalker. The movie's starting."

Despite the fact that I've seen *Lonesome Dove* dozens of times, every interaction between Robert Duvall's character, Gus, and Diane Lane's character, Lori, kills me, which Porter finds ridiculous.

"That's why I love Robert Duvall so much," I said, stopping the movie when Gus reached out and stroked the side of Lori's face. "That little gesture is so tender and so complete."

"Listen, I agree with you that Duvall's a great actor, Beth, but what I don't get is what it is about this particular character that you love so much?"

"Gus McCrae? Oh, that's easy. He's super masculine, but he's also incredibly loyal and has a huge heart. He's been in love with Anjelica Huston's character for years, but she's married and her husband is injured, remember? And when Gus goes to see her, he takes care of her husband," I said. "It's a selfless love. Plus he protects Lori."

"Well, thank God we have our own copy now so we can watch it every night."

Little did we know then that the lockdown would stretch on and on, and we'd end up watching all of our movies multiple times.

But Italians are creative, and their spirit is resilient, and every night the news features some new way that people are coping—singing out of their apartment windows, playing tennis on rooftops, sending cheerful messages from apartment to apartment on a system of pulleys. It's enough to make Jeremiah Denton proud.

Of course, Italians are also natural rule-breakers, and some people are bucking the system, causing Italian mayors to take to video with hilarious effect. Our favorite was the mayor of Campania, a grandfatherly type who, upon hearing reports of a graduation party, promised to send the police with flamethrowers. It really wasn't funny at all, but the outlook was so bleak at the time that gallows humor was all that kept us going.

Yesterday I took advantage of the rain to drag my dad's police academy trunk out of the closet and start going through it. There were concert ticket stubs and Playbills, papers and articles I'd written, our list of band names, letters from Jenny and David, drawings and cards you'd made for me over the years, the photograph of Jeremiah Denton I inherited from my dad, and several cards from your father.

I didn't read them, but I did keep them. I still love him, and despite all that's happened, I try to concentrate on being grateful for the years we had together. When Crawford asked me to marry him that night in Durham, we hadn't seen each other for nearly four years. We'd had dinner and a lot of drinks, and I was surprised by his declaration of love, but at the same time, it seemed right, and logical, and kind of obvious. Now I understand that even if we hadn't had the issue of his sexuality, we were wrong for each other, with totally different ideas of what marriage should look like. Crawford could never get past the icy detachment he'd learned from Blythe, and I needed something different, and deeper.

But I never doubted your father's fierce love for you, Mia, and I hope you didn't, either. He put work before you, just as Number Three had done to him, but he loved you in the best way he knew how, and for that reason alone, I consider the years we spent together a success.

It's been a long road to get to this point, though. After we split up, when I would be destroyed by every interaction with Crawford, David told me something that really helped. He said that to get through this, I would need to insulate myself.

"You can't take on board other people's opinions, Beth," he said. "And that includes Crawford's. You have to know who you are and continue to behave in a way that is consistent with your core values and let everything else fall away."

"It seems like he's trying to rewrite history, though, and make me the enemy."

"That's about him," David said. "Not you. Stay the course."

Mostly I succeeded. But there were times when the weight of what I'd lost with Crawford, the friendship that had spanned so many decades and the family we'd created, brought me to my knees. I once heard *Wichita Lineman* while I was picking up David's dry cleaning in Chapel Hill and had to walk outside and lean against the wall until the dagger-sharp pain in my chest eased up enough that I could stand upright.

But I try, every day, to stay focused on what's good, no matter how small it is. Like yesterday, when I was sorting through the trunk, I came across something I thought I'd lost long ago. A silver Cross pen with my name engraved on it, a gift from the first boy I ever loved. I immediately emailed Jenny.

I can't believe I found it, Jen! For years I thought it was gone, and of all the material things I've ever lost, this pen was the one thing I really wanted back.

Oh wow! I lost track of him ages ago, Jenny replied. *But I always thought he was the sweetest guy. Are you still in touch with him?*

Sadly, no. Maybe someday I'll hunt him down and tell him what his gift meant to me. Tell him he was right, that I did become a writer.

The way things are going in the world, I wouldn't wait too long, Bits.

One of the most difficult things I've had to come to terms with is the feeling of guilt I carry that you're not here to enjoy your life, too. The injustice of it all has often overwhelmed me, sometimes with fury, sometimes with sadness, but more often than not, with a tremendous sense that I don't deserve to be happy.

"But life isn't a zero-sum game," Porter said one night, when I explained to him how I felt. "There's not a finite amount of suffering in the world, so your taking on more of it doesn't lessen anyone else's burden."

"I know."

"You were a good mother, Beth. What happened to Mia was not your fault. And making your life smaller won't bring her back."

I nodded.

"And from what you've told me, she would hate that you're unhappy."

"She would," I said. "Mia always looked for the good in everything. She wanted everyone to be happy."

"Okay, so let's make a deal," Porter said. "Let's honor Mia by trying to be more like her. We'll be sun-seekers. Will you do that with me?"

"What do you mean? Like people who go to the beach?"

"No." He shook his head. "When you said that Mia always looked for the good in everything, it made me think about how sunflowers stay turned towards the sun. Maybe if we remind each other to just keep turning towards the sun and away from the shadows, we can stay focused on what's good. Not just for us, but for Mia, too."

"I get it," I said. "It's a deal. *Squadra girasole.*"

He pulled me towards him. "Team sunflower. I like it," he said, and kissed the top of my head. Then he stepped back and cupped my chin. "This is a great deal for me because it means I just get to look at you. You're my sunshine, you know?"

"And you're my Robert Duvall. My Gus McCrae."

He laughed. "That may be the nicest thing anyone has ever said to me."

Being with Porter again after all these years, being loved by him, will become normal at some point, I know. As slowly as we are moving right now, I can already feel myself forgetting to marvel at the twists and turns that brought us back together, forgetting to appreciate the million ways he is kind and thoughtful. But I do my best to not take any of it for granted.

He'll be fifty-four soon, and I'll be fifty-three. We have gray hair and lines around our eyes, and we've seen our share of heartache. But probably more than anyone else, Porter has influenced who I've become, our stories overlapping and intersecting in ways that neither of us could have imagined. I'm learning to trust what's between us, to trust that even if I say something he doesn't agree with, Porter's not going to punish me with silence or walk away, because he's just as invested as I am in making this work. He's not going anywhere. The emotional intimacy that I envied so much in other couples is a work in progress, but it seems like a real possibility with Porter.

I've been reading a book called *The Anatomy of Hope* on my Kindle this week. David recommended it to me ages ago, but I've been so distracted with house projects that I've just now gotten around to it. The author is a Harvard hematologist named Jerome Groopman, and in the introduction to the book, he makes an important distinction between optimism and hope. Hope, he explains, isn't just some pie-eyed way of looking at things. Instead, it's seeing a possible path forward, despite all of the pitfalls that lie along the way.

I've been thinking a lot about hope as I read Groopman's book. There have been debilitating periods of hopelessness in my life, more than I would have imagined possible, but it comforts me to know that the process of losing and rediscovering hope has always been part of the human condition. Long before the biblical stories were being told, Aesop wrote that Zeus crammed all of the useful things in the universe together in a jar and then put the lid down tight. He left the jar with humans, who, having no self-control, pried the lid off to see what was inside. When they did, all of the good things in the jar flew out and returned to the pantheon of the gods, but one thing was left behind. *Elpis*, hope. Aesop said that hope was left as collateral, to assure the humans that all of the good things that had flown away would come back to us over time. Around the same time, Theognis wrote that *Elpis* had indeed remained with humans, as an act of faithfulness, and because of this, humans could depend on the enduring presence of hope.

Be hopeful.

That's our charge, handed down from the Greeks, reinterpreted by the Bible, reiterated by a million works of art and music and literature.

Part of what keeps me hopeful, Mia, is that I firmly believe that you are in heaven, alongside my parents and Celia and your kitty Bandit, and, after his heart attack on the twelfth hole of the Bedford Hills golf course this past spring, your grandfather, Crawford William Campbell III, Lion of Wall Street. Good ol' Number Three.

And because you're in heaven, I suspect that you now know the answer to all the great mysteries, and that nothing you ever wanted to understand has been left unexplained, and no dilemma has been left unresolved. I believe that you are completely free of pain, both psychic and physical, because heaven is the one place where everything we've ever done or left undone has been forgiven, and then forgotten forever.

David says that my heart will grow around the hole left by your absence, and I am sure that's true, but I have accepted that the pain will never go away completely, and that my task is to learn how to cope.

So when grief overwhelms me, when I've soaked Oliver's fur with tears and have to lie down until the pain in my chest subsides, I make myself get up and walk out to the olive tree. I run my hand over her gnarled and twisted trunk and feel all of the cumulative effects of time, all of the scars left by life giving her too little of what she needed and too much of what she didn't, and I marvel that she is still standing, still serving as a promise of peace, like the branch of her ancestor that signaled an end to the flood and the return of hope to mankind.

And while I'm not sure that I can answer Mother Teresa's question just yet with any sort of precision, I do know that in spite of everything, I still have fruit to yield. There is still a place where my talents and God's will meet, where that divine spark, the *schekinah*, still burns.

I'm staking my claim among the olive trees, Mia.

I've made thousands of mistakes. I've been hurt by the people I love, and I've inflicted damage on those I valued most, and I've lost too much to bear...but here I am, bearing it. And just like the *Desiderata* says, I am no less than the trees and the stars, and I have a right to be here.

I trust that all of this is true.

And most of all, I trust that I'll see you again, when the time is right.

Until then, *Mia, cara mia,*

All my love,

Mom

Acknowledgments

No one deserves more thanks for this book coming to fruition than Lisa Paul Hodges, who read countless iterations with unflagging enthusiasm and lent her support, opinion, and editorial eye again and again and again. I owe you a vat of gratitude and guacamole, salty and with a hit of Tabasco, just the way we like it.

To the Davids, my gratitude for your friendship is only outweighed by my love. To the Jennys, chief among them Cristen W. Matilainen, who let me sleep on her couch and cry on her shoulder when the chips were way, way down, I'll chop up a cross and make us some cookies.

Tremendous thanks to the team at DartFrog Books, particularly my old friend Gordon McClellan, for their patient guidance and expertise.

To the very real Father Michael, thank you from the bottom of my heart for allowing me to share the story of your encounter with Mother Teresa. Nearly forty years later, the question she posed to you on that dark Nairobi evening still contains the power to redirect lives. I am forever grateful for you and for Miguel.

E come potrei mai ringraziare Marco per tutti i chilometri in Toscana e in Umbria e le risate che li hanno accompagnati, anche quando la macchina era in un fosso? Grazie di cuore!

Lastly, a huge thank you to my family and friends who value a turn of phrase and a well-told story in the same way that other people value air.

About the Author

Corey Stewart's award-winning writing includes everything from victim's impact statements to keynote speeches, with the pinnacle of her career being a collection of off-color beer descriptions for her favorite brewery, *That Damn Mary....* or perhaps the titillating global messaging around a corporate *Policy on Policies*. It's a toss-up and both ultimately drive the reader to drink.

Stewart received a master's in theology and literature from the University of the South, where her presence led her academic advisor to question his life choices, and a bachelor's at UNC-Chapel Hill in peace, war, and defense, where all of her disposable income and most of her time went to the good people at Troll's (RIP) and He's Not Here.

Her work explores what is required to believe in something—whether that something is God, the future, or the healing power of hops and barley—and retain a sense of purpose in the face of life's calamities.

The Wisdom of the Olive Tree is her first novel.

Made in the USA
Columbia, SC
16 December 2022

74196363R00178